THE THING EXTENDED ITS FURRY TENTACLE TOWARD THEM.

For the first time, Lysandra noticed that the end of its manipulative organ could be splayed into several dozen slender, almost hair-fine, foot-long tendrils.

What the tendrils held was a scuffed and dirty scrap of notepaper. As she read it, she frowned:

YOU HAVE IGNORED THE WARNING. PREPARE NOW TO PERISH.

Other Avon Books by
L. Neil Smith

BRIGHTSUIT MACBEAR

TAFLAK LYSANDRA

L. NEIL SMITH

AVON BOOKS ◆ NEW YORK

AVON BOOKS
A division of
The Hearst Corporation
105 Madison Avenue
New York, New York 10016

First Avon Books Printing: December 1988

AVON TRADEMARK REG. U.S. PAT. OFF. AND IN OTHER COUNTRIES, MARCA REGISTRADA, HECHO EN U.S.A.

Printed in the U.S.A.

K–R   10   9   8   7   6   5   4   3   2   1

THIS BOOK IS FOR
Steve Heller, part-time wizard and full-time friend

CONTENTS

CHAPTER I:

Table Manners

"Mmmmmm . . ."

Elsie Nahuatl's spoon bit deep into the dark ice cream with its peculiar crimson topping. It was her first day on the planet Majesty, almost her first hour, and she was glad to see that the Majestans had developed (or imported) all of the civilized amenities. All of the amenities *she* considered civilized, anyway.

The local equivalent of a housefly landed on the smooth, spotless surface of the table where Elsie sat, was recognized at once by the table's built-in circuitry, and began to be drawn downward, into the selectively permeable substance of the table top to its destruction. It was a horrible sight in its own way, Elsie thought, although no less so, she supposed, than flypaper or electric bug zappers. She always expected to hear a high, thin voice crying, *"Help me! Help me!"*

As the ice cream melted in her mouth, hurting her teeth in the exact way she'd looked forward to, she glanced over the wire rims of her glasses and around the hovercraft terminal's little restaurant. The place seemed brand-new, no doubt the brainchild of some immigrant entrepreneur. After closing —unless it was open twenty-four hours (no, make that twenty-three hours on Majesty) a day—hundreds of tiny chromium "housemice," no larger than her own small fist, would emerge from the baseboards around the room to collect the day's debris, scour the tables and chairs, and polish the floor until it was clean enough to eat from.

Unless you happened to be a fly.

At the moment, however, the restaurant—more of a snack bar, to tell the truth—was crowded with a mixture of "natives" and tourists sitting at the small, round, plastic tables, sharing Elsie's idea of an enjoyable way to spend the afternoon. Some sort of music—if that was what it was; too many hundreds of inhabited planets, too many thousands of cultures had been discovered already for any one person to keep track of what was popular in all of them—lent an old-fashioned touch. It could be heard above the general racket, playing from acoustic radiators mounted in the ceiling panels overhead, instead of being transmitted in the usual way, directly to the listener's brain.

It was easy telling at least some of the tourists from the "natives." In addition to human beings of every size, color, and description, they included gorillas of both the lowland and highland varieties, several large, noisy families of chimpanzees, a long-armed gibbon (a scholar, Elsie guessed from the cut of his clothing and his thoughtful, abstracted expression, perhaps on sabbatical), two auburn-haired orangutans holding hands, obvious honeymooners, even a porpoise—*delphinus delphus*—resting in a wheeled, motorized contraption that resembled a pair of undersized bicycles bolted side-by-side, enjoying an aromatic plate of live mackerel (which had to have been imported, Elsie thought, as Majesty possessed no real oceans) with the help of a servo-mechanical arm.

Each of the "natives," of course, was human, descended from interstellar colonists who'd landed here by accidental good fortune what seemed to them—

owing to a confusing peculiarity of physics—thousands of years ago. For the rest of the galaxy it had been less than a century. She was disappointed (but not at all surprised, given what she'd been told) to see none of the taflak, the real natives of Majesty, in the restaurant. Word of some sort of trouble between two warring tribes of human locals, with some possible involvement by the taflak, had added a certain edge to the buzz of conversation among the Confederate tourists—all of them accustomed to living in a much more peaceable universe—now contemplating going into harm's way.

She did see a freenie, no more than fifteen inches tall, looking a bit like a cross between a fluorescent pink army helmet and a crook-topped plumber's friend—one of the rescued former inhabitants of a planet that had been called Yamaguchi 523-C until its sun had exploded—sitting atop a table, drinking what she assumed was a cup of coffee in its characteristic, embarrassing manner.

Like most other offworlders here, Elsie and her father had just arrived—by shuttlecraft, rather than the customary down-Broach—from the giant orbiting starship *Tom Sowell Maru*, a vast, snow white inverted bowl-shape almost eight miles in diameter and more than two miles from rounded top to flattish bottom, which had been their home for months. Now, unlike the vacationers all around her, she and her father had a job to do, and, adding to a certain personal problem she'd been worrying about, Elsie was not looking forward to it.

It was bad enough, she thought, to be stuck for days, possibly for weeks, in the middle of nowhere on a mundane, boring technical test-run (Elsie was unaware that almost any other young person her age might have jumped at such an adventure), but she wouldn't even be working in her own specialty. The education she'd worked so hard to acquire might as well have been a hobby, and her degree—she was the youngest person from Earth ever to have won such an honor—only a merit badge.

Her gaze, no less abstracted than the gibbon professor's (although, she assumed, for very different reasons—she almost giggled at the alternative possibility, until memory of her personal problem sobered her up again), extended past the restaurant's odd assorted collection of customers, a collection she'd been used to all her life and regarded as normal. Through the broad, self-cleaning (and, if need be, self-repairing) windows, she looked out where a yellow sun, which had never shone upon the Earth where she'd been born fifteen years earlier, beat down hard and hot on a rubberized parking apron.

At one end of the apron, a road led back to Talisman, the original colonial settlement occupying the southernmost of the Majestan poles, and which—like the village of Geislinger, its North Polar counterpart—had more than doubled its population in the not-too-distant past with the rediscovery of Majesty and the regular arrival of star-traveling vessels like *Tom Sowell Maru*.

Between the road and the other end of the parking apron, Elsie could have counted hundreds of small hovercraft if she'd felt like taking the trouble, taxis, charter buses, private vehicles out from the nearby town, well kept and enameled in a cheerful array of bright metallic colors, but, for the most part, several years out of date, and dwarfed by the half dozen much larger excursion craft that were their reason for having come here in the first place.

At the apron's other end, the sunbaked, resilient surface gently tilted and disappeared into the "shallows" of the Sea of Leaves. From there to the ruler-straight horizon, except for one or two excursion craft already showing the wonders of the planet to loads of goggle-eyed tourists, lay the unbroken expanse of vegetation—of reasonable proportions here at the relatively cool, dry South Pole, but reaching depths of six metric miles at the hotter, damper equator—which Elsie and her father had come to explore in a more scientific manner.

Overhead, a squadron of armed aerocraft, small, swift, flying disks, suspended in the air by their electrostatic impellers, kept watch over the larger, slower vessels, looking out for monstrous equatorial wildlife that burrowed beneath the surface of the vegetation further north, but were often observed wandering close to the pole when they became old or sick, unable to withstand the savage competition of the greater depths, but still dangerous to smaller life-forms.

It was bright inside the restaurant, and Elsie, had she altered her focus a bit, might have seen her own reflection in the window. If she had, she'd have observed a young human female, rather small for her age, with large brown eyes, medium dark brown skin, straight shoulder-length blond hair, and a nose her father asserted was "cute"—to her inevitable annoyance. The wire-rimmed spectacles perched atop that nose might have indicated she was allergic or otherwise maladapted to the usual correction techniques. As it was, Elsie was in the habit of saying she simply preferred them to surgery or contact lenses, avoiding the thought that they provided a convenient barrier to hide behind.

The truth was, Elsie didn't like the way she looked. In fact, she considered herself unlovely. The nose her father regarded as cute she saw as broad and flat, suitable accompaniment to lips that were far too full, and the coarse, straight hair of a garish yellow which reminded her (if no one else) of the thatching she'd seen on cottages during a brief tourist trip to Stratford-on-Avon.

What she hated worst was that it looked like this unfortunate condition was permanent. As a small child, she'd been able to tell herself that someday she'd outgrow her skinny ankles and knobby knees, but now . . . well, the time required for that sort of transformation, she felt, was beginning to run just a bit short.

At the moment she was dressed in the height of fashion for her time and place, the middle of what some termed the twenty-first century, in a rubbery silver smartsuit capable of performing many functions for its wearer, including maintaining comfortable temperature and humidity, even air pressure on more hostile worlds. It was programmable, using rows of colored buttons running along both forearms, to resemble other clothing. Resigned to spending the rest of her life short and shapeless, Elsie chose to let her smartsuit look like what it was.

Elsie was aware that her Australian heritage was interesting and unusual. But, on those occasions when she gave the matter any consideration, she thought of herself first as an Earth-person, no different, no more remarkable than the humans, gorillas, orangutans, chimpanzees, gibbons, porpoises, killer whales, and assorted other entities of both natural and artificial intelligence among whom she'd grown up, and who, along with a variety of alien life-forms—the real natives of an increasing number of planets like Majesty—comprised the Galactic Confederacy. Like them, she had her own special interests and aspirations. Like them, she had her own special problems.

Elsie sighed a discontented sigh.

How was she going to tell her father what she'd done?

A flicker of movement caught her eye, distracting her from her survey of the restaurant and its environs. A sizzling mammothburger—her father's favorite—was emerging from the surface of the table with fries, dill slices, and all the trimmings. Its molecules mingled with those of the furniture (she tried not to think about the fly) as they had throughout the short journey through the walls and floor from the fabricator in the restaurant's automated kitchen where they'd been assembled an atom at a time, until it rose above the tabletop.

Across the table from her, sitting on its haunches in a cheerful-colored plastic chair just like the one she occupied, a furry gray-tan canine-shape had one of its legs up, scratching with some energy at the base of its ear with a jiggling hind foot.

Elsie frowned, pushing her glasses back up on her nose.

"Do you have to do that in public?" she whispered at the doglike creature. "Don't you know it embarrasses me to be seen with you when you do that?"

The coyote stopped scratching, put its leg down, and tilted its head at the girl.

"You don't know the meaning of embarrassment," it replied. "You don't have to be seen in public with a daughter who puts barbecue sauce on chocolate ice cream!"

CHAPTER II:

The Subfoline *Victor Appleton*

"Excuse me, sir . . ."

The towering smartsuited hulk shambling along the rubbery sidewalk dropped its jaw and stared, unaccustomed as it was to being addressed, however politely, by a coyote.

G. Howell Nahuatl wasn't any ordinary coyote. To his knowledge—and his deep, lifelong regret—he was the only thinking member of his species in the entire Galactic Confederacy. Selected from what would have been a line of thoroughbreds—had it ever occurred to anyone to hold coyote shows and hand out ribbons to exceptional representatives of what the dictionary calls "a small wolf of the North American plains"—as a puppy, he'd been the experimental recipient of an early "cerebro-cortical implant," a small, powerful computer surgically attached to the surface of his baby brain and hard-wired into his developing nervous system, with the idea of enhancing his already considerable intelligence from the level of an extraordinarily bright canine to whatever was required to perform the specific task he'd been bred and modified at enormous expense to perform: protecting sheep on a Wyoming ranch from his unenhanced relatives.

The operation was a failure, but the patient had lived. Rather, the operation had been altogether too successful, for, once modified, Howell had aston-

8

ished his creators by displaying the intelligence, not of an extraordinarily bright canine, but of a human being. Under a Confederate custom far stronger than any law, this meant he wasn't anybody's property but his own. His former owner, having lost a substantial investment, had vowed never to make another such mistake (as it turned out, the next time he made an altogether different mistake instead), dooming the coyote to a degree of loneliness unprecedented in the history of sentient life.

But that was then.

This was now.

As Howell and his adopted daughter Elsie had emerged from the air-conditioned hovercraft terminal into the broiling South Polar heat of the Majestan sun, the coyote had found himself wondering— although he'd seen the textbook figures long before agreeing to come to the planet—what it must be like on the equator.

The individual he'd addressed glowered down suspiciously at the coyote and the girl.

"You talkin' t'me, pilgrim?"

The terminal building was a prefabricated titanium-framed geodesic of obvious Confederate manufacture, with a scattering of transparent panels, the upper third of which was occupied by the restaurant. Within sight were numerous other domes, a handful of half-cylindrical quonsets, and a clutter of other structures and large pieces of machinery, associated with housing and maintaining the excursion craft. No rational plan seemed to be discernable in the way the buildings had been laid out. What Howell had thought would be a short, simple walk to their destination now looked like a long, confusing, sweaty expedition.

"Why, er, yes. I was. Could you—"

In any other civilization, this might have been a dangerous encounter in a dangerous section of a dangerous port city. However, about Elsie's waist, on a lightweight belt of the same remarkable material as her suit, she wore a pair of tiny Walther Electric .01 caliber Model UVPs reversed—the floorplates of their magazines faced forward—secure in their open-topped holster-rechargers. The pistols' size was deceptive. They could accelerate a half-inch trajectile, alloyed of iron and depleted uranium and a mere ten thousandths of an inch in diameter—less than the thickness of a business card—to a quarter million feet per second, yielding not quite seventy tons of destructive energy at their miniscule muzzles.

Although his lack of thumbs (and hands to wear them on) had led him to some unusual measures, Howell was similarly prepared, as was everyone else around them this fine sunny morning, tourists and terminal personnel alike. If all Confederates agreed upon a single thing (in general, being the independent sort, they didn't), it was that self-defense meant just that: a task it was impossible to delegate to anybody else. This may have been why, judging from talk he'd overheard in the restaurant, the reported battle further north on the Sea of Leaves was being regarded by most of the visitors as no more than an added entertainment attraction.

The giant grinned, addressing Elsie.

"I get it, it's a gag! You're a ventry . . . you're throwin' your voice, ain'tcha, little girl?"

Elsie removed her spectacles and polished them with a handkerchief pulled from a pocket of her smartsuit, looking embarrassed. Just as their lenses had darkened upon entering the harsh sunlight, her suit had begun working in its own efficient, automatic manner to keep her comfortable. Howell, who'd been known to wear a smartsuit only when it was absolutely necessary (on the surface of an airless planet like Earth's moon, for example) complained about the way the close-fitting garment matted his fur, and preferred the insulation of his long-haired thick pelt, relying on that and his species' millions of years of adaptation to the merciless extremes of the American Great Plains to keep him cool. He did wear a small knapsack on his back, however, containing a number of necessities.

Canines are unable to sweat like human beings, and must do so through the bottoms of their feet and their tongues. Howell wondered if his panting, an involuntary doggy reflex, embarrassed his daughter, too. Despite the degree of intellectual maturity she often demonstrated, she seemed to be of an age at which everything embarrassed her. It was a simple matter, he was certain, of adolescent blood chemistry overcoming powerful inborn mental faculties and superior education. Nothing in his own peculiar background offered to help him cope with the phenomenon, or to make his daughter's progress through it easier. He just tried to be even more understanding of her feelings than usual.

"I'm *not* a ventriloquist!"

"She's *not* a ventriloquist!"

Howell and Elsie spoke at the same time, demolishing the giant's theory. That individual was attired in a worn smartsuit adjusted to give the appearance of coveralls, emblazoned across the back with a logo, the speeding hovercraft of one of the excursion companies, and decorated further with a coating of engine lubricant. It was belted to support a steam-fusion Sebastian Mark IX, old-fashioned and underpowered for its size, fitted with oversized grips.

He recovered from surprise and looked down at them.

"Er, then what can I do y'for?"

"Well," Howell answered, "you could point us toward Slip 23 of the private docking facility."

The mechanic blinked, reached up, removed an outsized billed cap, and scratched his shaggy head where his hair had been parted in the middle with meticulous care. For anybody else, it would have been a long reach, since the creature was better than eight feet tall, and covered, where his smartsuit let it show, with long, yellowish white fur he'd somehow managed to keep free of the same grease that stained his suit.

His eyes were a deep and beautiful shade of blue.

"Why sure, pilgrim. Just go down this here alleyway an' turn right at the Shrine of Our Lady of Discord. Can't miss the big golden apple. You're a coyote, ain'tcha?"

Howell nodded.

"I was the last time I looked. And you, sir, unless I'm greatly mistaken, are a yeti."

"One sixteenth Sasquatch on m'daddy's side of the family, an' born within the sound of the Dalai Lama's temple bells, as the sayin' goes. 'Cept I grew up in Hinsdale County in the good ol' N.A.C., as a matter of plain unromantic fact. An' thanks for not sayin' 'abominable snowman.' It'd be my guess you two're the folks from Hellertech I was s'posed t'meet. The guy your principals hired got taken a little drunk an' needed replacin' at the last minute. Obregon Grossfuss, master mechanic an' volunteer copilot, at yer service."

He bowed until his hair brushed the pavement and extended a broad, furry hand that would have made four of Elsie's. Prompted by a signal from his cerebro-cortical implant, Howell's knapsack stirred, its synthetic cover unzippering down the middle to release a long, thin, complicated-looking arm that unfolded and reached up to accept and shake the hand Grossfuss had offered.

"G. Howell Nahuatl, Mr. Grossfuss, and equally at yours, I assure you. I'm quite pleased to make your acquaintance. It was my understanding that your people are usually too retiring to mingle much in what we optimistically term 'civilization,' and, indeed, you are the first yeti I've ever met in person.

"This is my daughter, Miss Elsa Lysandra Nahuatl. She's just recently taken a Scholarate of Praxeology, and is here to have a scientific look at Majesty while she helps us wring out Hellertech's newest, most expensive toy—which you'd greatly oblige me by showing us to."

The yeti replaced the cap on his head and grinned down at the girl.

"Talks perty, don't he, kid?"

His blue eyes twinkled—his wide jaws were full of pointed and intimidating teeth—eliciting an answering grin from Elsie. He turned to Howell.

"Right glad to, pil—Mr. Nahuatl—if you'll follow me. She's right this way."

With this, he pivoted on his heel and proceeded with the gigantic strides his people, on both sides of the family, were famous for, down the service street he'd first pointed out. The coyote beckoned to his daughter, let his mechanical arm refold itself into the knapsack, and followed at what he'd have resented anyone else calling a dogtrot.

Majesty's South Pole, Elsie thought to herself, was enjoying a bumper crop of visitors at the moment. This could change at any time if the reported trouble between the local human tribes was the beginning of a trend. Confederates may have been an adventurous lot, but they weren't foolhardy. As it was, notices had been posted inside the terminal building: excursions were being rerouted to avoid the danger, schedules were subject to change without warning. Charters into the combat zone could be arranged, but at an extra charge, and—the Confederacy had few lawyers, none of whom would ever have dared suggest that an individual was responsible for any but his own mistakes—entirely at the customer's risk.

Meanwhile, even here in what was—in name, at least—a private docking area, where owners of noncommercial hovercraft were accustomed to stowing and launching their yachtlike pleasure vehicles, room had been made, no doubt at a premium, for extra passenger machines intended for those special excursions. The yeti, the coyote, and his daughter were forced to slow their businesslike pace (to the secret relief of the girl, who'd been having a hard time keeping up with the long-legged Himalayan and her fleet-footed father) as they became stuck behind a flock of tourists lined up to climb a boarding ramp at the dock.

Waiting without patience behind the clump of gorillas, chimpanzees, porpoises, and assorted other Earth beings, the three watched yet another huge hovercraft, a Blackmon Sante Fe, skate up with a graceful, side-sliding motion to the parking apron, meet a set of motorized stairs, and begin disgorging passengers—more Confederates, Elsie realized, as she indicated one individual who could have been neither a Majestan "native" nor one of the indigenous taflak.

"Father, that's a lamviin, isn't it," she asked, pushing her glasses back to the bridge of her nose and peering through them, "over there with that boy?"

Elsie envied boys. They always had adventures, and *did* things.

The coyote glanced in the direction she was looking. (He'd brought her up knowing it was impolite to point, even if he was incapable of it himself). Elsie was sure the creature she was asking about, walking along the apron deep in conversation with a boy about her own age, was one of the yard-tall

nine-legged natives of the planet Sodde Lydfe. Years
ago, Howell and Elsie had visited that desert world,
in particular the Empire of Great Foddu, a short
while after it had been discovered by the Confederacy—just in time to stop an atomic war between
the Fodduans and their archenemies the Hegemony
of Podfet—and had found they liked the furry,
crablike beings. Following the arrival of the starships, many of the lamviin had begun to spread
with enthusiasm among the Confederate worlds,
yet so many of those worlds existed—and just one
planetful, as yet, of lamviin—that seeing one anywhere but Sodde Lydfe was still as rare an experience as seeing a yeti.

Elsie wondered if this one was anybody they knew.

"Yes, dear, I believe you're right. Perhaps if we've
time, later, and he, she, or rhe—"

" 'He,' " Elsie interrupted. "He's much too tall to
be a female or surmale."

"—is still around, we'll have a chance to catch up
on the latest Fodduan gossip. I wonder what that
rascal Agot Edmoot *Mav*'s been up to lately. Meantime, my dear, we've work to do, if Mr. Grossfuss
will be good enough to lead the way."

The crowd ahead had cleared at last, having filed
aboard the waiting excursion vessel. It revved its
impellers, stirring up a miniature hurricane, and
slid off across the Sea of Leaves. The three continued along the walkway, which, as the level of the
vegetation beneath it fell away, began to resemble
an elevated pier extending outward onto a still,
green lake. They came to a halt at a point along the
pier marked *Slip 23* in several languages and al-
phabets. Elsie and Grossfuss craned their necks
and peered over the side at what lay below.

"This proud, innovative vessel," Howell informed
them with a proprietary flourish of his manipulator—
which seemed to have sprouted from his knapsack

of its own accord—"prefabricated in the Old Solar Asteroids and assembled aboard the starship *Tom Sowell Maru,* is the H.P.S. *Victor Appleton*—our *subfoline!*"

Grossfuss removed his cap and scratched his head. Elsie pushed her glasses back and frowned at the awkward, unfamiliar word. She'd been thinking of it all along as a sort of mechnical mole, or perhaps a leaf—and Elsie—borer. Occupied with other more important personal matters aboard the starship— one of which still worried her—this was her first look at the machine in question, whatever name it went by.

"Our—make that *your*—what?"

"Subfoline," her father replied. "From the Latin *sub,* meaning 'under,' and *folia,* meaning 'leaves.' The expression's analogous to 'submarine': *subfoline.*"

Elsie looked down at the long, narrow craft half-submerged (a better term might have been *subfoliated,* she thought) beside the elevated jetty. At least a hundred feet long and twenty in diameter, it was the basic, streamlined, cigar-shape she'd expected, colored to match the sea it rested upon, without visible hatches, conning tower, fins, or any other traditional protrusion. A covering of what seemed like millions of stiff wires the diameter of coat-hanger stock, about a foot long, swept backward, like the coarse fur of a seal (although the individual bristles reminded her more of elephant hair), from what Elsie assumed was the needle-pointed bow of the machine, to its somewhat blunter stern.

She poked her spectacles back where they belonged again and looked up at Howell.

"What's Latin for 'fuzzy pickle'?"

"Stand where you are," a shrill voice demanded, *"and put your hands in the air!"*

"That couldn't be right," Elsie mused to herself. "Something must have gotten lost in the translation."

Without being entirely aware of the process, she found she had a Walther UVP in each of her hands, their safeties snapped off, their ready-lights burning. She looked back at the subfoline to see what had triggered her self-defensive reflexes.

The slender figure of a girl in a tattered uniform stood astride the vessel near the bow.

The outsized military handgun clamped in both her hands was pointed straight at them.

CHAPTER III:
Goldberry MacRame

It was one of those frozen moments.

"I told you to stand where you are!" the girl with the military pistol shouted. "Put your hands up!"

Two of the three on the dock complied, an annoyed and grumbling Grossfuss adding several feet to his already impressive height; Howell, as might have been expected, with all four feet on the dock, the mechanical arm between his shoulder blades raised to the vertical. Elsie stood with her elbows near her hips, her forearms level, her twin Walther Electrics held at a subtle angle that would cross their lines of fire—paired and furious streams of ultravelocity trajectiles—at the solar plexus of the individual who threatened them.

Elsie's voice was quiet and firm: "Drop your weapon."

"You drop yours!"

"Well, whaddaya know," laughed Grossfuss, "a Majestan standoff. Good work, kid, I didn't even see y'draw."

The girl aboard the subfoline might have been attractive, Elsie thought, if it hadn't been for her dirty and bedraggled clothing, her tangled hair, and the dark circles under her eyes. Something serious was wrong with her, however, for the muzzle of her big ominous-looking handgun—an actual chemical-powered firearm, if Elsie knew her history —made figure eights as her hands shook.

Grossfuss spoke again, his voice as level and calm this time as Elsie's.

"It's all right, Goldberry, these here are the vessel's owners. You can relax, now."

"Hunh?"

The girl leaned forward, peering at Grossfuss, suspicion and confusion battling for domination of her face, exhaustion serving as a sort of referee.

"At ease, Leftenant MacRame." The yeti put an edge in his voice: "Stand down—*dismissed!*"

For a moment, Elsie thought the girl was going to shoot. Then, as weary comprehension won an upset victory over her features, the weapon's muzzle dropped. She collapsed in a sprawling heap across the curved hull of the *Victor Appleton*.

Elsie holstered her Walthers. She and Grossfuss hurried down a nearby ladder to a small, unbristled area at the subfoline's bow that served as its upper deck, with Howell—his four feet something of a disadvantage, where ladders were concerned—following. Elsie reached the older girl and knelt, feeling for the pulse at the base of her throat—it was strong and regular—and trying to remember her first aid.

"I take it, then, that you know this person?" Howell asked the yeti, catching up.

Grossfuss looked down, shaking his great head.

"Yeah, that's Leftenant Commander Goldberry MacRame, or so she says, late of the Antimacassarite Navy. Her screwmaran-of-war got sorta eighty-sixed in that big tussle up north, which put her on the beach an' outa luck. I promised her a few silver ounces t'watch the *Victor Appleton*, here—too many strangers in port—while I went t'look for you."

Howell considered this.

"Later I'll ask you what in Benjamin Tucker's

name a screwmaran is. For now, I'd be satisfied knowing how she got down here to the Pole, when, according to the reports, the battle happened on the equator only yesterday, six thousand metric miles away."

To be certain of his facts, Howell had checked with his cerebro-cortical implant—which performed other functions besides enhancing his intelligence—tuning it to one of the local news services. The conflict was still being given what another medium would have called "front page" treatment. His memory had been correct.

"It would have taken the speediest hovercraft I'm familiar with," the coyote estimated, "at least all night to make such a trip. And I believe the colonists don't have aerocraft. How do you suppose she got all the way down here?"

Grossfuss shrugged.

"Dunno," replied the yeti, scratching his head. "Claims she got concussed in the dustup an' don't remember a thing between that an' when I put her on the payroll."

Elsie looked up from the unconscious Goldberry MacRame, her nose wrinkled with annoyance. She gave the nosepiece of her glasses a tap with her forefinger to push them back into place.

"While you detectives figure out her itinerary, maybe you can help me get her in out of the sun and treated for shock, exhaustion, and probably malnutrition."

She turned to her father.

"How do we get inboard—the usual way?"

Howell blinked.

"Quite right, my dear, yes. I'm sorry."

Again the coyote issued certain mental commands to his implant, this time to emit a short-range signal called a key code, the same means by which any Confederate might have unlocked his hovercar or the front door of his home. His effort was rewarded with a yelp from Elsie as the deck beneath her knees began to absorb her, just as the restaurant table had earlier absorbed the fly. It was also, of course, a reversal of the process by which his food had come to the table. Elsie, as familiar with this method of transportation as she was with walking, had been startled only by its suddenness and the location of the "door" beneath her.

Inch by inch, the molecules of her body interpenetrated those of the hull. Some help from Grossfuss was required, folding the helpless Majestan officer's legs at the knees and tucking her arms at her sides. Together, he and Elsie let the permeable surface lower them and the unconscious girl into the cool dark of the subfoline's interior, where it became a deck beneath their feet (the ceiling closing in over their heads), and, following Howell's directions, they passed in a more conventional manner—walking under their own power—through the control area and the small dining facility and galley, to place Goldberry MacRame in one of the half dozen closet-sized cabins intended for passengers and crew.

"An Antimacassarite, you say?"

Howell's auxiliary arm held the primitive cartridge pistol before his eyes, turning it over for examination. He'd returned to questioning Grossfuss as soon as his daughter had seen to the colonial girl's needs—which had included a sponge bath and the business end of a glucose drip inserted into one limp, unresisting arm—and tucked her into the bunk under an extra blanket. The three sat in the dining area, where Grossfuss had let one of the chairs dissolve into the deck because its available range of sizes were all too small for him, and sat, instead, in the space it had occupied. Even so, he was still taller than Elsie. Howell had found makings and machinery for coffee and brewed a pot. Now three steaming mugs—two steaming mugs and a steaming mixing bowl for Grossfuss—rested on the table before them.

The Himalayan nodded.

"I reckon you know there was two old-fashioned nation-states here on Majesty when the first Confederates arrived. Still are, for that matter—Antimacassar an' Securitas by name."

"Yes," the coyote answered, "with regressive cultures and technologies, as is usually the case with the First Wave. So far they've climbed back, after nobody knows how many cycles, to relatively sophisticated mechanics—gear trains, differential hoists—but neither to heat-engines nor electricity, as yet."

"Prob'ly coulda had steam engines, if slaves wasn't so cheap an' easy t'come by."

"I see." Howell's voice was grim. "Go on."

"Natcherly," the yeti continued, "they been sluggin' it out with each other—barrin' occasional unavoidable outbreaks of peace—for the last several centuries. What else is nation-states for, I ask you? What I don't understand's the taflak gettin' involved. They're usually smart enough t'stay well out of it."

"I gather," Howell inquired, "that their participation in the recent battle is unprecedented?"

The giant primate nodded, taking a quart-sized sip of his coffee.

Listening, for the moment without comment, Elsie shook her own head. Her world, although she was in no position to realize it, had always been built inside out. Within the fuzzy but ever-expanding borders of the Galactic Confederacy, peace, personal freedom, and prosperity predominated. Outside those borders, thousands of petty, primitive empires and dictatorships—like Antimacassar and Securitas—resisted its expansion to the best of their limited ability. This might have been easier to understand had the Confederacy possessed anything resembling a central government, bent on interstellar conquest, but it didn't. The Confederacy consisted, in the main, of scientists, explorers, and merchants, out to profit (this was no less true of the scientists and explorers, in their own way, than of the merchants) by trading whatever they had too much of, for things that other beings produced in surplus, guaranteeing satisfaction all around.

Enjoying, in her absent, thoughtful way, Howell's conversation with the giant mechanic, Elsie poured herself another cup of coffee, warmed her father's, and went to start another pot for Grossfuss.

From a different perspective, of course, the Confederacy's lack of authority and territorial ambition, its interest in trading goods and information, rather than missiles and death rays, were the very reason its expansion was resisted. Throughout the sad, violent history of her native planet, those rare individuals who valued liberty above all else had always been forced to flee—most of the time westward—across the battle-scarred face of the globe, in an attempt to escape either from outright tyranny or from cultures they regarded as cramped and "overcivilized." All this had changed, however, with the advent of what at first had been the North American Confederacy, the concrete political expression of a logical process which had led from Thomas Jefferson's observation that "the government that governs best governs least" to the realization that the government which governs least is no government at all.

As this realization began spreading, those individuals (not quite so rare) whose livelihood depended on stealing what others had labored to create—burglars and bureaucrats, pickpockets and politicians—reacted with alarm. At first they opposed the inevitable changes by traditional means—ballots and bullets—but in the end, reversing thousands of years of history, they came to understand that it was their turn to flee. Thus the desperate and disaster-plagued "First Wave" of interstellar immigration from Earth had taken place: not courageous frontiersmen seeking new liberties and opportunities, as fiction writers had always imagined, but frightened authoritarians anxious to prolong their ancient and corrupt regimes.

Excusing herself, Elsie looked in on Goldberry MacRame, who continued sleeping, all indications from the medical panel in her cabin in the figurative green. With nothing better to do until Grossfuss and her father finished discussing current events and began planning the subfoline's first experimental run (it had been delivered here by the shuttlecraft that brought them; their job was to test and "install" it) she wandered aft to examine what she could of the *Victor Appleton*'s revolutionary superconducting power plant.

Lights came on overhead as she melted through one bulkhead membrane after another, separating different compartments, and winked out behind her as she passed.

Despite her curiosity about the new technology, her thoughts, almost despite her wishes, were still concerned with history.

The technology with which the refugees had chosen to expedite their escape from Earth had proven as imperfect as their political philosophies, scattering the would-be escapees at random, not only in the depths of space, but—and more important—in the mists of time, as well. A decade later by any "objective" calendar, when the *Solar* Confederacy, with the aid of a technology that worked better, had started transforming itself into a *Galactic* Confederacy, launching a more successful "Second Wave" of immigration and exploration, its participants discovered human populations already long established among the stars. Their civilizations had risen and fallen countless times, over an historical period that, for the people trapped in those rising and falling civilizations, had been as long, in some cases, as five thousand subjective years.

Majesty was home to one such population, divided throughout its history into warring cultures that had burgeoned and collapsed in cycles. Warfare's senseless waste of lives and money and time had kept them primitive by comparison with the younger Confederacy. Like her father, Elsie wasn't certain what a "screwmaran" was, but she knew it would be handmade, capable, after a fashion, of navigating the Sea of Leaves armed with large versions of Goldberry MacRame's crude pistol (cannon, or perhaps flamethrowers), and powered by human suffering.

Examining the subfoline's power-plant controls, Elsie shuddered at the thought. The emotional rejection of technology, she knew from her studies, at some arbitrary level of complexity—and comprehensibility, she suspected—between the bicycle and the combustion engine (or the bow and arrow, and the repeating rifle) was a feature common to many authoritarian pseudo-philosophies. Over the course of history, its ultimate consequences (intended or not) were always a drastic reduction in living standards, a shortening of individual life spans, the creation of an aristocratic elite, and the revival of slavery.

Some of these dismal facts of Majestan history Elsie had absorbed without much thought during the voyage here. Like almost all Confederates, she possessed one of the cerebro-cortical implants her father had pioneered. It served her, as it served trillions of her co-sapients, as an alarm clock, calculator, computer, library, telephone, stereo, radio, and personal movie theater. No telltale lights glowed, for instance, on the medical machinery in Goldberry MacRame's cabin, any more than on the controls of the superconducting engines. Both communicated directly with her implant. The one thing it couldn't do, placed where it was when she was a baby, on the surface of her brain inside her skull, was light her cigarettes, which was all right with Elsie. She didn't smoke.

And Confederate cigarettes lit themselves.

Elsie dreaded the boredom and inactivity it would entail, but now she was grateful that the job her father had accepted would keep them below the surface of the Sea of Leaves, where no intelligent life ever ventured. (She decided to avoid thinking about the full implications of that statement until later.) It would be her task to study certain scientifically confusing phenomena reported there, while Howell and his monstrous mechanic tested the subfoline itself.

"Herself," she corrected: the *Victor Appleton,* like all ships, was a "she."

Elsie's own life was confusing enough at present, she reflected, without the extra complication of intra-Majestan politics. She was something of a scientific phenomenon herself, even in her own phenomenal civilization, having won the Scholarate of Praxeology her father had mentioned—her "Sc.Prax.," as she thought of it, a degree more difficult to obtain than any mere doctorate—from the University of Mexico's Von Mises College, at the age of fourteen. She was discovering, however, as young men and women had discovered to their dismay for thousands of years (as the sleeping Goldberry MacRame had no doubt discovered in her own turn, perhaps no more than four or five years ago), that no amount of formal education ever quite prepared a person for a life outside of academia—or the many personal problems real life presents.

Again Elsie considered the unconscious First-Waver.

Tidied up, Goldberry MacRame had turned out, in the younger girl's envious estimation, quite beautiful, with lustrous honey-colored hair, and a soft, milky complexion touched, as a probable result of her profession—naval officer, hadn't Grossfuss claimed? —by the Majestan sun. For some reason she couldn't identify, this caused Elsie to think about the boy she'd seen earlier, the one with the lamviin. Although she didn't understand why, she became angry with herself.

And struggled to control it.

If this was what it meant to grow up—not knowing from one moment to the next what you were going to feel, or why—she didn't want any part of it.

How was she going to tell her father what she'd done aboard *Tom Sowell Maru*?

"Elsie?"

Her thoughts were interrupted by the sound of her father's voice, and she heard his nails clicking on the deck before she saw him. She turned in the narrow companionway, away from the floor-to-ceiling panel she'd come here with the intention of examining.

"Yes, Father, I'm here."

He sat on his haunches and looked up at her.

"Woolgathering? Well, I suppose there's no harm in it—as they say in Wyoming, fifty million coyotes can't be wrong. However, I did wish to consult with you in your paramedical capacity. If our young Antimacassarite guest's going to remain asleep for at least another couple of hours, Obregon and I thought we'd take the *Victor Appleton* out for a trial spin. What do you think?"

Grinning, Elsie hunkered down beside Howell and put both arms around his neck. Despite her many accomplishments, she had no medical capacity beyond what she'd learned of first aid in the Galactic Girl Guerrillas, supplemented by some veterinary stuff she'd thought it a good idea to learn on her father's account. She was grinning for another reason, as well, having just discovered she looked forward to putting the subfoline through its paces a bit more than she'd realized.

She readjusted her glasses and, folding her smart-suited legs beneath her, sat down on the deck.

"The medical panel in the cabin says she's suffering from exhaustion, mild hunger, dehydration, maybe a touch of emotional trauma. I can understand that, if she lost her ship. The news service says both—maybe all three—sides lost the engagement up on the equator and a lot of people are dead or unaccounted for. I didn't want to try to sedate her, but I think she'll sleep."

Howell's eyes crinkled in a manner Elsie knew represented an answering grin. She resolved then and there to confront him with the thing that had been troubling her.

"Very well," he began, "shall we be upon our—"

"Before we do, Father, there's something—"

"Mr. Nahuatl!"

The voice belonged to Grossfuss, coming from the bow of the subfoline, and it rang with panic.

Holding her glasses to the bridge of her nose with a hand—the other resting on the handle of one of her pistols—Elsie hurried forward behind her father. When they got as far as the cabins, they saw Grossfuss standing at one end of the corridor. Between him and them, Goldberry MacRame leaned against the frame of the dilated cabin door membrane, swaying, her intravenous tube trailing from one wrist. In one hand she waved a gleaming scalpel she'd taken from the first-aid kit.

"Mr. Nahuatl," Grossfuss complained from one corner of his mouth, the tone of his voice hinting that all this was somehow Howell's fault, "this is gettin' t'be a real bad habit with her."

"Where have you hidden my sidearm, animal?" the girl demanded. "I shall see every one of you foul creatures broken and sent to the Steps! But first we must abandon this machine . . . It is about to be destroyed!"

CHAPTER IV:

Bristles Aweigh

Howell attempted not to show it as he tensed to seize the scalpel with his manipulator, already at full vertical extension, as if in token of surrender.

"What do you mean, young woman, 'This ship's about to be destroyed'?"

Elsie stood impatient, her arms folded, one rubber-covered toe tapping with annoyance on the rubber-covered deck-plates. It was a measure of her contempt, more than restraint, that this time she didn't bother to draw a weapon.

"You'd better lie down, Leftenant Commander, before you have another collapse."

Grossfuss, if such a thing was possible, was backing forward, toward the control console and out of harm's way.

"What're 'the Steps'?"

"Nobody hid your sidearm." Toe still tapping, Elsie pushed her glasses back into place with an angry gesture. "Can't you see it lying there on the galley table?"

The scalpel shook in Goldberry's hand. She glanced from face to face with a look of utter confusion and something she'd never have acknowledged was terror. Elsie could tell what she was thinking: she was trapped in a closed-in, unfamiliar passageway; only one of the faces staring back at her was human, and even that was rather different from faces she

was used to seeing; her life had been a hazy nightmare since the battle—was it only yesterday?—and
nothing seemed to make sense anymore. The Earth
girl watched as the Leftenant Commander breathed
in and exhaled several times, sanity returning slowly
to her eyes.

"This is not the *Compassionate.*"

It was a statement, not a question. Elsie could
almost hear the bone and sinew creaking as she
and her companions relaxed. But it wasn't all over
yet, she reminded herself, trying to remain alert, as
concern filled Howell's voice.

"No, my dear, it's the subfoline H.S.P. *Victor
Appleton,* at rest in her berth at Talisman. I take it
you don't remember being paid to stand guard over
her?"

The Antimacassarite nodded, staring at the floor,
too weary to do anything else.

"Yes, I remember now. Being offered money to
guard her. Nobody ever paid me."

Howell threw a glance at Grossfuss. The yeti,
who by this time had backed up well past the little
galley, almost to the imagined safety of the control
area—and the hatchway even further forward—
returned a sheepish expression, having almost to
shout his answer along the narrow length of companionway.

"Well, I wasn't gonna pay her in advance, that
wouldn'ta been good business, would it?"

Fur swelling outward about his neck, Howell advanced on the primate, his muzzle wrinkled and his
teeth bared. It appeared that he only just managed
to suppress a snarl.

Grossfuss put both hands in front of him, palms
outward.

"Okay, okay! I'll pay her! I'll pay her!"

Ruffled fur smoothed in an instant. Naked fangs
and fury-contorted canine features became only a

memory. Elsie suppressed a giggle. She'd watched her father practice this display, hours at a time, in front of a mirror, claiming it was a second line of self-defense and part of his "ethnic heritage." At home they were never bothered by the same door-to-door salesman or religious proselyte twice.

"There's a good fellow," Howell answered Grossfuss in his most cultured Etonian accent, "see that you do. Leftenant Commander MacRame—my dear Goldberry—you really ought to lie down before you fall down. Please, will you let us help you?"

Goldberry sighed, looked at the razor-sharp surgical knife in her hand as if she'd never seen it before, tossed it onto the galley table beside her pistol, and shuddered.

"I shall do as you say, sir. Please accept my sincerest apologies. I believe I had some sort of nightmare. I was back aboard the *Compassionate*, sir, just as she was—oh, it is too horrible to contemplate, sir, let alone tell!"

She put her hands over her face, I.V. tube still dangling, and began to sob. Elsie, beginning to feel some sympathy for the girl—despite herself, and wishing Goldberry could limit it to one *sir* per sentence—stepped forward, took her by an arm, and steered her back into the cabin and onto her bunk.

"It's called a flashback," Elsie explained. "Let me get you a cup of—maybe you'd prefer tea—and you can tell me all about it. Believe me, Goldberry, it helps to tell."

As she turned in the door, she heard relays clatter into place, felt the deck beneath her feet give a gentle lurch, and knew the *Victor Appleton* was under way.

"I am—was—third officer in charge of security aboard the frigate A.L.N. *Compassionate* of Her

Imperial Kindness' Leafnavy, in service to Her Government-in-Exile. The *Compassionate* is—was— what I heard your servant call a 'screwmaran.' Now that noble vessel and all who served aboard her are no more. And to think the whole affair began as a simple punitive expedition against Securitasian pirates!"

Still badly shaken, the colonial girl had begun her story as soon as she'd settled back in her bunk with a hot mug of tea. Consulting the medical panel, Elsie removed the tube from Goldberry's wrist and cleaned up the mess the dripping baggie had cre- ated, all the while mumbling sympathetic denials to the chagrined leftenant commander's repeated apologies for what she termed her "unbecoming dis- play of weakness."

Now the younger of the two girls sat on a stool, using all the remaining room in the cabin, holding a mug of her own on her lap, nodding more sympa- thy and understanding, trying—although she knew the effort itself constituted an indictment—not to take the older girl's golden curly hair and turned-up nose as a personal affront.

"I guess you Antimacassarites mount that sort of expedition all the time?"

"These lowborn brigands style themselves official naval vessels of the Securitasian government. As if barbaric savages like that could have a navy, let alone a government! They make frequent, cowardly, thieving sorties into our territory and must be driven off before they do harm to our smaller vessels."

Elsie sipped her tea, rising vapors from the hot liquid rendering the lenses of her glasses opaque for a moment. She tried hard not to feel grateful. Even sick and exhausted, Goldberry was everything Elsie wished to look like—and didn't.

"How did it turn into a major war?"

Goldberry shook her head, tossing her curls.

"I am not altogether certain, child."

"Elsie," replied the "child," her efforts focused now on trying not to grit her teeth.

"In any event, word came to my captain-mother of a Confederate presence upon the Sea of Leaves, far from where Confederates might normally be expected. Ordinarily, the Leafnavy would, in Her Kindness' name, overlook such an intrusion."

She leaned forward and sipped her tea, looking at Elsie over the rim of the cup.

" 'Word' consisting of furtive messages relayed vessel to vessel by spark-gap radio"—Elsie couldn't resist grinning—"which you Antimacassarites and the Securitasians regard as a military secret? Our radio-astronomers, the only Confederates with any use remaining for the electromagnetic spectrum, have another word for it."

Goldberry sat back, her tea forgotten, startled by Elsie's vehemence. Elsie was startled, too, aware she was being unpleasant for no good reason, but unable to help herself.

"Anyway, that's probably a good policy, Goldberry. Muzzle-loading cannon—or is it flamethrowers? —wouldn't last long against lasers and plasma guns, would they?"

Goldberry lifted a well-formed and defiant chin. When she lowered her naturally violet-shaded eyelids, momentarily laying her long, dark lashes against her creamy cheeks, and smiled a superior smile, she displayed—by Elsie's envious estimate—no more than seventy or eighty white and perfect teeth.

"Securitasian primitives use flamethrowers aboard their crude vessels, child. We of the Leafnavy have the latest, most advanced catapults Antimacassarite science can devise, capable of hurling greekfire more than three hundred—"

Elsie put a hand up, trusting it not to become a fist of its own accord. She wondered whether Goldberry appreciated the fact that, by revered and long-established custom, Confederates were forbidden only one act: the initiation of physical force. That custom alone would have sent any "intruder" packing, had the Antimacassarites simply thought to claim right-of-property on the Sea of Leaves. That custom alone was what kept Elsie now from rearranging Goldberry's white and perfect teeth, every time she heard herself being called "child."

"Okay, Goldberry, okay. I promise I'm appropriately impressed. So what happened?"

"We learned these Confederates possessed some object, some item of gimcrackery, in my captain-mother's words, that the Securitasians desired. Something that might have given them an unfair military advantage. Naturally we could not permit this."

Aside from the question of what tourists were doing that close to the equator, Elsie wondered what they had that the Securitasians wanted. It wasn't so much a matter of advanced technology. Confederates never tried to keep that kind of hopeless, unprofitable secret. It had to be something the colonists could comprehend (unlike the lasers and plasma guns she'd mentioned) and keep in repair. Floodlights, maybe, for night assaults, or even antique cartridge machine guns.

"And naturally," Elsie suggested, "you tried to beat the Securitasians to it. And naturally, whoever you attempted to hold up busted your little red wagon for good and probably treated the Securitasians to a dose of the same medicine."

"These things never used to happen," Goldberry wailed, back to the ragged edge and close to tears, "before you—before your Confederacy—came to Majesty!"

"I understand," Elsie replied, keeping one inward eye on the girl's medical readouts, but unable to hide her sarcasm. "It's the victim's fault because two muggers injure themselves quarreling over something they both want from him?"

"Those murderers cut my ship in half before my very eyes! Mercy knows what befell the captain-mother!"

Elsie opened her mouth, but whatever protest she planned was interrupted by polite scratching at the doorframe. Her father stuck his head through the membrane, making him look like a taxidermist's trophy hanging somewhat lower on the wall than was customary.

"As you've no doubt realized," he informed the two females, "we're under way. We'd only intended running out a few miles on the surface and returning to Talisman, but things are going so well, there's no reason not to continue the full range of tests. I came to see whether Goldberry mightn't appreciate a lift home."

Elsie suppressed an expression of gratitude, glancing at the girl. The latter shook her pretty head.

"That is good of you, sir. The only home I have ever known is with the Fleet and the Government-in-Exile, sir, scattered over the Sea of Leaves precisely so they may not be discovered. I seriously doubt that you will ever find them, sir."

"I was aware of that, Leftenant Commander," Howell answered.

He was aware of more than that, Elsie knew. When Confederates had arrived on Majesty, willing to treat the rights of their predecessors—who'd been living at the poles and nowhere else—as moral absolutes, offering to purchase whatever land they needed, they'd been astonished when the "natives" had refused to bargain, but had packed up their entire small nation-state aboard vehicles intended for travel on the Sea of Leaves and departed to a self-imposed, unnecessary exile.

"However," the coyote continued, "we'll be sur-

veying the area between here and the equator as a
part of our tests and Elsie's scientific commission.
Perhaps we'll run into some Antimacassarite vessel
that can take you home. Meantime—"

"Meantime, I accept your generous offer, sir,"
Goldberry interrupted, throwing back the blankets,
having forgotten she had nothing on, "provided you
direct me to some useful task aboard this vessel so I
shall not remain beholden to you and your little
daughter for your kindness. I have rested. I am
healthy. I am strong. I can work. Sir."

"Dear me."

It was all Howell could think of to say. He may
have been a coyote, but he'd been raised among
"naked apes" and was as subject to embarrassment
as any human. He averted his eyes and turned his
back, creating a different sort of taxidermist's trophy.

Elsie started to laugh, but caught herself wincing
at the sight of Goldberry's long, smooth legs. This
envy business was getting out of hand, turning her
into a very unpleasant sort of person. Sooner or
later, she was going to have to give herself a good,
stern talking-to. "Little daughter," indeed! It didn't
help that the graceful, slender officer was also a
head taller than the Earth girl.

Elsie was also about to disagree with the leftenant
commander's diagnosis, when a glance at the medical readouts—rather, at the images they sent her
implant—told her what the older girl had claimed
was true. Her readings were normal. Her rate of
recovery was astonishing. Maybe a life of military
discipline had something going for it. Despite the
fair, full, female form she'd just revealed, it had
certainly made a man of Goldberry MacRame.

"As we saw when we came aboard," Howell observed, "the *Victor Appleton* is covered with thou-

sands of bristles, rooted in the hull and slanting sharply backward."

"Tea and sympathy," as Elsie found herself thinking of it, which had begun in Goldberry's cabin, had by now moved to the galley, where Howell and Grossfuss had joined Elsie and the leftenant commander, leaving the subfoline on its own to circle on the featureless surface of the Sea of Leaves at low speed.

The Antimacassarite wore the tatters of her uniform again, laundered in the *Victor Appleton*'s modest facilities. She had also, with evidence of relief, strapped her pistol back around her slender waist. Elsie had hopes of getting her into one of the spare smartsuits aboard. It would monitor her health and could be programmed to resemble any weird regalia she desired. But that could wait. At the moment, Howell was explaining the operating basics of the odd vehicle they occupied.

"These bristles can be rotated 180 degrees, theoretically reversing our direction of travel—that's one of the novel features we're here to test. When she's under way, however, they do nothing but vibrate very rapidly, and with such a slight motion it can scarcely be seen, rendering the subfoline 'slippery' in one direction only. This is what makes her move forward, the so-called 'Tente Principle' which first appeared in toys of the twentieth-century United States—"

Elsie nodded.

"Like the ancient Aztecs, who never developed any grown up use for wheels."

"Quite so," her father answered, "and like those pre-Columbian wheels, this principle was never applied to full-scale vehicles before the opportunity represented by the Sea of Leaves."

"Vibratin' bristles, you say?" Grossfuss scratched his head. "I don't think I get it."

Elsie watched Howell trying to remain patient with the yeti, remembering he'd been a last-minute substitute for the mechanic Hellertech had hired, one reason they'd thought it a good idea to enlist Goldberry's additional assistance.

"It's difficult to explain," he told Grossfuss, "but simple enough, once understood. The bristles push away the leaves that surround the *Victor Appleton*, loosening their hold on her, opening a place for her, as it were. Normally, such vibration would move her back and forth, side to side, in any random direction."

"But for the backward slant of the bristles?" Goldberry offered.

"Which ensures"—Howell gave her a pleased and toothy grin—"she'll only move in one direction: forward."

Grossfuss asked, "Do we steer with the bristles, too?"

"Why, no. Her prow, as I'm sure you've noticed, is almost like a needle, capable of swiveling in any direction, threading her way through the vegetable tangle."

Seeing a possible flaw for the first time, an odd expression came over Elsie's face, as if she were the first person who'd ever noticed the Tower of Pisa was leaning.

"Can they overcome gravity, as well?"

Grossfuss elevated his white, shaggy eyebrows, but the effect was lost on his three companions because the rest of his forehead was white and shaggy, as well.

"Does she expect the *Victor Appleton* to fly?"

"No, my friend." Howell chuckled. "I believe she wonders whether, once she's submerged—"

"Subfoliated," insisted his daughter, "from the Latin—"

"Very well, once she's *subfoliated,* will her bristles bring her back to the surface? Yes, in theory, working against the resistance of the medium she travels in."

Goldberry's brow wrinkled prettily. Everything she did was like that. Why in Henry Louis Mencken's name, thought Elsie, did she have to be so darned beautiful?

"I am afraid it is I who does not altogether understand you now, Captain."

"Captain?" Howell paused before he replied. "I hadn't thought of it that way before. I believe I rather like it. Captain . . ."

"I suggest that you answer her, Captain-Father, before you become drunk with newfound authority."

Howell cleared his throat, a peculiar habit, since he didn't use his real voice to speak, but a vocal synthesizer driven by his implant and attached to his backpack harness.

"Well, you see, my dear, there are so many of the bristles, each bearing only a fraction of our weight. Their slant, of course, prevents us moving backward."

"This much, I have understood, Captain."

"Yes, well, as they vibrate, some wobble up over various leaves and twigs, supporting a bit more than their share, while others follow suit, gradually working the vessel forward, bit by bit, even if 'forward' happens also to be 'upward.' Because there are so many bristles, it should be a rather smooth and rapid process. But it's something we want to test most thoroughly."

Goldberry nodded with considerable enthusiasm. "I should think so!"

"Ciliae!" Elsie blurted, surprising even herself.

Howell gave her a concerned look.

"You understand the principle well enough, my dear. I don't believe you're silly, at all."

"I meant, *Captain*"—Elsie peered hard at her father, trying to determine whether this last remark had been serious or was another one of what he considered jokes—"she propels herself with vibrating hairs, like a microscopic animal."

"What keeps us," asked Grossfuss, "from bein' vibrated t'pieces?"

"An excellent question, my dear fellow. The bristles, you see, vibrate out of phase, canceling any such tendency. We're running on one-tenth power, now, and in dead silence. I seriously doubt whether even at full power we should hear the faintest humming. She certainly made no noise on the test stand, on Ceres."

This evoked nodding around the table, even from Goldberry, unaware that Ceres was the largest of the Old Solar Asteroids.

"However," Howell's tone changed a bit, "we've not, as yet, discussed the power plant. The first thing you should all understand thoroughly is that nothing must ever interrupt the flow of energy through its superconducting coils."

"Why not, sir?" Goldberry asked.

"Because, my dear, if it ever does, we shall all die in a most spectacular manner."

CHAPTER V:
Girl Talk

"Puccini . . ."

Goldberry MacRame's voice was muffled, and her features concealed, by the opaque-visored smarthelmet she was using to scan the Sea of Leaves. The paratronic device relayed more than a dozen kinds of information to the eyes, ears, and other senses, almost as if the wearer had a cerebro-cortical implant.

"Verdi," she continued, "Mozart, Wagner, Mercury, Townshend, and Parsons."

The morning was brightly sunlit, fresh with sweet-smelling breezes. Overhead, the sky was an unbroken bowl of blue, although at the eastern horizon, contrasting with the glowing emerald of the sea, a low palisade of purple-gray promised another of the afternoon thundershowers that were a daily feature at this latitude. Meanwhile, the vessel plowed along at a leisured thirty miles per hour.

Over the past few days, Goldberry and her shipmates had discovered that, despite her returning health, a result of rest and good food, and the best intentions on the part of the Antimacassarite to make some payment for her passage aboard the experimental subfoline, there wasn't a great deal she *could* do. Like most Confederate structures the *Victor Appleton* was, from tapered stem to blunted stern, self-cleaning—even more so than the restau-

42

rant Elsie and Howell had visited their first day on Majesty, since cleanliness was more than just desirable from an aesthetic standpoint—it was vital to the vessel's proper function.

Even the galley was automated, and a person can only make so many pots of coffee.

Elsie found herself likewise unemployed. Howell and Grossfuss had decided to wring the new machinery out on the surface before burrowing beneath it. Her part of the bargain was to report on subsurface biology, although the task fell beyond her expertise as a student of intelligent life. What made the situation worse was that, either they'd chosen an area of the planet remarkable for barrenness (discounting the living sea itself, an incredible mass consisting of a single species of plant life that filled the view from horizon to horizon), or, test results to the contrary, the *Victor Appleton* made some noise, at some frequency, which frightened the wildlife away before it could be observed.

Consequently, once the girls had made the happy discovery that, while no area on the hull was devoid of bristles, shallow, foot-long slots grooved the entire surface, into which the bristles could be programmed to fold flat when it was convenient, nothing could confine them to the comparative indoor gloom of the subfoline, where the only outside view available was relayed from sensors on the hull.

Aft of the subfoline, Elsie could see a wake of disturbed vegetation writhing back into place. She'd read that the sea was unusually mobile for plant life, but until now hadn't believed it. Of course, the smarthelmet operated indoors as well as out. Back in the Old Solar Asteroids, Howell had anticipated the necessity of recruiting a native guide, human or otherwise, and had made appropriate provisions for non-implanted individuals. It was even possible to program sections of the inner walls as viewscreens, conveying full-color three-dimensional pictures of what the vessel's sensors saw. Many architectural surfaces in the Confederacy possessed this capability. The restaurant table could have functioned in this manner, just as it had disposed of insect pests.

Still, Goldberry had insisted, and Elsie had agreed, that it just wasn't the same.

Any amount of uncluttered "deckspace" could be created by folding unused bristles, and the pair rode outside for hours at a time. This made Elsie's latest task much easier.

"*Hoedons allniiwdytiip,* I would appreciate your keeping an eye on the leftenant commander for me," Howell had told her. "As long as her qualities as an individual are unknown—"

Elsie had snorted.

"*Ku sro kmexytiip piimadu al Pah,* you can say *that* again and file it in triplicate!"

They had sat together in the galley. To confer in private—though the measure struck the coyote and his daughter as impolite—they used Fodduan, one of the lamviin languages, which they were certain neither Goldberry, her head presently covered by the smarthelmet, nor Grossfuss, doing his turn at the controls, understood.

"Once ought to be sufficient," Howell answered. "I wish I understood why you've taken such a dislike to the young lady. *Waad heipiiriisod,* it's quite unlike you."

"Maybe"—Elsie pushed her glasses back—"because she's always going on about that stupid, *eisavdesyv* empire she belongs to. Or because she's condescending, contemptuous, haughty—without any quality to justify it—and basically a mean person."

"Elsie—"

"You asked, Daddy, now let me finish—*komyobo fo,* I need this! Maybe it's because she's all teeth, hair, and legs, with no brains or *vedevsod* at all.

Maybe it's because she's a classic authoritarian personality who sucks up disgustingly to whomever she perceives to be in power—you—while treating Grossfuss as a *woenets* menial. That is, when she acknowledges his existence at all."

She sighed, looking down, unfocused, at her hands where they rested on the tabletop.

"Or maybe it's because, although I'm only four years younger than she is—at the most—and have a degree worth a brace of doctorates, let alone half a dozen *Student Prince* commissions like hers, she never calls me anything but 'child.' "

"You don't resent it," Howell observed, "when our *faitseytain* friend calls you 'kid.' "

"*Ta, Y hatas.* Not much, anyway. He doesn't mean anything but affection by it, you know that. He'd probably scratch you on the head and call you 'pooch' if he—"

Howell stiffened comically.

"*Grrr!* He does and I'll give him a dose of rabies!"

Elsie laughed, as she always did, sooner or later, during one of these "serious" conversations. Her father was a pretty fair country praxeologist himself, she thought.

"Maybe I resent Goldberry most because, despite her miserable condescension—and *uoer,* the fact that she's taller and prettier than I'll ever be—now I'm supposed to keep her company, put up with her militant ignorance, and be polite to her. Father, why do you always have to be so blasted polite?"

The Fodduan idiom Elsie had used, "*livvytiip tyno,*" meant "damply courteous," appropriate to a planet whose natives regarded water as a poison. She had a natural fascination with, and understanding of, alien life-forms. Now, although she'd seen no animal larger than a cockroach—she was hoping for a glimpse, however brief and far away, of the real Majestan natives, the taflak—Goldberry told her stories of huge and terrifying monsters she'd encountered. Thrown together by idleness, and despite their differences, the two had begun to enjoy a sort of "girl talk," concerning the leftenant commander's career, matters of scientific interest to both, and Elsie's tales of life in the Confederacy.

"You are—I cannot remember, how did you call it, child?—a *praxeologist?*"

This had been the topic earlier that morning, as they examined the country they passed through, Goldberry from within the helmet, Elsie raising the face-covering of her hood in order to employ the sensory-enhancing powers of her smartsuit. Her implant required data to work with; her suit enjoyed a better vantage than the sensors in the low-lying hull. Looking like an old-fashioned scuba diver's wetsuit—with the hood turned backwards so that, when it wasn't in use, it hung at the wearer's chest like a bib—its rubbery surface was capable, not just of deceiving the eye by adopting any appearance its wearer desired, but of absorbing and processing optical information in a wider range than the visible spectrum.

"Praxeologist, that's right."

The Antimacassarite rolled the word around in her mouth as if she didn't like its taste.

"And your—the captain, I mean—is . . . I cannot remember what you called that, either, child. In any case, I have never heard of either occupation."

Be nice, Lysandra, thought Elsie, calling herself by the middle name she liked better than her first, *no matter what it costs. Even if she is an ignorant* niimis, *Goldberry's our guest.* Despite the lack, so far, of anything constructive to do, she hadn't had time—hadn't made it yet—for the good, stern talking-to she'd promised herself. She smiled, deriving comfort from the fact that she was better at certain things than Goldberry, but as things stood now, it would take more than educated familiarity with a word or two to make up for natural advantages (at what, she didn't dare ask herself) she felt Goldberry enjoyed.

"Don't be afraid to mention that Howell's my father. The arrangement's unusual even in the Confederacy. We're proud of it. He's also a dagnystician—the word you wanted—a specialized kind of entrepreneur. The field's named for one of its early practitioners."

"Yes"—Goldberry nodded—"but what is an entrepreneur?"

Elsie sighed. "I guess the best way is to explain how he got to be a dagnystician. The first thing he says he remembers wanting to be was an operatic tenor."

Elsie paused, waiting for a response.

"You do savvy opera?"

Goldberry had nodded, but then, she'd done that before asking what an entrepreneur was. Elsie braced herself to explain a subject she knew nothing about.

"Puccini," the Majestan officer had offered before Elsie could think of what to say, or even how to begin, "Verdi, Mozart, Wagner, Mercury, Townshend, and Parsons."

Goldberry shrugged off the helmet, shook her hair out, blinked her eyes into focus. Elsie laughed: she'd forgotten they shared a common cultural heritage, although, from Goldberry's viewpoint—skewed by the physics of her ancestors' voyage here—the culture was thousands of years old. The original vessels would have departed the Solar System stocked to the gunwales with music, movies, history and science recordings, edited, of course, to suit the bias of colonial leaders. That any memory of Earth's achievements had survived that, and dozens of centuries of warfare and collapse, was something of a phenomenon in itself.

Before she could answer, another distraction: Grossfuss had taken them in a sweeping circle ten miles in extent. Facing east—and the clouds—again, for the first time in several minutes, Elsie thought she could discern a difference. She raised the hood of her suit to cover her face. According to a magnified image on its inner surface, she hadn't been mistaken. The stormclouds were higher on the horizon, billowy at the top, forming a black-purple cliff-face toward which the subfoline was headed. They were headed toward the subfoline, as well. Bad afternoon weather was moving in faster than it had the day before.

She thought back to the orbital atmospheric patterns she'd studied before leaving the *Tom Sowell Maru*. Given the low topography of the Sea of Leaves, much like the plains where her father had been born, tornados weren't unlikely. She hoped Howell, busy with his tests, was keeping an eye on the weather.

"For that matter," she told Goldberry, picking up the thread of conversation, "Howell still wants to be an operatic tenor, but . . . well, in the beginning he blamed it on a lack of suitable roles, even on costuming. It's difficult finding a suit of armor his size. In the end, he was honest enough to realize that nobody likes to listen to a coyote howling, not even another coyote."

Goldberry shook her head, a touch of genuine sympathy softening her superior expression. She sat down on the deck, folding her legs in front of her, spread a cloth she'd brought with her, unholstered and unloaded her pistol—a peculiar magazine-fed revolver-automatic hybrid; Elsie noticed its cartridges were of white plastic, triangular in cross section—and drew a small hex wrench from a belt pouch. Watching the Antimacassarite remove paired sheet-metal housings to clean the magazine well, barrel, and rotor with a small brush, she shrugged.

"Don't feel too bad. He's *directed* two operas, amateur productions: Rothbard's *John Galt* at the Coprates Civic Auditorium and Lube Shoppe on Mars, before I was born; and Schulman's *Die Lasermaus* in the Centaurus System just before we came here."

In her mind, Elsie could hear the score of the more somber of the twentieth-century works, remembering the words from her father's old bubble recording. " *'I swear, by my life and my love of it'*," she caught herself humming, " *'that I will never—'*

"That was after he began his second career, if you count flopping as a singer his first, hiring himself out as what a detective friend, who helped him get started, called a 'private nose.' "

She shivered as the breeze of their passage increased, accompanied by a sudden temperature drop. Her suit compensated, but the front was moving in, and nothing could be done about that.

Goldberry proved as unfamiliar with private investigation as she was with praxeology and dagnystics. Antimacassarite investigations were carried out by Her Kindness' (whoever she was) military police. Elsie had to explain how, in the Confederacy, no government existed to hunt down criminals. Even murder was pursued in civil courts. Individuals were as responsible for carrying out whatever notion of justice they believed in, as they were for their own physical security. The older girl was scandalized, her cleaning brush hanging suspended in midair, her pistol forgotten in her other hand, while she attempted to absorb and deal with another person's peculiar customs. She hadn't had much practice.

"Individuals taking the law into their own hands? That leads only to chaos!"

"Any other kind of law's a dangerous illusion, Goldberry. Where can anything ever be, the law included, except in the hands of individuals? What else is there? Besides, life *is* chaos. And one thing you can say about chaos is that it works."

Goldberry shook her head sadly. Elsie went on.

"Anyway, the P.I. biz led Howell to discover his talent for dagnystics. As I said, that's a form of entrepreneurship, you might even say applied praxeology, consisting of bringing especially diverse elements together into a coherent, profitable whole."

Goldberry scratched her head, looking for a moment a bit like Grossfuss. She returned, as if seeking refuge, to her task, paying careful attention to the small spaces around the hammer and trigger of her old-fashioned weapon. By now her brush was gray-black with powder soot and dirtied lubricant.

She looked up again.

"Profit is theft."

"I guess I should have expected that. Your culture's not very ethically or economically sophisticated, is it? No offense, but can't you see that's why it *stays* primitive and doesn't have anything better to do than fight wars?"

From the look on Goldberry's face, Elsie could see her struggling, just as Elsie did with her, to remain polite, and hurried on against the chance she might lose her struggle—and against the failing daylight, losing its own struggle with the overcast.

"Okay, here we have a world that, discovered millenia ago, remains almost unexplored. Follow me? Unexplored means unexploited; zillions in untapped potential profit, pardon a dirty word. My father learns of this, and looks up a small research company—we're keeping the name secret for the time being—willing to do the exploring, in hopes of doing some of the exploiting."

She awaited objections, expecting to explain private venture capitalism. Goldberry, still exercising restraint, made more work of replacing the halves of her pistol than necessary and used a heavier hand with the L-shaped wrench than was perhaps wise.

"Right. Now, another company, Hellertech, is interested in testing its new power plant, and a third outfit, until now limited to toy manufacture, is brought in, and what do you get?"

Goldberry looked resigned: "Dagnystics."

"Right"—Elsie smiled—"as manifested in the *Victor Appleton*."

"You mentioned 'applied praxeology.' Tell me again, child, what praxeology is."

"*Grrr*—it's a disciplined, nonquantitative study of the actions of intelligent beings. Historically, the discipline concerned itself with humans. Since we've had a chance to see that the same rules apply to all sentients—think about it; they must—it's come to include all consciously self-aware species."

Goldberry used the now-sooty, oil-stained cloth to wipe off her wrench and brush, restoring them to their pouch on her belt, and reloaded her pistol in a practiced motion, using a stripper clip from another pouch. She fed the plastic cartridges she'd removed from the pistol, one by one, into the emptied stripper before putting it away, and began wiping down the outside of the weapon.

"Such as the taflak?"

Elsie couldn't decide—was that a raindrop that had fallen on her hand?—what mixture of contempt and curiosity colored the Antimacassarite's tone.

"Lamviin, freenies, yeti—and my dad. Thus the discipline subsumes all those earlier, pseudoscientific subjects like anthropology, sociology, political science, economics . . ."

"Those I have heard of."

"You have my sympathy. Its prime tenet is that

the behavior of sentient beings arises from a complex mix of billions of hereditary and environmental inputs, plus uncountable acts of free will, containing too many variables to be reduced to numbers."

"But statistically"—Goldberry nodded—"if you put enough individual units together—"

"Asimov's fallacy—one of them, anyway." Elsie shook her head, certain now that she'd felt a raindrop spatter her cheek. "Aggregate sentient behavior involves more variables, and any attempt to quantify it is even sillier. It can be predicted only poorly, and only by logic, rather than mathematics."

Goldberry frowned.

"It isn't that bad," Elsie told her. "To any extent it's a science (and unlike discredited pursuits like behaviorism, Keynesianism, or astrology, nobody claims it is), the place praxeology begins, its equivalent to the atom or quark, is individual action."

"We are taught," Goldberry mused, "that individuals count for nothing against the well-being of others. When I was a child, my captain-mother showed me a bucket of water, ordered me to thrust my hand into it. When I removed it, no hole remained."

"Proving?"

Without question, rain had begun to fall. She could see it making leaves nod all around her, darkening the surface of the deck. Goldberry reholstered her pistol not a moment too soon, fastening the military flap over it, and began wiping her hands off.

"That no individual," she asserted, "is indispensable."

Elsie nodded. She wouldn't have mentioned it—at the moment she might have traded the fact straight across for any of what she conceived to be the older girl's undeniable charms—but she'd become one of the Confederacy's most respected praxeologists at an incredible age, and was now in her own element.

"It might if life were a bucket of water. I have a coffee mug at home that claims it's 'just a chair of bowlies.' The parable's common throughout the galaxy and supports collectivism in many primitive societies. Sodde Lydfan savages use a tightly woven basket filled with sand. But figure it out for yourself, Goldberry: the individual exists without the group. The group can't exist without individuals, the concept has no meaning. In praxeology, nothing proceeds without consideration of the individual as an indispensable element, the one element early 'social sciences' overlooked—or sneered at—and the reason why nothing they had to say was ever very useful, or even made much sense."

Elsie gave the other girl a close look, wondering whether she was making a dent. This wasn't their first such discussion. She was beginning to feel discouraged about prospects for dragging Goldberry into the twenty-first century. She wouldn't, however, give up without a—

"Excuse me, ladies . . ."

Elsie glanced toward the permeable spot on the deck they'd been using as a hatch. Howell's disembodied head was sticking up through the hull. Elsie turned back to grimace at Goldberry.

"Ladies, he calls us?"

Goldberry shrugged.

"Crewpersons," Howell amended. "I suggest you come in out of the rain, since this disturbance seems severe even for Majesty. The news services are saying it will turn into a flock of tornados, so I intend taking us below the surface sometime in the next ten minutes."

CHAPTER VI:

The Dancing Leviathan

In the galactic history of transportation, nothing had ever been quite like the H.S.P. *Victor Appleton*.

Prefabricated on Ceres, largest of the Old Solar Asteroids, in the inky blackness of Earth's metaphorical backyard between Mars and Jupiter, she'd been assembled under Howell's supervision aboard the starship, *Tom Sowell Maru*, and, having passed the surface trials to which he had subjected her, was about to burrow into the miles-thick vegetation covering the surface of the planet Majesty.

At Howell's urging, the females gathered their belongings and followed him down through the permeability in the hull, hurrying forward to catch a glimpse of viewscreen as he gave the order to dive.

It is a law of the universe that everything takes longer than it ought to in order to make good drama (except for those occasional, horrible events which take place much too fast) and carrying out Howell's order, especially this first time, was governed by that law. He and the grumbling Grossfuss had a lengthy checklist to work through, one item at a time—had it been printed out and bound between covers, it would have been five inches thick—including such details as verifying the proper function of the experimental power plant, reversing any overlooked permeabilities remaining in the hull (the expression "screen doors in a submarine" kept coming to Elsie's mind), monitoring life-support systems, and calibrating the subfoline's rudimentary navigational instruments.

Before every indicator had transformed itself from red to green—the *Victor Appleton*'s equivalent of a submarine's "Christmas tree" panel was purely imaginary, consisting of an implant-generated display that was literally "all in their heads"—the Sea of Leaves unveiled a last surprise for them. As the subfoline's needle prow began to tilt downward, toward Majesty's hidden surface, one of the predicted tornados gave her a playful farewell slap on the rump which set her spinning—the motion was actually a yaw—like a pestle in a mortar.

Inboard, her occupants were saved by wrist-thick tendrils that instantly extruded themselves from the rubbery walls and under-decking, part of the vessel's safety systems, snapped out and wrapped themselves around four bodies and assorted arms and legs, and afterward, when the danger of being dashed around like a bean in a can had passed, slumped and melted back into the floor and bulkheads. As they "subfoliated," the calm and quiet that followed seemed almost as noisy, in its own way, as the storm they had only just escaped.

"The *Victor Appleton* was designed to solve a number of mysteries about your planet."

Howell spoke to Goldberry as she settled into one of the pair of extra jump seats that had sprouted from the floor at his mental command, but without taking his eyes off the screen above the broad control panel in the subfoline's bow. Like the smarthelmet, it too had been rigged for the Antimacassarite's benefit, and the visual attention Howell paid it was, in fact, unnecessary. He could have supervised proceedings by means of his implant—he was monitoring the performance of the vessel's unusual engines in that manner—but it was hard for anyone to ignore the sight before them. Scientists and non-scientists alike, along with both kinds of natives, had long wondered what lay in the mysterious depths—in particular at the bottom—of the sea. Now, perhaps, they were going to get a chance to satisfy their wondering.

"The taflak," Goldberry responded, "believe a mighty civilization far below—the source of their myths and legends—was by the gods found wanting in some unnamed virtue, and, as punishment, was overwhelmed and covered by the leaves."

Elsie grinned, surprised the leftenant commander knew anything about the beliefs of the nonhuman dwellers upon the sea. The young Confederate had understood that the First Wavers, having discovered when they first arrived on Majesty that they couldn't exterminate the taflak, had resolved, forever afterward, to ignore them.

"Nobody can dispute the theory," she told Goldberry. "Sonar and radar, as well as devices peculiar to the paratronic spectrum, are useless for exploring the depths. Not much is known about the soil below, but the leaves seem to absorb a high metallic content from it."

Goldberry accepted this lack of information in silence. She understood that the subfoline must feel its way along, a yard at a time. It would be quite a strain on the pilots. Howell and Grossfuss would be alternating duty, pausing for frequent rest-breaks. Already the Himalayan, with his huge hands on the controls, refrained from joining the conversation, as he guided the *Victor Appleton*'s prow through what looked like a passable opening in the leaves.

The machine pitched forward—Goldberry and Elsie braced themselves on the slanted deck—intruding itself further into the vegetation. As they slipped deeper below the surface, the last light of the sky disappeared behind them. Onscreen, leaves, stems, twigs, and branches parted before the bow. Visibility was limited—Grossfuss switched on powerful lamps mounted along the outer hull—to a couple of feet and no more. Soon, the explorers had lost contact with the surface altogether, and entered a world of predation, parasitism, and decay.

"Two fathoms," Grossfuss muttered.

"Twelve feet," Howell translated for Goldberry's benefit, adding, "or, if you prefer, just under four meters. Hold her here, if you please, Obregon, forward dead slow."

He turned to the two girls.

"We're quite near the equator, at the deepest point in the leaves. Our first excursion will be carried out, as on the surface, along a shallow, descending spiral ten miles in diameter. We'll take our time and see what we can see."

Already, the viewscreen was filled with weird and wonderful—and frightening—sights. Until now, Elsie had been disappointed over the lack of wildlife. Now many a strange organism could be observed, some driven away, others attracted by the lights.

"Look at that!" Elsie pushed her glasses back into place and fought to keep herself from shouting. "Doesn't it look like a big transparent blue-green spider? There's another! Ugh!"

Goldberry laughed. "A *tugwush*, child, no bigger than your hand. They migrate to the surface at night and may be caught with nets. Very tasty steamed over a fermented liquid."

"Like soft-shelled crab," Howell offered, "or lobster?"

Unacquainted with ocean animals, Goldberry shrugged, peering at the screen.

"I'll stick with crab and lobster"—Elsie shuddered—"if that's okay. What in Lysander's name is *that?*"

What had been a vague reptile-shape now was no

more than a sharp-toothed mouth as a creature
tried to chew a video pickup from the hull.

"Zoom-snake."

Grossfuss tossed a glance over his shoulder. He
was beginning to get a feel for the unusual vessel
and could afford to relax a bit.

"Surface-dwellers, too, most times. Comes season
t'spawn, once a year, they leap into the air an' fly
on foldin' membranes which I'm told, once in their
evolutionary history, were gills. Impressive as all
get-out, but they can be a nuisance when you're
paintin' a house or hovercraft. Like sea gulls, if
y'get my meanin'."

Goldberry reddened while Elsie giggled.

"Be that as it may, we've completed our initial
circle," Howell announced. "Take her down another
couple of fathoms, if you please, Mr. Grossfuss."

"Aye, aye, Cap'n, steady as she goes!"

The yeti turned to the girls, a broad grin spreading across his furry features.

"I just love talk like that."

Over the next several hours, the travelers continued their sight-seeing from a unique new perspective, observing not just the strange and wonderful
wildlife of the planet, but, with their instruments,
the passage of various surface craft. Most were Confederate hovercraft, speeding by at several hundred
miles per hour, unaware of the subfoline below.
Despite their size, their weight was so well distri-
buted on broad air-cushions, they only rippled the
vegetation overhead.

"Okay, explain this, if you can."

Elsie spoke after a long silence. She'd just returned from the galley a few steps aft with a mug of
chocolate in each hand, intended for herself and
Grossfuss. Her father and the leftenant commander
had turned down chances at a fourth—or was it

fifth?—both of them far more fascinated with what was to be seen on the screen.

"Y'got me, kiddo," Grossfuss yawned. "Any ideas, Cap'n?"

The image they referred to was a view back toward the surface. Whatever moved up there, crawling at a pitiable three or four miles per hour, was hidden by the leaves. But it compressed vegetation and left a detectable track that could be elaborated on by the subfoline's computer. The simulation resembled a worm the size of a small ocean liner, or worse, a centipede twice the length of the *Victor Appleton*. With an absent, human gesture of his retractable arm, Howell scratched his head.

"I'm afraid it has me stumped, Obregon. Leftenant Commander?"

Goldberry peered at the screen, frowning and shaking her head.

"I'm glad," Elsie offered, "it's up there and we're down here. I hope it doesn't decide to get in out of the sun! Anybody want anything else from the galley?"

"Galley!" came a shout from Grossfuss.

"Some significance," Howell inquired blandly, "attends this outburst?"

"That's a crankapillar we're seein' from underneath," the yeti informed the coyote, "or I'm a Neanderthaler's nephew."

Elsie understood at once why the word *galley* had set him off. The "crankapillar," a leaf-traversing vehicle devised by pre-Confederate colonials, was a sort of galley—in the sense of a big oceangoing vessel propelled by muscle power. Nodding at the screen, she summoned up the image of just such a machine.

"That's right!"

Grossfuss' observation was unnecessary. They examined a long train of primitive wagons, woven from dried sea-branches and connected by a wooden crankshaft turned, at the cost of backbreaking effort, by pairs of sweating, naked men chained by the ankles in each section. The crank was geared to tires three times a man's height, two on either side of each cart, which carried the machine along at a snail's pace. The rearmost was armed with crude, gigantic flamethrowers and had a broad, railed deck where overseers in fancy uniforms, protected by an awning from the sun, cracked whips over the heads of unprotected slaves.

"Disgusting!"

The hateful, fascinating image vanished as Elsie spoke, replaced by the original simulation. They could make out the depressions and compressions on the surface made by the vehicle's enormous wheels. The girl had hoped it was a machine from the leftenant commander's nation-state, but unfortunately, both for Elsie and Goldberry, crankapillars were used only by Securitasians, the latter's mortal enemies.

"I agree, child," Goldberry told her. "Let us destroy it!"

"I'm sorry," Howell replied, "but we Confederates can't just—"

"These animals raid us, murder our people, steal or destroy what we build. Did your Confederacy not eradicate the evil barons and bishops of the planet Sca?" Goldberry demanded tearfully. "Did it not alter the culture of Vespucci beyond recognizability?"

"Great Lysander's ghost," Howell exclaimed. "She's done her homework."

"Did you not infiltrate and subvert the Queendom of Afdiar?" the leftenant commander persisted, "and put a stop to human sacrifice on Obsidian?"

Elsie shook her head.

"Somebody's done her homework for her, anyway." With a finger-tap she shoved her glasses into

place and turned to face the Antimacassarite:
"Goldberry, we can't just jump in and interfere. The
Vespuccians altered their own culture—admittedly
with Confederate help—and none of the rest of those
things was done without a great deal of study and
planning."

"This was the case"—Goldberry gave an angry
sniff—"with the lamviin of Sodde Lydfe?"

Turning to her, Howell made a gesture that was
the closest he could come to a shrug.

"Whoever taught you these things told you the
truth, Goldberry, but the lamviin were about twenty
minutes away from a thermonuclear war. Even so,
the case is still debated. It's true Confederate custom allows us to interfere in order to preserve the
lives and rights of intelligent beings, but the grounds,
in this instance, would have to be slavery, and . . ."

"And?"

"And," Elsie put in, "although the mechanical
details differ, your people force slaves to propel
your screwmarans, just as the Securitasians do, don't
you?"

As if of its own accord, another brilliant, colorful
three-dimensional image took form on the screen,
acquired by Elsie from the subfoline's databanks,
updated by local news services on a continuing basis up to the moment they had subfoliated.

A pair of fat, gigantic woodscrew-shapes, each at
least a hundred yards in length, wound their way
across the Sea of Leaves. They were connected at
their large ends by a sort of flying bridge on which
a glint of window glass indicated a wheelhouse and
captain's cabin. Another, lighter structure connected
the pointed ends of the screws, so that they were
held rigidly parallel to one another.

In endless succession, long lines of men, no less
sweaty than the Securitasian galley slaves, no less
naked, marched along a central catwalk leading

from the vessel's double stern to its double bow, climbing onto treads—these were the "Steps" Goldberry had threatened them all with—cut along the vast screw-threads which, as the screws turned in opposite directions with the weight of the laborers rising upon them, pulled the screwmaran across the surface. When they reached the larger, rear end of the giant screws, the men climbed off the treads and back onto the catwalk, only to begin their terrible journey all over again.

The Antimacassarite ship represented an advance over the crankapillar, managing perhaps ten miles per hour to the Securitasians' three or four across the Sea of Leaves.

The image flared, searing itself into their minds, and vanished.

Goldberry was indignant: "Her Kindness' volunteer servitors are penitentials, child, *not* slaves!"

"What's in a name?" Grossfuss shook his head. "That's what they usta say about conscriptees an' taxpayers. Guess we'd hafta ask them, an' they might say different, mightn't they?"

Goldberry scowled, but failed to answer. The opening vocal line of Rothbard's opera *John Galt* came to Elsie's lips: " *'A is A—a thing is itself . . .' "*

Howell gave her a warning look, but not a word of admonition.

"Now that's settled"—Grossfuss cleared his throat—"think I'll— *Acceleratin' avalanche, what now?"*

Elsie experienced a bizarre flash of nostalgia for the lifeless surface. On the screen, before the widened eyes of the adventurers, a creature more gigantic than the crankapillar overhead insinuated itself through the leaves, heading straight for the subfoline. Its front end seemed to be all mouth. Its long flanks, dwindling in the perspective offered by the pickup, seemed to be all legs. It was the subfoline's instruments, limited as they were by the composition of the vegetation, which told them the animal was over two hundred yards in length.

Howell and Elsie glanced at Grossfuss; the yeti shrugged.

"Can-can."

It was Goldberry who spoke. Her companions could see at once how the thing on the screen had gotten its name. Its hundreds of legs were arranged in three long rows—trilateral symmetry dominated the native biology of Majesty—which, looked at a certain way, could have been a chorus line kicking up its heels. Any humor in the allusion was lost on them, however. The subfoline's crew had more than just the usual reasons to be anxious. In their journey across and through the Sea of Leaves, each of them—with the exception of the Antimacassarite— had found himself worrying from time to time about the huge, ferocious creatures reputed to live deep in the vegetation.

"They will eat anything"—she pointed at the toothy, triangular mouth—"anything at all."

"By Spooner's beard, I believe that specimen's jaws must be thirty feet across." To Elsie's surprise, as the monster grew steadily in the viewscreen, her father's calm, analytical voice was beginning to get on her nerves. "Ah well, anything big and strong enough to bite through our hull will receive a terrible surprise—"

"Not," his daughter argued, "that it would give us much satisfaction!"

Grossfuss grimaced; Goldberry looked a question at Howell.

"Indeed," the coyote replied, "for within the *Victor Appleton*'s powerful locomotory system, every electron she absorbs is stored in a superconducting toroid, to circle until the end of time—or until drawn off by induction."

Voice betraying annoyance, she prompted the pedantic canine.

"And . . ."

"And I'm afraid damaging that system—that is, interrupting the flow that races, ceaseless and without resistance, around its coils—would release the energy of a medium-sized atomic bomb."

"System's got advantages," Grossfuss apologized for the subfoline, "but if that circuit back there ever gets broke—"

"By the jaws," Howell added, "of some leviathan of the leaves, for example—"

"Yeah, for example, all that stored-up energy'll get set loose all at once, an'. . ."

"Kablooie?" Elsie suggested.

He waggled eyebrows at Goldberry and pointed a huge thumb at Elsie.

"What she said."

Goldberry eyed the creature in the viewscreen, coming closer and closer to the subfoline.

"What are we to do?"

"I'd given this matter some thought," Howell explained to the others. "You all know the *Victor Appleton*'s prow is needle-sharp and may be swiveled to steer the ship."

Three heads nodded as one.

"It had occurred to me it might also serve to threaten wild things in the depths and drive them away."

Somehow, despite his lack of human expression, the coyote managed to look pleased with himself.

"I have no idea who Victor Appleton was," Elsie told her father, "but, with all due respect, if the idea works, maybe this thing ought to be rechristened *Narwhal*."

"After Earth's long-tusked cetacean unicorn of the watery deep," Howell added because of Goldberry's expression. "I even believe it might prove easier than I first expected. Enormous creatures can afford more circumspection than smaller, more easily ingested organisms."

Goldberry nodded, uncertain.

"Oh yeah?" Panic had begun to bubble upward in Grossfuss' voice, "Well, y'better check your theory out with the can-can, Cap'n Nahuatl, 'cause here it comes!"

Nothing but mouth—surrounded by three clashing, saw-toothed jaws—could be seen ahead.

CHAPTER VII:

The Vacuole

Without warning or explanation, the huge jaws of the can-can closed before they'd reached the subfoline. The four aboard her watched as a sudden turn by the animal showed them a blurred and sweeping view of its hundreds of legs.

Before they knew it, the thing was gone.

"Close." Elsie blinked. Her glasses were down at the end of her nose again, but she forgot to push them back. "I wonder what made it change its mind."

"It has no mind to change, child"—Goldberry shook her head, curls bobbing—"but thinks only with its appetites and its fears. Something frightened it."

Grossfuss' jaw dropped. "What in the hairy Himalayas could scare that thing?" Apparently he hadn't believed Howell's theory about larger animals being more timid.

By now, neither did Howell.

"It is whispered"—the leftenant commander took a deep breath—"although I do not know who could have survived to tell the tale, that, in the Sea of Leaves, the deeper one goes, the larger and more ferocious the animals become."

"That's comfortin'," answered the yeti, his skin pale beneath his fur. "I think we're comin' to my stop pretty soon an' I'll get off. Anybody wanna join me?"

"Do not display your unseemly cowardice, man-like creature!"

Goldberry's voice changed; it no longer seemed like her own.

"The can-can too is a surface-dweller, at least part of the time. It may, with sufficient courage and cunning, be slain, as I have seen many a captain-mother do, commanding aboard the several noble vessels—I will remind you, only you Confederates belittle them with the appellation *screwmaran* —which I have been proud and privileged to serve upon. Many products of the can-can's body are use-ful to us, and, as the species goes, this was but a small one."

"'Manlike creature,' is it?"

For the first time, Grossfuss turned in his seat and looked directly at Howell and Elsie.

"You two gotta right t'know," he cautioned, "that all these here imposin' figgers of august authority she keeps goin' on about are little old grandmoth-erly ladies."

Goldberry's eyes flared, her voice still that of someone else.

"Uncouth animal! This is not the manner in which one speaks of the captain-mothers of Antimacassar and their supreme commander, the Great Grand-Admiral of the Fleet!"

"Yeah?" Grossfuss laughed. "Then how come their symbols of office are rockin' chairs, shawls, an' bifo-cal glasses?"

"These are merely the traditional symbols of dig-nity, wisdom, and—"

"Advanced senility," the yeti finished for her. "Now be a good little human an' lay off me for a while. We may be outa hot water with that can-can thingie, but this here vegetation's so dense an' fulla metal-lic compounds, we'll be lucky if the instruments're able t'see a lot deeper'n your pancake makeup, sweetie."

Goldberry turned to Howell, her cheeks flushed and her lips tight with anger, but it was in her own voice that she spoke, not that of the old women who had raised her.

"I am an officer and a warrior, Captain, is this—this *organism* to be permitted to speak to me in such a manner?"

Shrugging, Howell began a syllable, but was interrupted.

"Lookit, Leftenant Commander, warrior-lady, whatever you like: rather'n drag this out, I apologize."

She opened her mouth, outraged at such an easy, empty victory, but he pointed to the depth indicator.

"Sincerely. Now back off, if y'please—we're down almost a hundred feet, an' from here on, we ain't gonna get much warnin' in advance of what's ahead."

This, of course, was the reason it had been necessary to build the *Victor Appleton* in the first place. The importance of letting Grossfuss concentrate on his driving was something even a furious Goldberry could appreciate. By unspoken agreement, she and Elsie left the yeti to his navigation, with the coyote to assist, and retreated to the cabin where the Antimacassarite had been quartered.

There, as Elsie monitored the subfoline wildlife of Majesty with her implant, and with the aid of a repeater screen she'd summoned up on one wall of the miniature stateroom, she made notes while Goldberry talked. As she had up on deck, the leftenant commander spoke openly and at length of her life aboard ship, and of the endless war these old ladies of whom Grossfuss had been so contemptuous had waged against their bitter ememies for a thousand years before the coming of the Confederacy. From time to time, Elsie grinned, wondering whether her own wire-rimmed glasses might be a reason Goldberry spoke so freely and, however condescendingly, had begun to listen to her ideas, as well.

"Word came to us," she told Elsie, elaborating on her previous story of the three-sided battle, "of a fabulous treasure being offered Antimacassar by one of your Confederates. None but the captain-mothers knew what that treasure was."

If, in fact, even they knew, Elsie thought. *Any* item of Confederate technology might seem like a treasure to the backward nation-states ruling this portion of Majesty.

"But the signal came from within our territory, and we hastened in the direction indicated. To our regret and anger, others had heard the signal and were there first."

Elsie raised an eyebrow: "Securitasians?"

"No better than pirates—a brutal, male-dominated culture of crude barbarians!"

"So"—Elsie nodded—"you've told us before."

"And shall again, if need arise. Tell me, child, is Confederate civilization afflicted with pirates?"

Puzzled, Elsie looked away from the vegetation-filled viewscreen and into Goldberry's eyes.

"Yes, I suppose it is, in a small way." She patted one of the pistols she carried at her waist. "They certainly don't last long, and we don't worry about them much. Occasional crime's a sort of natural tax we all pay for being free."

Goldberry nodded. "As you, child, have told me before." She stared up at the overhead, as if musing to herself. "However, it might explain what happened, if Confederate pirates were in league with those of Securitas. For the offered treasure proved a trap.

"A great battle ensued, in which all Antimacassarite hands fought long and valorously. Against

Securitas alone, the engagement would certainly have been ours, but in the end, our ship was cut in half—straight down the catwalk, from stem to stern, as if she were fashioned of nothing more than wax!—by some diabolical device I am certain could not have been operated, let alone invented, by our enemy."

Preoccupied with her observations and notes, Elsie made reflexive, sympathetic noises.

"It must have been terrible."

Goldberry, sitting on the edge of her bunk, leaned forward, toward Elsie's chair, and tapped the younger girl on the shoulder with a long, slender finger.

"It was more terrible than I can say! I myself was thrown overboard, captured by taflak even more savage than Securitasians, and almost cooked and eaten!"

"What?"

Surprised, Elsie dropped the 'Com pad, a clipboard-sized electronic device on which she'd been making her notes. She'd undertaken a detailed preliminary study of the taflak, a hunter-warrior people, gentle and fearsome by turns. Nowhere in any of her references had cannibalism—defined by Confederates as eating the flesh of another intelligent being—been mentioned.

"Child, I swear to you I speak the truth, although such a thing is outside my experience, for I saw almost every minute of it myself. Many others of my ship, scooped up by the natives after the battle, suffered far worse than I, for they were thrust into a great boiling pot but were unable to get out as I did. I heard their dying screams as I escaped the camp of the savages."

However that may have been, Goldberry had somehow managed to escape from the "savage" and uncharacteristically hungry Majestan aborigines, she explained, striking out on her own across the open

Sea of Leaves. This wasn't an easy thing, for an unsupported human body tended to sink into the vegetation until it floundered, helpless and immobile, easy prey for the many nonintelligent lifeforms whose all-consuming voraciousness nobody questioned.

"How was it"—the Earth girl's assigned chores forgotten now, Elsie pursued her real profession and questioned Goldberry—"that you didn't happen to sink?"

Goldberry nodded, as if grateful that someone— even a child—was taking her at least this seriously.

"Antimacassarite vessels are equipped with—what is the Confederate expression?—'moss-shoes,' broad, woven devices one straps upon one's feet and—"

"Like snowshoes," Elsie supplied, "but—what an interesting idea—stocked just like inflatable rubber rafts or life preservers aboard an oceangoing ship."

"If you say so, child. I know nothing of such things. I had removed a pair from a locker just before I was thrown overboard. I managed somehow to hang on to them through the whole ugly ordeal with the taflak. Perhaps, in their savage, alien ignorance, they believed they were my feet. In any case, afterward, some violent event upon the sea followed which I cannot now remember. It makes my head hurt when I try . . ."

Elsie frowned. "What do you think it was?"

"Child, in my unsupported opinion—for I have nothing more than that to go by—it must have been an encounter with a monster such as the one we saw earlier today. Afterward, when it was over with, I found myself afoot once more."

"I know about that," the Earth girl replied, "wandering around in the vicinity of the South Pole, a quarter of a world away from where the battle with the Securitasians—and these renegade Confederates of yours—had taken place."

"Child—Elsie—I beg you, please do not make sport of me." Goldberry was close to tears again. "I truly cannot remember, and I find that, in itself, unbearably disturbing. I believe I must have been seized by some big, fast, animal. Perhaps a can-can, or one of the even larger, fiercer animals that can-cans fear. You are familiar, perhaps, with the phenomenon we call battle exhaustion? I believe my mind, already stretched to its limits by the fighting, and by losing my ship in so terrible, treacherous, and unexpected a manner, may have blanked out at the horror of being taken by the beast."

"And afterward?"

"Afterward, I have theorized, before I was eaten, I was dropped for some unknown and unknowable reason. Perhaps my predator was sick—or injured in the battle—and died."

"Or perhaps it was threatened or attacked"—Elsie nodded—"distracted, by yet another monster. As I've already had time to observe, Majesty has plenty of those to go around. I've seen falcons drop their prey when set upon—'mobbed,' it's called—by other birds."

"Yes, Elsie, so have I."

Elsie gave her another nod. Many Earth creatures had been brought to Majesty by First and Second Wavers alike—both by accident and by design—and had prospered in the new environment. However, she knew that the organisms every First Waver on Majesty called falcons didn't at all resemble the Earthly avians they'd been named for, but were more like giant flying sponges—with teeth. She also knew what Grossfuss thought: the leftenant commander may have deserted her ship in the heat of battle, hitching a ride on a passing Confederate hovercraft.

The three Confederates had discussed it thoroughly

during that time, earlier in the voyage, when the First Wave girl was still unconscious and recovering.

"Indeed," Howell had admitted to the yeti, lapping delicately at his coffee, "the simplest explanation would be that Goldberry is lying. Although it occurs to me that a somewhat more innocent interpretation is also possible."

"Yeah?" Grossfuss had sneered. "An' what might that interpretation be, Your Captaincy?"

"Perhaps," he'd suggested, "Goldberry was run down by a Confederate machine involved in the battle. A lone human being on foot would be hard to see against the leaves at three hundred miles per hour. Involved in some shady dealing, it picked her up out of guilt, but left her off at Talisman when she turned out to be all right."

In private, Howell had suggested to Elsie that Goldberry may have been Broached to the pole for some reason she was unaware of and which they might never learn. Her ship being cut in half (if her story was to be believed) sounded like misapplied Confederate technology. Not illegal: no Confederate law existed against anything to speak of, except the custom forbidding initiation of force; this ethical consideration seemed academic, since all the battle's participants were apparently enthuiastic, and, at least in their own terms, well equipped for it. However, few decent individuals would have encouraged taking such an advantage.

Now Goldberry was speaking once again, and Elsie found she'd missed most of it.

"I'm not sure I—"

Whatever Elsie was about to say was interrupted by a polite scratching at the door. Howell poked his head through its substance, appearing, once again, like an entry for the Boone and Crockett award. It was a startling effect, one which Elsie's father, often a practical joker, enjoyed very much, to Elsie's frequent embarrassment.

"Ladies," the coyote announced with a grin evident in his voice if not on his face, "I trust it will add to your subfoline sight-seeing pleasure if I call your attention to the fact that we're now a full thousand feet below the surface of the Sea of Leaves. Further, in fact, than any known exploration's ever penetrated."

Out of reflex, Elsie consulted her implant, which confirmed what her father had told them.

"It's our intention," he added, "to pause here for a short while, for a smattering of scientific testing and perhaps a small feast in honor of this momentous—"

Without warning, the *Victor Appleton* gave a sudden, violent lurch, and Howell's trophy-head slid to one side, struck the doorframe, and sank to the floor.

"Howell!"

The coyote opened his eyes and blinked them as he shook his head. Both females were on their knees beside him, running their hands through the thick fur around his neck and head.

"Dear me," he told them, "we must do this more often. In the meantime, however, I believe we'd better—"

"Captain!"

This time it was Grossfuss shouting, his voice loud enough, even from the control-space forward, to hurt their ears.

"Better come up here in a hurry!"

All three obeyed the summons. In an instant they were where they'd all been earlier, with Howell in the left-hand copilot's seat, and the two girls occupying temporary jump seats behind him and the yeti. Grossfuss was frantic, slapping at the controls, as the viewscreen told them an incredible tale.

"At first it looked like a solid green brick wall ahead of us," the Himalayan explained. "Solid—'bout the consistency of plexiplast. But by the time I'd put on the brakes—which we ain't got none of— she'd poked her nose right through."

On the screen, Elsie and the rest examined a sight reminiscent of the hollow candy eggs many cultures make and sell on holidays, with miniature scenery inside them, fashioned from sugar crystals and colored icing. This scene was tinted green, poorly lit, and seemed to be enveloped in a thin fog.

"What we got here's a 'vacuole,' an open space in the vegetation, bounded by some kinda barrier of hard-pressed leaves. As you can see, her nose is hangin' right outa the wall like some kinda weird trophy. I didn't see it comin', but I got us stopped before we fell to the bottom. That first step's a killer!"

Grossfuss was correct. Although it was dim inside the cavernous space they'd stumbled upon, and the air was filled with mist, all of them could see the *Victor Appleton* would have dropped several hundred feet if the yeti hadn't acted.

Now such conveniences, however antiquated, as radar and sonar would have worked, and the vacuole's dimensions might have been determined with some accuracy, but the subfoline wasn't equipped with such instruments. As near as they could tell from the visual display, the *Victor Appleton*'s tapered bow hung out into a space at least several hundred yards across, but it might have been as much as a few miles.

What was even stranger, to their surprise, and judging from the motion of the long line of torches bobbing toward them in the distance, was that the vacuole was inhabited.

By human beings.

CHAPTER VIII:

The Realm of the Selfquelled

As the flickering, smoky lights drew nearer far below, Elsie began to believe her first guess, about the species of the torch bearers, had been incorrect. However, Grossfuss boosted the viewscreen's light amplification, increased its magnifying powers, and was even more horrified to discover she'd been right.

They were human.

It was at this moment—demonstrating once again that, whatever one's academic qualifications may be, nothing quite substitutes for concrete experience —that the young praxeologist received her first genuine dose of culture shock.

"You're the authority on intelligent life-forms, cookie." The yeti, as shaken and upset by what he saw as Elsie was, had turned to her. "Whatcha make of this?"

"I'd suggest," she replied, her voice frigid as she tried to overcome her emotions, "that it's the polite thing to go outside, say hello, and see what they have in mind."

She glanced to her father for confirmation, then swiveled back to Grossfuss.

"And don't call me 'cookie.'"

The yeti shook a hand at the end of a loose wrist. "Touchy all of a sudden, ain't we?"

Following certain adjustments to the subfoline's controls—plus preparations of their own, including suit check and personal inspections of the vessel's plumbing—the travelers gathered beneath the hatchway area and allowed themselves to be extruded upward, through the hull, onto the open space that Elsie and Goldberry had called, in an orgy of optimism, "the upper deck."

"You were certainly right," Howell told the Himalayan, "about that first step."

There was a musty, somewhat oppressive odor to the cavernous enclosure. Each was torn, though none of them mentioned it, between leaning out over the unrailed hull to get a better look at the approaching party, and avoiding too direct a downward view from the dizzying height at which the *Victor Appleton* had come to rest.

"Of course," Elsie informed them as she checked her pair of Walther Electrics, trying, all the while, to peer into the gloomy depths of the vacuole, "politeness doesn't preclude the precaution of keeping our powder dry."

Nodding approval of this martial sentiment, Goldberry made certain of her own revolving autopistol, while Grossfuss solemnly examined his huge Sebastian Mark IX. Howell's precautionary weapons-check was a somewhat more complicated operation, but he was soon as satisfied as the others that he was ready to defend himself.

As a praxeologist, Elsie understood that, whatever their species, most "primitives" (which those approaching appeared to be) carried weapons and respected those who carried them. Only "civilized" individuals were foolish enough to believe they could wander through the universe defenseless and not pay an eventual, terrible price.

"I'm sure you'll correct me"—despite the distance, Howell, fighting off the urge to sneeze, found he couldn't help keeping his voice low—"but unless

I'm very much mistaken, the group of individuals about to greet us consists entirely of . . . "

"Cripples," the undiplomatic Grossfuss supplied.

What the yeti lacked in finesse, he made up in acuity. He wasn't, at the moment, using the magnifying powers of his implant. Howell shrugged: it was the Confederate way to search out cures for ailments, rather than euphemisms for those forced to suffer them. It was this, in a bizarre way—thanks to Confederate medicine, she had never met an amputee or paralytic, seen a withered or useless appendage, or anyone, besides land-going porpoises, who used a wheelchair—which left Elsie unprepared for this spectacle. As they neared, she and her companions could see that it was made up of hunchbacks, people with clubfeet and other distortions of the limbs and body, hobbling in obvious pain with the aid of canes or crutches, leading others who were blind. Several were being carried in crude litters. To her, it was something out of the Dark Ages. Every one suffered disabilities—among them a spectacular skin disease—which had long since disappeared from the Confederacy, and which Elsie's generation (and many preceding it) had only read about in history recordings.

"He's right, Father." She had to swallow hard to make her voice work. "And so are you. I noticed this before, on the viewscreen, below. I'm afraid it disturbed me—which is why I snapped at you that way, Obregon. I'm sorry."

" 'Sokay, kiddo," the giant primate told her; he was no more used to such a sight than Elsie. "I'm havin' trouble with it, m'self. You figure maybe this place is fulla ionizin' radiation or something?"

She shook her head.

"More like no science and too small a genetic population. I raised a tankful of inbred guppies as a school project once. Ten generations. It looked like this." She shuddered at the memory. "I still have nightmares about it."

Three dozen bent and broken figures approached. The tarry odor of their torches carried upward. The Confederates and their Majestan friend had no choice but to inhale it. Elsie considered zipping up her suit and breathing the sanitized and filtered air it could provide when surrounded by even traces of a breathable atmosphere. Unlike the sharp-eyed Grossfuss, she was already compelled to rely on its paratronic senses in the lack of better light and at this distance. At last, the local inhabitants drew up before the foot of the wall of vegetation from which, several hundred feet above them, the prow of the subfoline projected. Their apparent leader—under appropriate magnification Elsie saw he was a middle-aged, skinny man in an unbecoming loincloth—raised the staff he leaned on and shouted up at the travelers in a voice as thin as he was.

"Whadidde say?" Grossfuss demanded.

"I don't know." Impatient, Elsie hushed the yeti, "Be quiet, please, so I can hear."

She tuned her implant to the powerful sound-receptors in the subfoline's hull.

"*. . . in ye name of ye Selfquelled People, we bid thee welcome, motley strangers!*"

"Selfquelled?" Elsie murmured to herself. "As in *defeated*? They call themselves 'the self-defeated'?"

Turning to his companions, Grossfuss demanded, "Who's he callin' motley, anyway?"

No one answered.

No one having answered her rhetorical question either, Elsie addressed Goldberry: "Like it or not, Leftenant Commander, you're the local expert. You've been awfully quiet about all of this. What, if anything, do you know about these people?"

The Antimacasarite answered her with silence, raised eyebrows, and an eloquent shrug. Elsie had already learned that this meant she didn't know a thing.

"It was English, anyway," Howell offered. "More pre-Confederate colonists, I should guess, a splinter group forgotten even by their fellow First Wavers. The question is, where did they come from, when did they diverge, and why?"

"That's three questions," insisted Grossfuss. "An' not even the important one—which is when're we gonna get outa here? This place gives me the jittering jim-jams."

"Not to mention"—despite herself, Elsie's tone was cynical—"the jabbering jelly-spines."

Goldberry nodded her agreement. Grossfuss stuck a great slab of a tongue out at both of them.

"Each of us," Howell defended the yeti, "experiences different limits to his courage, and varying notions of what's prudent. Obregon, my friend, we're here to explore, not flee every time we see something we aren't accustomed to. Tell me: we have an emergency hoist aboard, and, as I recall, several miles of stout, lightweight line; mightn't we lower ourselves to the vacuole floor in some manner?"

"Excuse me, Captain Nahuatl," interrupted Goldberry, "could you not back the *Victor Appleton* up, burrow down another few hundred feet, and re-emerge closer to the floor?"

"Why, no, my dear." The coyote turned to stare at her, grateful, for once, that his face didn't convey human emotions—chagrin, for example—very well. "That would be too simple and straightforward for a clever, complicated fellow like myself."

He glanced up at Grossfuss.

"Obregon, would you please do as Goldberry suggests? I don't think it should take long. And Elsie, signal to the people down below. Inform them, if you can, of our intentions. This is no time for any more surprises, on either side."

The Himalayan nodded, stepped to the appropriate spot, and sank though the hull with the coyote beside him. Goldberry stayed another moment to watch Elsie making exaggerated gestures, became bored, and followed Howell and the yeti inboard.

When the girl had completed her assignment as best she could, and allowed the substance of the hull to settle her to the deck below—it was good to breathe recirculated, filtered air again—she found another sort of delegation awaiting her. Instead of readying the vessel for the short journey the Antimacassarite had suggested, Howell, Grossfuss, and Goldberry stood facing her, peculiar expressions on the faces of the two upright anthropoid sentients, a crumpled piece of paper, local First Wave manufacture, in the yeti's outstretched fingers.

"I didn't wish to trouble you, my dear, while you were trying to communicate with those people," her father informed her, "but it seems we have another puzzle to solve."

That, thought Elsie, remembering the personal problem she hadn't had time to consider for hours, *is all we need.*

When the *Victor Appleton* poked her long, sharp nose into the haze of the vacuole again, 570 feet lower than before, it was if she'd emerged in an altogether different world. As her crew came back out on deck, the enormous cavern was flooded with a soft blue-green light. The so-called Selfquelled People were slipping hoods of some sort over their torches, snuffing out the flames.

"A new dawn," Goldberry marveled, despite a running nose and the latest worry she and her three companions now shared. "What time is it on the surface?"

"You'd know," Grossfuss answered irritably, "if you consulted your— Sorry, Leftenant Commander.

Same time as it is down here, just after seventeen o'clock."

"Five in the afternoon," a somewhat subdued Howell observed. "This isn't sunlight. It's some sort of bioluminescence."

The forward third of the subfoline, which extended through the wall and into the vacuole, rested on a gentle slope like a beached boat. The Selfquelled People were gesturing for them to climb down. Cursory inspection revealed no weapon more threatening than the staves and crutches that supported the lame among them. Howell transmitted a mental signal to the *Victor Appleton* that caused her to extrude a short length of ladder which rose from the deck, arched over the side, and lowered itself to the surface the vessel rested on.

"Look," Elsie remarked as she set foot on the floor of the vacuole, "nobody needs moss-shoes here. The leaves are all, well, sort of fused together into a hard surface."

Grossfuss followed her down the ladder, bending to touch the floor with a fingertip. "A hard, sanded surface you could roller-skate on." He tapped it with a blunted claw. "Kinda shiny, too. Looks like they've quelled more'n themselves."

"I wish"—Howell leaped the short distance to the ground—"you knew more about these people, Goldberry."

"More than the nothing at all I do know, Captain?" the Antimacassarite stepped off the last rung and slapped imaginary dust from her hands. "I tell you—I swear to you on the shawl of my captainmother—I have never so much as heard of them before."

"And I believe you, my dear. It's just that— Hello, my name is G. Howell Nahuatl, at present in command of the H.S.P. *Victor Appleton*. May I introduce my fellow travelers?"

The emaciated individual Howell had addressed
didn't reply, but turned to the others of his party.

"It speaketh! Ye ancient legends informed us
rightly!"

His voice rasped with the first coarsening of middle age, but his taut skin glowed with feverish good
health even in the odd light of the vacuole. He was
in exquisite shape for his age, not undernourished,
as they had believed, but without an extra ounce of
fat, despite the limp that slowed his movements.

This is a vigorous man, Howell thought, beginning to age in a way Confederates hadn't seen since
rejuvenative therapy had increased life expectancy
to four figures, but in admirable condition for his
apparent fifty-five or sixty, nonetheless. Trembling
with excitement, the man turned back to the coyote. His mouth was full of big, square, evenly spaced
teeth. His eyes had begun to fill with tears.

"I hight Humility ye Mortified, Eldest among ye
Selfquelled People and qualified to speak for them.
Is one among thee any elder? I am 123 years of age."

Humility the Mortified, supported by his super-
annuated gaggle—he claimed they ranged, despite
appearing half that age, from seventy to just under
his own century and a quarter—invited the travelers to accompany them into the misty, blue-lit
reaches of the vacuole, toward what Elsie, acting as
interpreter, understood to be their village. Feeling
cautious, Howell avoided answering questions about
his own age or those of his companions. Possibly
Elsie misunderstood: English, as spoken by this
people of contrasts—distorted bodies blessed with
inexplicable longevity—consisted of a mixture of
archaic forms inconsistent with what she knew of
their origin (all Lost Colonial expeditions had started
from Earth in what some still termed the twentieth
century) and local idioms.

The strange tribe living a thousand feet below the surface appeared to welcome the travelers in a manner friendly enough. They seemed fascinated, in a dull way that the four were about to learn was characteristic of them, with the coyote and the yeti, two nonhuman furry beings who nevertheless spoke and acted like "people." From what little the Selfquelled had to say about themselves—polite introductions—Howell and Elsie, as analytical a pair as ever existed, began forming theories about the vacuole-dwellers, independent of one another.

"And this is my half brother, Subjugation ye Selfconquered," Humility offered, pointing out a dwarfed, arthritic-looking youngster. "Selfconquered, this is Howell ye Nahuatl, Eldest of ye Victorappleton People, his daughter-by-ceremony, Elsie ye Lysandra, their voyaging-friends Goldberry ye MacRame and Obregon ye—"

"Ye gods!" the yeti interjected, stifling a sneeze. "—Grossfuss."

Elsie wasn't certain whether her father-by-ceremony was finishing for the Selfquelled leader, or interfering before the yeti got them all in some kind of trouble.

"A pleasure," continued Howell, "making your acquaintance, Subjugation, and your friends, Overmastered the Humble, Abasement the Subdued, Abjectitude the Downcast, Modesty the Vanquished, Abashedness the Broken, Meek the Reduced, the double-barreled Diminution the Diminished, and, last and without a doubt the least, Crush. . ."

"Crushidity the Debased," croaked one of the smaller litter-carried figures who, if Elsie's sickened guess was correct, had been born without any arms or legs. He was over eighty, but with a smooth, almost childlike face and twinkling eyes.

A shadow slipped by on the ground and some kind of bird passed with a dry whirring noise overhead.

Elsie glanced up—her eyes itched and burned in this paradise for pollen—but it was gone.

"Crushidity the Debased. Well, that's certainly a name you've got, isn't it? And this—"

"Thy pardon, Howell ye Nahuatl, but thou hast forgotten my sister-by-marriage."

"Forgive me! I seem to be a bit thick this morning. What was her name, again?"

"Mediocrity ye Abominable."

"I knew," the yeti complained to the universe in general, "I wasn't gonna like this place."

Howell cleared his electronic throat.

"As I was saying, I take it this is some of the special vegetation you spoke of, Humility?"

The conversation took place as they ambled at a pace slow enough for the litter-bearers. The coyote indicated a clump of phosphorescent berrylike growths that seemed responsible for the illumination filling the cavernous vacuole. They provided enough light to turn the thick covering of normal leaves, which formed the roof, walls, and landscaping of the vacuole, a healthy dark green.

"We were aware your planet is covered by a single species of vegetation. We knew it capable of enormous morphological specialization. But this surpasses anything I've ever heard about."

"Sorta like natural light-emittin' diodes," speculated Grossfuss.

Humility had a puzzled look, one which he'd worn through Howell's last speech, as well. Then he gave them both a broad, insipid smile, but said nothing, as if he knew something they didn't know—or didn't know anything at all, himself.

"Obregon's a technician," Howell explained, "with a technician's view. As a jackal-of-all-trades, and more interested in biology, I'd guess that, from time to time, the trillions of berries illuminating your world wink out, producing artificial night. Hothouse plants require a rest. We must have arrived at the end of one such."

"Thou art correct," responded Humility. "It is as it should be. We Selfquelled live 365 days a year, in harmony and accordance with Nature's plan."

"I'd have to say," Howell told the man, envying his immunity to the allergens that seemed to be floating all about them, "that it appears to agree with you."

There was that vacuous smile again, the knowing —or know-nothing—silence.

Elsie filed Humility's words away. The Selfquelled might descend from equalitarian environmentalists, a movement popular when Lost Colonists had fled Earth. Given the story Goldberry had told her of the bucket, they might be an offshoot of Antimacassar.

"It is we who agree with it," he answered the coyote at last. "We Selfquelled are enabled to obtain aught we may require by ye grace of ye bounteous life-form roundabout us. This we ensure through a process of Criticism."

Elsie could hear the capital C in the man's voice. Remembering some of the grimmer versions of Chinese history she'd heard, she looked suspiciously at Humility.

"Self-criticism?"

"No," he told her, "we live only to serve others, and that is who we Criticize."

The floor of the vacuole wasn't level. As they topped a low rise, they looked down on what must have been a village, although the four travelers saw it long before Humility, who seemed a bit nearsighted, pointed it out to them. Structures spaced at intervals resembled, more than anything, giant squatting rosebuds. As they entered the village, another seven or eight dozen individuals, much like those they'd already met, emerged to give the trav-

elers and the delegation sent to the *Victor Appleton*
a polite, low-key reception.

Humility invited the surface-dwellers into the small
podlike cottage he identified as his own. As they
followed him through the low entryway, Elsie took
the first fresh glance she'd had time for at the bit of
paper Grossfuss had found on the subfoline's deck
beneath the control console, placed there sometime
while he had gone off to meet them at the hovercraft terminal. He thought, and they all agreed,
that it had been swept off the console, unnoticed,
when they'd carried the unconscious Goldberry
aboard. There was a dirty footprint—that of Grossfuss' smartsuit—in the middle of the paper.

The trouble was that no one, not the leftenant
commander, not even the Himalayan, had possessed
the code-key to the *Victor Appleton* before Howell
had arrived to give it to them. No one could have
placed the note aboard the subfoline. Elsie read the
warning—it was English, in characterless block
letters—once again:

WHOSOEVER INTRUDES THIS MACHINE
OF EVIL NEATH THE SURFACE OF THE
HOLY SEA WILL BE DESTROYED WITH IT.
(signed, if that was the word for it)
THE HOODED SEVEN

CHAPTER IX:

The Rights of Broccoli

"This thing wasn't constructed," Grossfuss observed as he ran his fingers over the inside wall of Humility's rosebud cottage. "S'pose it grew here, complete with furniture?"

The structure was more hut than cottage, but it was indeed furnished, after a fashion, with a pair of chairlike objects, a sort of table, and a low cot, all of which resembled simple woven slings or hammocks, except that the mesh was all of a single piece, and they were rooted to a floor composed of the same substance as the "ground" outside, although perhaps a bit softer and more resilient.

With the Himalayan, Howell, Elsie, and Goldberry inside with their host, the place was crowded. Above their heads, the ceiling seemed equally so, with dozens, perhaps hundreds of rounded, hanging, multicolored excrescences ranging in size from that of marbles (or grapes, Elsie thought, might be more appropriate) to a couple of bulky objects the diameter and shape of watermelons.

Grossfuss sat on the floor, as did the coyote.

The girls each took a chairlike object.

"Wilt thou all partake of a refreshment?"

Still standing, and without waiting for an answer from them, Humility reached up toward the low ceiling overhead. As elsewhere in what he'd called the Realm of the Selfquelled, all the illumination originated at ground level—indoors, the source was flattened glow-berries, fused into the floor—casting everything in an eerie, sinister light. Stretching, he plucked several globular objects from the "rafters," distributing one of them to each of his guests.

Elsie took hers. It was, in essence, a rolled and cup-shaped leaf, something like a hollow, water-tight cabbage, except that the color was a pale violet. It was filled, as she discovered when she followed their host's example and peeled a section back, with a sweet-smelling golden liquid. Not being obvious about it, she dipped the end of one finger into the juice, watching the readouts generated by her multitalented smartsuit and transmitted to her implant.

"Mostly water," she reported to her Confederate companions, via the same silent, paratronic medium, "laced with complex natural sugars, a few simple proteins—and heavily vitamin-enriched. Barring specific individual allergies, which we're all supposed to have had shots for, I'd say it was safe to drink—even good for us, perish the thought. Be sure to brush your teeth afterward."

To her relief, she saw that Goldberry, unable to communicate with the others by implant, had waited for her friends to start before drinking her own juice. The taste was odd, something like a combination of room-temperature onion soup and liquid spearmint gum, but, even odder, not displeasing. And it was a welcome break from what they could prepare in the subfoline's limited galley—even filet mignon and broiled lobster pall with sufficient repetition.

Howell held his drink before his face, using his mechanical arm, and lapped at it with his tongue. They were all still suffering from the vacuole's assault on their respiratory and immune systems, and anything liquid was helpful.

Humility the Mortified was nothing if not a generous host. The strange drink was followed by something he called "breadfruit," also plucked from the hut's rather bulbous and complicated ceiling, looking and tasting more like fresh-baked bread than the bananalike Earth vegetable that had probably given it the name it bore. They were encouraged to spread it with what Elsie promptly dubbed "butter-and jellyfruit," squeezed like toothpaste from the grapelike objects Elsie had noticed. As side dishes, the travelers were offered something resembling smoked meat to the human eye, nose, tongue, and fingertips.

"*Ah ... succulent and tender portions of well-cured textured vegetable protein,*" the coyote commented over the circuit he and his daughter shared with Grossfuss.

With a canine's powerful olfactory sense—perhaps a million times more powerful than any human being's, even dulled, as Howell's was, by a bout with allergies—he wasn't quite as easily deceived as Elsie or Goldberry might have been if they hadn't watched Humility the Mortified strip pieces of the fibrous foodstuff from the rafters of the cottage as if they were covered with birch bark.

"*Umm, I'm a vegetarian,*" Grossfuss asserted. "*You think I oughta eat this stuff?*"

Howell responded, "*I should think that depends, my large and furry friend, on why you first became a vegetarian. If for physiological reasons, feel perfectly free: there's no more real meat here than in a carrot. The same holds if you're an ethical vegetarian, and for precisely the same reason.*"

"*And if you just want something to deprive yourself of,*" Elsie added, "*so you can feel guilty, that's another reason to go ahead. I didn't notice any vegetarian inclination on your part the other night when we were having lamb chops.*"

This was one of Howell's special favorites.

"Aww . . ."

At this range, Elsie and her father could almost feel the yeti's embarrassment.

"I just always seem t'have trouble eatin' strange food in strange places. Y'know, sometimes I don't feel like eatin' for a couple or three days at a time."

"Funny," Elsie replied, *"I've always felt the same way about strange bathrooms."*

As it happened, after the brief but satisfying meal, Humility pointed out another of the hut's facilities, to the well-concealed relief of at least one guest, who found her shyness overridden by more urgent necessity. Something else allergy shots couldn't prepare you for, Elsie thought as she retired to the indicated wall-niche and drew a drapery of large leaves—fig leaves, she supposed, seemingly glued together at the edges into place—was the sudden effect foreign food sometimes had on the metabolism. It appeared the Selfquelled refertilized their living homes on a regular basis, as much part of the process of "living in accord" with nature as eating and drinking what it produced. Thinking like a praxeologist, rather than the embarrassable teenager she also was, Elsie concluded that, ultimately, their mortal remains must feed the plant life, as well, and wondered what Selfquelled funeral customs were like.

Minutes later, after Elsie had returned, Humility went to some pains explaining at greater length than any of the Confederates cared about how, despite the fact he was both leader and spokesman for his people, owing to his great age and presumed wisdom, his dwelling differed in no respect from any other in the vacuole.

He did have one interested listener.

"Everyone here"—Goldberry reiterated the essence of Humility's lecture with obvious approval, startling Elsie, who hadn't noticed until now how reserved and silent the pretty Antimacassarite had been—"is taken care of, generously and equally, fed, housed, clothed?—I wondered about that—from birth to death?"

Humility grinned from ear to ear, smiling at her as if at a student who'd recited a lesson perfectly. To Elsie's ear, the leftenant commander sounded more than a bit intoxicated. She checked her suit's analytical readouts again, this time for alcohol or vegetable poisons, but detected nothing of the sort. Maybe it was one of those euphoric reactions to allergens people sometimes manifested.

"Did you watch the villagers when we arrived?" Goldberry asked her companions. "Did you see how quiet and polite they were, incurious and dignified? These are a people in repose, such as I have heard of before in legends of ancient Earth. No competition exists among the Selfquelled, they are completely equalitarian, they have no personal ambition and, I would wager, no conflict at all. See for yourself: Humility does not even know what evils we speak of, do you?"

The vacuolite grinned again, like a cheerful idiot, Elsie thought, spreading his hands in a shrug.

"It is a clean and efficient closed cycle in which these people live," the leftenant commander concluded, "one which I find somehow strangely appealing."

"Welcome t'my share," Grossfuss shuddered. "I'd give a copper t'know why previous Confederate surveys turned up no hint of these folks. Kinda creepy an' suspicious, if y'ask me."

Addressing her captain more than the yeti, Goldberry admitted that knowledge of the Selfquelled People would come as a surprise to her own civilization as well, a pleasant one, validating many of their own beliefs.

Since it wasn't carried out paratronically, Humility had followed this exchange with his usual cheerful, vacant look when the subject was outside his expertise. Goldberry's remarks, however, seemed to be something he could comprehend.

"We Selfquelled live," he told them, "as have uncounted generations, under a gentle, watchful eye of Criticism, in good accord with fellow man and all that which surrounds us. We do no harm. We are neither seen nor heard. Unlike those evil others whom Ancient Song says failed to live by Nature's Plan, and perished."

Elsie raised her eyebrows at her father. She'd noticed, not for the first time, that their host's expression of his philosophy seemed a bit stilted, rendered in singsong tones and rhythms like a ritual, as if it had beem memorized by rote a long time ago and now had little actual meaning for the speaker.

Half seriously, she was reminded of the red-tailed African Gray parrot, Earth's avian rhetorical genius, capable of reciting poems as long as a thousand words—although no one would dispute that it was a literal "birdbrain." She wondered—this being the test, she knew, of real intelligence—how Humility the Mortified would fare in a situation he hadn't been prepared for.

Outside, as the assorted beings visited, the blue-green berry-light began to fail again. Humility explained, with a yawn, that it did this in the vacuole two hours out of every five. They were welcome, he told them, to remain in his home, during this customary period of rest. Since it was his understanding—based on what, Elsie wondered, more ancient legends?—that the surface-beings needed and desired to be by themselves (alien, he admitted, as the notion seemed to him) he'd respect their wishes and join friends in a nearby cottage.

With these words, he backed toward the door of the hut, and began to take his leave.

Elsie sighed. Goldberry's fascination with the Selfquelled annoyed the Confederate girl. The leftenant commander had been plucked from among one collection of barbarians by another, had been lucky to escape into a real civilization, only to become fascinated with a third bunch of barbarians! From the beginning, Elsie had entertained doubts about the wonderfulness of life in the vacuole. What she'd noticed about the villagers wasn't that they were quiet, polite, incurious, or dignified, but that they seemed listless, a bit stupid like their spokesman, and even more deformed than the original welcoming committee.

At first she'd dismissed her feelings as a trace of xenophobia she hadn't known about. How could she, surrounded all her life by porpoises, gorillas, killer whales, chimpanzees, assorted extraterrestrials, and a coyote for a father? Perhaps it was no more than a claustrophobic reaction to the idea of cave-dwelling —which this was of a sort—or any sort of troglodytic existence. However, she knew that people of all species made their homes in enclosed spaces everywhere in the galaxy, from the undersea domes of Piper's World to the opal mines of her ancestral Australia, and had never objected to it before.

No, something else was bothering her, and while the others prepared themselves to rest, she groped around inside herself to discover what it was. Whatever else her unprecedented scholarate indicated about her, the most important way in which she'd surpassed other girls (and boys) her age was by acquiring the knack of listening to her feelings without letting them dictate to her.

For starters these "Selfquelled People," or at least Humility the Whatchamacallit who acted as their spokesbeing, claimed they lived as an integral part in "Nature's Plan." As young as Elsie was, she'd observed that intelligent life always forces nature to operate according to *its* plans. This inclination seemed to be the one definition of intelligence that worked everywhere in the galaxy.

Humility was right about the need for privacy. Elsie wished she could confer with her father, without being overheard, even by Grossfuss. For years she and Howell had discussed working out some kind of family code, but, as with most such ideas, had never gotten around to doing anything about it. Now, as she listened to her friends say goodnight to one another, she set the electronic portion of her brain to that task: searching through the miniature library all Confederates carried with them for a cyphering system that might serve her purpose.

Seconds later, Elsie had fulfilled her own wish. Leaning over, she touched an edge of Howell's backpack with a finger of her smartsuit, transmitting to him in a direct manner that couldn't be intercepted by a third party. Neither Howell's tone nor expression changed, but his implant accepted the trapdoor code-key she was sending, a long prime number her own implant had generated, and they were soon able to speak together by means of scrambled impulses.

She told Howell about her uneasy feelings.

"I quite agree, my dear. Nature's 'plan' for mankind, and coyotekind, is that we should still be shivering in a damp cave on Earth somewhere, gnawing wormy berries, sandy tubers, and raw meat, and dying of old age before we turn thirty."

"I don't think their longevity's up to Confederate standards," Elsie replied, free, now that she'd placed her worries in her father's paws, to play devil's advocate, *"but they seem to be doing something right here. Otherwise they wouldn't live so long."*

"Indeed," Howell told his daughter. *"However that may be, I suspect you and I are more or less alone in our negative speculations about this place. Despite its drawbacks—I'm having my worst case of hay fever since I left Wyoming—Goldberry's clearly enamored with life as it appears to be lived among the Selfquelled."*

"Why shouldn't she be?" Elsie snorted. *"From all she's had to say about Antimacassar, 'Selfquelledism' is just her own culture's social philosophy piled higher and deeper!"*

Some sense of the expression Howell might have assumed, if he'd had a human face, was perceptible by implant. Elsie felt her father shake his head ruefully.

"There's more to it, I fear. Like anyone who can't, or won't, confront her own shortcomings, the poor child yearns to avoid them by throwing herself into some effort to help these unfortunates with their obvious physical afflictions. Much the same thing always motivates what Humility calls 'Criticism': ignore your own failings, pick on somebody else instead, and call it serving others."

"I wasn't aware," Elsie replied more fiercely than she intended, *"you knew she had any shortcomings."*

Howell sighed. *"Oh dear . . . it would appear there's something else I wasn't aware of, anyway. I'd hoped you'd realize, without my having to tell you, that, in my opinion, and whatever other qualities she may possess, our leftenant commander's a narrow, ignorant, rigid, and authority-bound personality."*

"Father, I—"

Perhaps this was the time to tell him.

"Kindly don't interrupt. By now she's persuaded herself that the afflictions of the Selfquelled result from nothing more than their small, inbred population, rather than their failure—a failure her own

culture shares—to create a society in which incentive exists to make sufficient material progress to prevent them. We may have trouble persuading her to leave with us."

Elsie transmitted a sly chuckle.

"Why try? As long as she's happy being miserable, it's a free galaxy. We won't have that problem with our trusty master mechanic and part-time pilot."

"Obregon," Howell answered, *"is as disturbed at what he sees as you or I, although he may not know why. 'There ain't,' he informed me* sotto voce *at dinner, 'no such thing as a free lunch, even bread-an' butterfruit!' But he refuses to discuss it over an open circuit—as if he fears the vegetation might overhear."*

"A plant with an implant?"

"I believe that's precisely what worries him. I wonder myself, sometimes, how aware plants are. Certain experiments along that line, in the U.S. last century, offered reason to believe vegetarianism's even sillier than it always seemed."

"You mean broccoli," Elsie giggled, *"might object as strenuously to being eaten as beefsteak?"*

It was an old family joke. Along with cauliflower and Brussels sprouts, he loathed broccoli, which seemed appropriate, predator that he was, calling it "The Green Death."

"I mean," her father asserted, *"I see no logical reason to assume broccoli has any fewer rights than beefsteak, or that someone who refrains from ingesting beefsteak is more virtuous than someone who refrains from ingesting broccoli. However that may be, and however rustically he puts it, Obregon's correct about something else: the life cycle in this vacuole can't be closed, as advertised. Among other things, this violates the law of thermodynamics."*

"The planet's covered with a single species of plant life, Father. For all we know, maybe it's one big

organism, powered, even down here, by sunlight from the surface."

She felt her father's mental nod.

"True, the Sea of Leaves absorbs massive amounts of solar energy at the surface. However, as you're also aware, that surface is a temporary phenomenon. The entire sea churns, turning over constantly in a complex annual cycle."

Elsie nodded back. *"Sort of like a self-tossing salad?"*

"There's raising a growing daughter for you. Are you hungry again, already? So as many individual leaves receive exposure to the sun as possible."

Now that he'd mentioned it, she was hungry. The sniffles always did that to her: feed a cold, starve a fever, *gorge* an allergy. Would it be polite, she wondered to herself, to raid another person's ceiling for a midnight snack?

"Everywhere," she answered, *"but here, the stuffiest place in the known universe."*

"The vacuole wall prevents it. Providing light, clothing, dwellings, food, and so forth, for the Selfquelled, implies far greater energy than appears available."

"In addition to," his daughter suggested, *"very specialized high-energy chemistry."*

"Indeed. All of which must come from somewhere." He yawned.

"Well, one problem at a time. You and I haven't even had a chance yet to discuss that note Grossfuss found. I don't imagine we'll solve this puzzle tonight. Strange, I'm positively exhausted. I suggest we emulate Goldberry in one respect—"

"Not to mention the Abominable Snoreman over there . . ."

Howell yawned again.

"With only a two-hour night before us, morning will come rather soon, wouldn't you say?"

He received silence for an answer. Elsie's carrier-wave told him she'd fallen asleep.

He curled himself up, covered his long nose with his bushy tail, and followed her example.

CHAPTER X:

The Green Death

"What . . . ?"

Elsie awoke with her eyeglasses neatly folded and clutched in her hand, which meant she'd fallen asleep before taking them off. It wasn't the first time this had happened—more like the thousandth—nor was it likely to be the last.

For a long moment that was all she was certain of . . .

Then with a sudden flash of panic she realized she didn't know where she was!

Lifting her head a couple of inches from the resilient floor of the living hut of Humility the Mortified, it all came back to her in a rush. Her father was awake already and gone somewhere. He'd always been an early riser. Grossfuss still lay unconscious, sprawled on his back, arms flung wide, snoring like a chain-saw motor, one enormous foot up on a chair. The leaf curtain had been drawn across the alcove, and the hammock Goldberry had occupied was empty.

Elsie tried to get up.

A lightning bolt of pain blasted across her eyes, answered by a thundering ache in the back of her head. She gasped, weakened and short of breath, fighting nausea, her vision reduced to a narrow, gray-walled tunnel. She lay sideways on the floor, supported by her left hand and right elbow, until the throbbing at the base of her skull faded and she could control her stomach.

"Elsie?"

The leaf curtain slid to one side, revealing Goldberry, who, for some peculiar reason, seemed to be on her knees. Elsie realized it was only the second time the leftenant commander had called her by her proper name. Obviously something was wrong.

She struggled against pain to turn her head and focus on the Antimacassarite's face.

"Yeah, Goldberry. You feeling bad, too?"

The Majestan nodded, pale-faced and gulping. Not even attempting to rise, she approached on her hands and knees and sat down on the floor beside the Earth girl.

"Do you know where my father went? I'll tell you, if he felt like me, he crawled off somewhere to die in privacy. I sure hate to wake Grossfuss up, he looks so . . . so . . ."

"Natural?"

Howell stuck his head in through the door of the hut.

"I'm not altogether certain he'll be pleased to hear it," the coyote observed, in what seemed like an ordinary tone for him. "It rather strikes me as the sort of remark one customarily reserves for the guest of honor at a funeral."

"Which," Goldberry offered, "is what I feel like. I do not recall ever being so ill, not even as a midshipperson on my first cruise during a spring turnover storm."

"Me too," was the best Elsie could manage, and that much in a croak. Her powerful imagination had gotten carried away with Goldberry's seagoing allusion, and, despite its obvious attraction, the curtained niche seemed a long way away.

"Which is why," Howell answered, stepping into the hut, "I attempted to let you all slumber on while I went for help. Our Himalayan friend, in particular. I didn't fancy having four hundred pounds of travel-sick yeti on my hands, so to speak."

"But didn't you—"

"But did you not—"

Elsie and Goldberry had spoken at the same time.

"I did by all means, my dears. Quite as unpleasant as anything I've ever experienced. Goldberry, if you can get up, I suggest you try one of those large, yellow fruit up there—that's right—they taste a bit like mangoes, but the important thing is, they'll bring you right back to normal in no more than a few minutes."

Elsie was content to wait while the leftenant commander climbed to her feet to fetch the fruit. Meantime, she checked her suit and implant to see what was wrong with her. To her astonishment, she couldn't find a trace of any toxin. Her blood sugar, however, proved as depleted as if she'd scaled a mountain in her sleep.

"I feel like someone threw me down a flight of concrete stairs," she told her father, "and not in a nice way. When we get back, I'm going to speak to somebody about those allergy shots we took. It's even possible I'll let them live."

"I know the feeling. I went to see Humility the Mortified about it, first thing." Howell nodded. "He admitted it was a common complaint among his people as well—some residual physiological inability of Earth organisms to adapt to the vacuole—but the pseudo-mangoes, one of which he gave me, are a sovereign remedy."

Which turned out to be the truth. Within just a few moments of biting into the fruit Goldberry handed her, she began feeling better. The leftenant commander's color returned and she actually smiled at Elsie as she finished her "breakfast."

"Well," Howell told the girls, "now at last I suppose we can contemplate awakening Grossfuss. Better have at least a couple of those fruit handy, however—"

"Or wet sheets and a set of leg irons," his daughter suggested.

"I never eat breakfast," the yeti offered in a cheerful tone, startling his three companions. "I s'pose we gotta go back to the sub t'get some coffee."

They stared at him, their jaws hanging.

"How do you feel?" Elsie asked.

The yeti, sitting up, stretched his arms, and yawned in a manner that reminded Howell and Elsie of Carlsbad Caverns. His fingertips brushed opposite walls of the hut.

"Pretty good for just a nap. Most times they make me cranky. Nice of you t'ask. How 'bout yourself?"

For the first time, Elsie realized she'd slept for no more than an hour at most. After all, she'd spent half of the two-hour dark period talking with her father. The "nap" that had followed now felt like a much longer interval to her.

"As if I'd spent a couple of centuries in a mausoleum—as one of the prepaid guests."

With Howell and Goldberry, she took part in explaining the "morning's" events to the yeti.

Grossfuss shook his head.

"Well I'll be darned. Dunno why I feel so good. Almost enough t'make a body feel guilty."

"Almost," replied the other three together.

Once assured Elsie was better, Howell decided to spend part of the "day" on a solitary walk. He had some thinking to do, mostly about his daughter, who was busy at the moment learning more—and enjoying it less—of social life among the Selfquelled.

It wasn't like Elsie to let a personal distaste for a people or their customs interfere with her work. On the other hand, it wasn't like her to keep secrets, either. Part of it, he knew, was healthy. Like any self-respecting caterpillar with hopes of becoming a butterfly, a girl becoming a woman needed privacy in which to work the transformation. But there was something else . . .

Overhead, the coyote heard the raspy flapping he'd noticed the day before. When he looked up, he spotted a green, ropy creature supported by outspread wings with the texture of corn shucks. The thing appeared more vegetable than animal. Howell suspected it was examining him with the same curiosity that he examined it. Before he could get a closer look, the plant-bird swooped, diving on some small, squeaking animal amidst the berries, and vanished from sight.

Elsie came back to mind: never had he felt so inadequate, as a parent, or a thinking being in general. Perhaps he should consult Grossfuss, who claimed several children of his own, grown and married. One never argues with success, but learns from it where possible. The yeti had expressed an intention to visit the *Victor Appleton*, and that was the way Howell happened to be heading. The decision made, his four feet took him along faster than the casual stroll he'd intended.

"Good morning," he told the Himalayan, who was inspecting the subfoline's exterior.

"Afternoon already, Cap'n. Dunno how I'll ever get used t'these here abbreviated days. Makes me feel like kindergarten where y'had t'take a nap whether y'wanted to or not. I hadda make sure the sub was okay, though. Crashin' her through a wall was bad enough. Doin' it twicet got me t'worryin' about her hull a mite."

Neither of them mentioned the threatening note, although it was on both their minds.

Howell made a show of looking over the craft with Grossfuss. Hellertech had built well: not so much as a single bristle was damaged or out of place. If anyone intended sabotaging her, it would be a labor-intensive undertaking. He asked the primate whether he'd ever had the cup of coffee he'd wanted. Receiving a negative answer, he invited the other inboard, and put on a pot for both of them.

Soon the conversation turned to daughters.

"At Elsie's somewhat tender age," Howell told the yeti, "she's sensitive about a great many things."

"The bashful stage," the Himalayan nodded. "Y'know, Cap'n, it's always been kinda hard t'see your daughter as a little girl, her bein' a scientist, an' all."

"Difficult for me at times, as well. I tend to forget—until something like this. One thing, of course, is her appearance: her need for old-fashioned glasses, what she imagines to be her unattractive face and figure. Despite herself, I know Elsie envies Leftenant Commander MacRame her tall, slim, mature good looks."

Grossfuss chuckled.

"I'd envy her, too, in Elsie's place. I like 'em bigger, better-rounded, an' a lot hairier, but even I can see Goldberry's a fine specimen of a female nake."

Howell let the yeti's impolite reference to human beings—"naked apes"—pass. The fellow meant no harm by the turn of phrase, which chimpanzees, gorillas, even human beings themselves sometimes, and equally naked cetaceans often used.

"Elsie doesn't know it"—he hoped he was making allowance for a father's pride—"and wouldn't believe it if I told her (I made the mistake once of saying her nose is 'cute'; she's never gotten over it) but by anybody's standard she's a pretty girl and will be a beautiful woman."

Grossfuss nodded.

"Sure, I'd noticed, Cap'n. Trouble is, somebody else gotta tell her. Somebody human, male, an' about her age. I don't think you're ready for that."

"I'm not sure I ever will be."

"You'll be relieved, in the long run. It's gettin' to that point that's troublesome."

"Well, odious as comparisons may be, they're also instructive."

Perhaps Howell didn't realize that, if he wasn't being altogether objective about his daughter, he was placing his employee in an awkward position.

"Unlike Goldberry, Elsie possesses the energizing spirit of a free and independent being."

"No argument, Cap'n. First Wavers always treat us like we was subsimian or somethin'."

Howell nodded, having had the same experience on other Lost Colony worlds.

"A far better, more flexible, and, without question, more benign intelligence than Goldberry's, I warrant, resides behind Elsie's eyes. All she needs—although, thanks to her age, she's in no condition to realize it just yet—is the benefit of two or three more years of growing and learning."

The yeti laughed.

"Don't worry, Cap'n, take it from a veteran. You'll both survive it somehow."

When the glow within the vacuole began to dim again, three hours after Elsie had fought back to consciousness the first time, she was ready for it. She'd felt better as the brief day wore on, but now she was exhausted. This time she'd sleep instead of staying up half the night—one hour out of two—in conversation. Another two-hour nap couldn't do any harm. She'd read somewhere that sleeping in short installments was healthier than a single unbroken eight-hour stretch. She wondered if this accounted for the amazing longevity of the Selfquelled.

Goldberry returned to their borrowed quarters as the strange dusk started settling. She'd spent her "day" exploring, speaking with as many of the natives as she could, observing their ways. This was the activity Elsie might have pursued in normal circumstances. On this occasion, she'd remained in the hut, organizing her notes for transcription into the *Victor Appleton*'s computer, transmission back to Talisman, and up to whatever vessel of the Fleet next happened by. At some point they'd find their way back to her alma mater in Mexico City.

She made another note to ask her colleagues about references to a "Hooded Seven"—although by the time any information got back it might be too late—and, just in case, to brace Humility on the same topic at the next opportunity.

Howell and Grossfuss followed Goldberry. Humility stopped to offer them another meal, inquire whether they'd had an interesting day, and promise them a surprise tomorrow. Preparations were being made by something called the Council of Criticism, in honor of the travelers. The Selfquelled leader was as enthusiastic as they'd seen him.

"But not a great deal smarter," Elsie told her friends after he'd left and they began to settle in.

She ignored what only she could have known was a disapproving look from her father.

"Sorta like a little kid the night before his birthday," Grossfuss offered.

"If," Elsie answered, "he was on veterinary tranquilizers. What does it take to get these people stirred up?"

"They are a people of repose," Goldberry repeated this earlier observation. "You—"

Howell interrupted: "You mightn't like seeing them stirred up. Recall the saying about sleeping dragons."

"Thought it was sleeping dogs," Grossfuss told him, "no offense."

"None taken—except that I believe it to be an excellent idea," he yawned, exposing teeth. " 'Let sleeping dogs lie'—and yetis a sixteenth Sasquatch on their fathers' side, and human beings of the more interesting gender."

He yawned again: "Goodnight, ladies, goodnight to you all."

Despite a resolution to the contrary, Elsie found she had trouble getting to sleep. This time, she folded her glasses and slid them into a padded pocket of her smartsuit, pillowed her head on her arms, and tried to make her mind a blank . . .

The trouble with being an intelligent being is that your mind can never truly be a blank, especially when it's been preoccupied for days with self-disapproval, envy, guilt, threatening messages from nowhere, and certain overwhelming personal worries. It's easy to shove all of that aside during the day, when work must be done, but much harder at night, when you're not quite so active. And the fact that "night" came to the vacuole every three hours made things worse.

It's true—and Elsie knew it was—for young people in particular, that what may seem to be "overwhelming personal worries" often turn out, in the estimation of others, to be relatively minor matters. It's also true that knowing this usually doesn't help. Sometimes the very triviality of what bothers you makes it all the more difficult to discuss with someone who might be able to help—if only they could see how serious such a "trivial matter" could be.

Annoyed at herself, Elsie rolled over onto her back. She tried to ignore the sound of Goldberry grinding her teeth and whimpering in her sleep. To make matters even worse, Grossfuss was snoring once again, shaking the entire hut with the thunderous fury of a Himalayan blizzard. The lump made by the glasses in her pocket was bothering her—along with the lump made by the problem in her mind.

She understood that in some respects she was no different from any other adolescent. What she'd been worrying about telling her father all this time was simple. Almost anyone—except Elsie and Howell—would have regarded it as trivial.

She wanted to stop being called "Elsie."

With a quiet grunt of annoyed resignation, she pulled her glasses from her pocket. She felt she could think much better with them on, in any case. And it didn't look, after all, as if she were going to be doing that much sleeping. At least they stayed where they belonged when she was lying on her back.

Without waking, Howell rolled over, stretched, and curled up into a furry canine ball again.

It was like someone had once observed about being hanged in public, she supposed: if it weren't for the honor of the thing, she'd have just as soon skipped it. The problem was that "Elsa" had been the name of Howell's long-dead coyote wife, the one other member of his species to wear an implant and suffer the consequences. When his owners had discovered their mistake with him—and realized the loneliness to which circumstances sentenced him—they'd attempted to provide him with a mate. Something had gone wrong, terribly wrong, something of which Elsie had never been able to get Howell to speak.

From nothing more than reflex, Elsie pushed at the bridge of her glasses, although they hadn't moved. She was unaware that this too was part of her thinking process.

Years later, Howell had adopted a human daughter, naming her for his lost Elsa. Now that human

daughter, Elsie, was afraid Howell's feelings might
be hurt by the change she desired. Being named for
someone he'd loved was an honor. But she felt—and
knew almost anyone else would disagree with her—
she bore an undistinguished, undignified name for
a fifteen-year-old human female. She might not have
put words to the feeling, but it was also insult
added to injury when the fifteen-year-old human
female didn't feel good about herself to begin with.

Elsie wanted (although almost anyone else would
have regarded the alternative as worse) to be called
by her middle name, which Howell had also given
her—"Lysandra," for Lysander Spooner, statesman
and philosopher to be admired, President of the old
North American Confederacy in what some still
called the nineteenth century.

What made her problem most severe was that—in
what she now felt was a moment of moral weakness
—she'd already legally changed it while aboard *Tom
Sowell Maru.*

She removed her glasses, taking an absent nibble
at the end of one earpiece. The oddest thing about
the vacuole was that it fell silent when the lights
went out. Elsie was used to night noises, at home
on Earth, and aboard starships which boasted gar-
dens, parks, street traffic, and a certain amount of
wildlife.

"Legally," in Confederate terms, meant posting a
conspicuous public notice, something you could hire
done at a reasonable rate. Elsie had money of her
own—among other things, she'd sold her scholar's
thesis to a publisher—but now she felt she'd been a
coward to set the process in motion just as they'd
left the ship, so that her father wouldn't know about
it until she was ready (or she'd somehow worked up
the intestinal fortitude) to tell him.

At last the combination of toss-turning coyote,
whimpering, tooth-grinding leftenant commander,

abominably snoring Himalayan, and unnerving quiet outside the hut became too much for Elsie. She wished they were back aboard the *Victor Appleton* for many reasons, in this instance because each of them had his—or, more important, her—own state-closet. She put her glasses away again, zipped up the facepiece of her smartsuit, and adjusted it to exclude all extraneous noise. She was in the process of selecting some Mozart from the music stored in her implant, when she realized she was hungry again.

Without lowering her facepiece, Elsie increased its light amplification until the inside of the hut appeared illuminated by full daylight. To her sur-prise it seemed better that way. Lying on her back, she was perusing the cluttered ceiling for some edible tidbit, when something among the clutter moved!

She peered upward, trying to convince herself it was a trick of the light, or perhaps the local equiva-lent of mice raiding the pantry. This became diffi-cult when she watched a dark, sinuous object—some sort of cross between a tree root and a long, thin snake—lower itself inch by quarter-inch, to creep, without a whisper, along the taut supports of Goldberry's hammock.

It was seeking the girl's pale, vulnerable neck!

CHAPTER XI:

Dancing Cheek to Cheek

Paralyzed with horror and disgust—and with the sudden, sickening understanding that this must have happened to all of them the previous "night"—Elsie watched the dangling obscenity attach itself to Goldberry's throat, pulse for a short time with her heartbeat, and detach itself to seek a new victim.

There was nothing else to call it but a "vampire root." Hanging from the ceiling—she was certain it was part of the hut, not some independent organism —it lowered its business end further and began groping about for the other occupants. She wasn't sure what to do—all sorts of ideas and theories began forming in her mind unbidden—until the thick tendril reached for her father.

Without thinking, Elsie seized the evil thing in her smartsuit-gloved hands.

It surprised her with its enormous strength, just like a huge snake in that regard. At once it began a wild thrashing, desperate to free itself, a sense of shock and outrage somehow transmitted by its struggles. In a corner of her mind, Elsie considered drawing one of her Walther UVPs and blasting into the ceiling of the cottage where the base of the thing was rooted, but found she didn't dare let go long enough, even if she'd been convinced it would do her any good.

In some final desperation of her own, she gave

her smartsuit a series of rapid mental orders, rendering one hand positively charged, the other negative, with as much electrical potential between them on their outside surfaces—some three or four thousand volts she thought; she was too busy to scan the readouts—as the smartsuit could muster. Power thrummed and surged between her palms.

The electrocuted vampire root thrashed harder, tossing the terrified but determined girl around like a predator with prey in its jaws too big to swallow in a single gulp. They were shaking the entire hut. Only her suit's tendency to stiffen with a blow protected her, but that safety measure was meant to withstand a single strike—a bullet, a careering hovercraft in the street, even a micrometeor in space—and had never been intended for repeated impacts. As it was, the smartsuit began screaming dire warnings to her implant that its energies were draining away faster than they could be replaced.

And Elsie too was running out of strength.

All of a sudden she was aware of her father on his feet beside her, holding her down, snatching at the thing with his mechanical arm, his thick fur standing erect. Fat blue sparks leaped between Howell and the monstrous growth, but he appeared to ignore them, as he did the scorch marks and gaping holes they were leaving in his pelt. His wolflike features were twisted into a snarl of rage.

Goldberry was awake as well, weak from the blood the vampire root had taken from her, but batting at it with one unprotected hand. She was coughing and tears streamed down her cheeks. Elsie could see she was afraid to grab the thing as the Earth girl had, but the leftenant commander, pistol in her other hand, was looking for a place to put one of her big .40 caliber projectiles.

Inside her facepiece, Elsie's smartsuit gave a final moan. The air she was breathing already tasted used and stale, and her amplified vision began fading to gray.

The thrashing stopped.

Everything went quiet.

As she ordered her smartsuit's exterior voltage shut down, Elsie found she'd been locked in a life-and-death struggle with what now appeared to be nothing more than a piece of inert rope. In the dim, foggy vision provided by her suit's slowly self-regenerating power supply, she saw Grossfuss towering over her, his great daggerlike fangs exposed in a ferocious grin. On one pants leg he was wiping what looked like human blood—no doubt mixed with plant juices—from a huge and gleaming Rezin Bowie knife she hadn't even realized he was carrying.

He bent down, mouthing words she couldn't hear.

You gonna be all right now, cookie?

Trying to suppress the urge to vomit, she threw the severed vampire root away from herself, sat up, and unfastened her facepiece. The room was filled with a noxious, acrid smell that people of another place and time might have recognized as tear gas.

Goldberry was wheezing audibly.

Her father unleashed sneeze after violent sneeze.

Protected by her anger, Elsie ignored the smell and let the facepiece dangle in front of her.

"Don't," she told her rescuer, "call me 'cookie.' "

The mighty Grossfuss threw back his shaggy head and guffawed, which in turn, as the irritating fumes began to thin, drew an urbane chuckle from Howell.

"And before this goes any further"—Elsie wrapped both arms around her knees and shivered, too exhausted as yet to attempt standing—"I've something I've got to tell you, Father."

Howell cocked his head at her, looking like a record-company logo—and probably knowing it.

"What might that be, my dear?"

"Hey, Cap'n," Grossfuss interrupted, tossing a

thumb at Goldberry, "you want we should step out-side? We could use a breath of fresh air, in any case."

It was Elsie who replied, shaking her head.

"I'm not sure that would be safe just now, Obregon. Besides, almost getting killed by that . . . that *thing* has drastically rearranged my perspective."

He raised his eyebrows, but again, due to lack of contrast, no one noticed.

"Oh?"

"Yeah. For one thing, I'll never ever laugh at *Attack of the Killer Tomatoes,* ever again. For another—and this may not be quite as private or important a matter as I thought—Father, just be-fore we left the *Tom Sowell Maru* I published offi-cial notice I was changing my name. From Elsie to Lysandra."

After a brief silence, Howell padded over to the girl and nuzzled her shoulder.

"Yes, dear, I know."

She opened her mouth, closed it, and opened it again.

"You knew? You knew all the time?"

Her father sighed.

"Yes, dear, I did. The last thing I did before debarking was update my implant. For you, the problem was working up to telling me. For me, it was waiting until you could. Don't worry, I think I understand, and it's quite all right."

For various reasons that seemed sensible to them, the four travelers decided not to mention what had happened in the hut that night to any of the Selfquelled.

They also decided to go back to the *Victor Appleton* and sleep aboard her from now on—with someone wakeful and on guard at all times. In the eerie darkness, they made their way to the subfoline with weapons drawn and every sense alert. Almost to their disappointment, the Earth girl thought, nothing happened. They didn't see a solitary human being, although the ominous papery rustle of corn-shuck wings overhead told them they didn't travel altogether unobserved.

Inboard the subfoline, where the filtered and recycled air felt cleaner and they could make some coffee, a muttering Goldberry began rummaging through the galley, pulling one drawer out after another, scattering their contents, slamming them shut in disgust, and giving the overhead cabinets the same treatment.

"Hey, y'know I just straightened all that up day before yesterday. Real days, I mean, not these here vacuole blinks. Whatcha doin', Leftenant Commander?"

She whirled on the yeti.

"What does it look like I am doing, you abominable annoyance? Doubting somewhat the efficacy of mere bullets against nightmare horrors like that vine back there, and not having had the foresight to provide myself with a shortsword such as you carry, I intend to arm myself with the biggest kitchen knife I can find."

With a puzzled expression, Grossfuss looked down at the handle of the massive edged weapon he carried in a flat thigh-pocket of his smartsuit—in his mighty hand it must have seemed no larger than a letter opener—and shrugged.

Without waiting for a reply, Goldberry turned back to her search.

Howell, up until this moment lost in thought, left his daughter's side near the subfoline's control console to join the angry, frightened First Waver, plunging his furry gray forequarters into a low cupboard beside the vessel's food synthesizer. In a moment he had backed out again, an enormous pair of plastic-handled utility scissors opening and closing ominously in his mechanical hand.

"Not an inestimable notion, that of our young Antimacassarite friend," he told his daughter and Grossfuss. "I do detest having been caught off guard like that. I believe I'll just carry these dainties—this poultry notch seems exactly the right size for that root—in my little rucksack from now on."

His mechanical arm folded and disappeared into the pack, taking the shears with it.

Elsie—now Lysandra—grinned, giving the glasses on her nose an absent shove.

"Well, I just realized"—she yawned—"that while all of you were busy making Zs, I never got any sleep at all tonight—say, can you find anything in that cupboard for me? A big can of napalm would be nice—so let's leave any other analysis or planning you had in mind until tomorrow, okay, Father? Grossfuss? Goldberry?"

"I hate to be the one to point it out," Howell told her, "but it's already morning."

Before they'd even decided what to have for breakfast—Elsie/Lysandra and Goldberry had to fight nausea again when they recalled having eaten what the hut provided—the subfoline's computer informed them they had visitors waiting outside.

It was a watchful four who emerged through the subfoline's upper hull to peer down at the ground.

"Greetings and salutations," Humility addressed them, as if nothing untoward had happened. "I come this day in the name of the Selfquelled People and their Council of Criticism to invite you all to witness our most ancient and honored competition, a monathlon, which we hold in honor of our esteemed guests."

"It sounds a whole lot like 'your tax dollars at work,'" Lysandra whispered to Goldberry, "and by the way, so much for Selfquelled being noncompetitive."

Aloud, she asked, "How about it, do we attend this event and record it on our implants for posterity—"

"Or do we make like sensible people," Grossfuss interjected, "an' bug outa here?"

"Was Christopher Columbus," Howell asked, "what you'd call a 'sensible person,' Obregon? Or Amerigo Vespucci? Or Charles Lindbergh? Or Edward William Bear?"

"Okay, since you're droppin' names, how 'bout Ferdinand Magellan, James Cook, an' Amelia Earhart?"

"I'm afraid I don't quite get the point you're trying to make," the coyote replied. "How do those explorers differ in principle from the others I mentioned?"

"They don't—'cept two got eaten by cannibals and the third disappeared 'thout a trace."

"You refer to Captain James *T*. Cook?" Lysandra asked. "As in 'Where no man has gone before'? And I thought Magellan died of a tropical plague or something."

Her father sighed. "I don't think you're making our case any stronger, Els—Lysandra, my dear. As I believe I mentioned earlier to our friend here, few worthwhile endeavors are without a certain measure of risk. I, for one, shall go and see this celebrated Selfquelled 'monathlon,' since it's given in our honor, and the rest of you won't disappoint me if you do exactly as you please."

More discussion took place. Magellan, it turned out, on consultation with stored information, had been killed by natives of the Philippines, while Cook, despite his name and that which the islands had borne at the time, had died presumably uneaten by the Hawaiians who murdered him. Lysandra, surprised to discover an ally in Goldberry, argued that, especially in light of the threatening note, the subfoline shouldn't be abandoned again. But one by one, they followed Howell down from the upper deck of the *Victor Appleton* and back to the village.

On the way, they passed the former site of Humility's cottage. (Or was it, Elsie wondered, the site of Humility's former cottage?) In either case, where it had once stood, now only a blackened hole marked the ground and a littering of decaying vegetable trash. Humility's empty smile appeared, right on schedule, but this time he spoke before any of the four could think of something to say.

"An incompatibility," he told them, indicating the rubble. "I suspected some such might come to pass, although it is truly said one never knoweth until one tryeth. Wouldst thou care to try another of our cottages this night?"

"Thank you," Howell answered the Selfquelled leader, "but our craft requires inspection, and I believe we'll be more comfortable sleeping aboard while it's attended to."

The vacuolite favored them with another of his silent, idiotically self-satisfied grins, and shrugged, as if mildly disappointed. He led the four through his people's village into a meadowlike quarter of the vacuole where none of them had so far ventured. Most of the population, it appeared—men, women, and children just as heartbreakingly distorted as their parents—had turned out for the athletic event and were already in the field, waiting for them.

A dozen of the younger men stood in an uneven, nervous row behind the starting line, a bit of thread held at each end by a couple of the village girls.

"Ready?"

At Humility's sudden, shouted word, the monathlon began in a peculiar manner, with each of the

contestants sitting down abruptly on the ground—
the girls knelt as well, lowering their string—which
seemed consistent to Lysandra, as they hadn't appeared all that enthusiastic to be competing in the
first place.

Grossfuss squinted his eyes and shook his head,
as if he couldn't believe what he was seeing.

Goldberry stood with one hand on her gun and
the other on the handle of the nine-inch butcher
knife thrust through her pistol belt, ready for
surprises.

None of the crowd of observing Selfquelled seemed
to think anything strange was happening, although,
like their leader, the native spectators were more
agitated than the travelers had ever thought to see
them.

"Go!"

"Well I'll be molassesed and feathered," exclaimed
Grossfuss.

Lysandra let out an astonished gasp.

Even Howell's jaw dropped.

Goldberry permitted a noise of contempt to escape her lips.

The contestants had begun inch-scooting along
on their bottoms, tilting first to one side, then the
other, proceeding at as slow a pace as they could, on
what must have been well-callused fundaments, toward the designated starting line. Lysandra wondered what she dared to call this sport in her report
back to the university. *Biathlon,* which seemed more
appropriate somehow, was taken.

At the same time, while making as little forward
progress as possible himself, each of the village
monathlon "runners" was kicking and pushing the
nearest opponent handy with his otherwise unoccu-
pied feet. They were all attempting to shove some
individual among their number through the starting thread. The spectators were frantic—for Self-

quelled People, anyway—commenting to one another
on various fine points of the competition which the
travelers couldn't make head or (Lysandra forgave
herself the unintentional pun) tail of.

"I will be *tarred* an' feathered," Grossfuss observed to no one in particular, "sit-down Sumo
wrestlin'!"

"It is forbidden"—Humility leaned toward them
to comment in loud tones against the noise of the
crowd—"upon pain of disqualification, to move
backwards."

At long last, some unlucky someone got shoved
under the thread by the rest of the competing mob.
The Selfquelled monathlon was over.

Before he could protest, the individual in question was declared the "winner" by Humility and
acclaimed by the watching nonparticipants. Despite
being the center of all this attention, he didn't seem
happy about his victory. On the other hand, all of
the monathlon's "losers" now appeared delighted.
Lysandra was reminded, once again, of the old saying
about public hangings.

Along with the spectators, the former competitors
jumped up, seized the winner and carried him on
their shoulders. Yelling and cheering every step
of the way—Lysandra had the feeling they were yelling and cheering to drown out his screams of protest
—they carried him across the meadow, through a
bordering line of what looked like gooseberry bushes,
inward, to the center of the vacuole.

Overhead, hundreds of plant-birds circled in a
thick flock, reminding her, as she knew they must
remind her prairie-born father, of starving vultures.

At Humility's urging, the four travelers followed
the noisy crowd at a discreet distance. This was a
direction in which, during previous hours, none of
them ventured. The one "day" any exploring had
gotten accomplished, Howell and Grossfuss had found

themselves back at the *Victor Appleton,* Goldberry had examined the village and its inhabitants, and Lysandra—Elsie, as she then was—had remained, she remembered with a shiver, in Humility's now-defunct cottage.

As with everything else she'd experienced in the Realm of the Selfquelled, she felt, rather than saw, a hazy, dreamlike atmosphere in which she wasn't quite sure why she was doing whatever it was she did, and didn't much care in any event. She strolled along with her friends, drawn more by whatever she was walking toward than pushed along by curiosity or Humility's encouragement.

Soon, although she didn't know it, she couldn't have turned back if she'd tried.

Another outlandish vegetable outgrowth awaited their inspection when they arrived at the place where all the villagers had halted. In general outline, it wasn't unlike one of the village huts—or even one of the edible fruits within it—but, as she stumbled half-aware around it, Lysandra realized it possessed no door, and had an opening at the top that appeared to be steaming, something like a large, green bell pepper stuffed with tomato sauce and rice.

Lysandra found that her field of vision had narrowed without her noticing it. It was a bit like looking through a tunnel with transparent but smudgy sides. All around her, things seemed to be less real, and she felt a long way from her friends.

The flock circled lower, making her more uneasy. As she had with the vampire root, she wondered if they were animal or vegetable, whether they were independent organisms or somehow functioned as the eyes and ears of . . . of the vacuole itself?

The huge growth in the center of the crowd groaned, spreading itself open. Inside, the thing was scarlet and bilious yellow, the edges of the sections serrated like great teeth.

The crowd grew noisier.

The plant-birds circled lower.

A stench of acid and decay arose, which they could smell even from this distance.

The birds now formed an almost solid green cloud above it, hovering like gnats.

Without further ceremony, and before the travelers could do anything to stop it—even if they'd been inclined or felt they had the right—the winner of the monathlon was lifted and tossed into what looked to three of the four travelers, at least, like a cross between a gigantic Venus flytrap and a ruptured pitcher plant.

Lysandra fought the urge to be sick.

Goldberry sank to her knees, motionless.

Howell too stood frozen, staring.

"Sure hate t'see what happens," Grossfuss observed dully, "if y'get disqualified."

idelberry and Howell, neither of whom was
on a summit, stood and watched. Their
d un...

CHAPTER XII:

Unnatural Selection

"No!"

As if an evil spell had been broken, a horrified
Lysandra found herself rushing forward, shoulder-
ing the crowd aside despite her small size, in an
attempt to rescue the winner of the monathlon. To
her surprise, Goldberry was beside her.

In an instant, they'd climbed to an opening in the
carnivorous growth and pulled the victim from its
vegetable grasp. His feet and ankles appeared covered with acid burns, no doubt the digestive juices
of the plant, but, especially considering possible
alternatives, he was otherwise unharmed. The Earth
girl and the leftenant commander lowered the man
to the ground as gently as possible.

"Are you all right?"

The man blinked up at Lysandra and offered her
one of Humility's meaningless smiles, accompanied
by a wordlessness that might have meant anything
—or nothing at all. He made a few goldfish motions
with his mouth, but remained silent.

"I believe," offered Howell, who'd joined the girls
at a more leisurely pace, "he's in a state of shock."

Lysandra was drawing on the storage capacity of
her suit—water reclaimed from her body and the
environment, held in a layer beneath the surface—to
wash the corrosive from the man's skin. Grossfuss,
who'd also joined them, followed Lysandra's exam-

ple. Goldberry and Howell, neither of whom was wearing a smartsuit, stood and watched. Elsie glanced up, wary of the other Selfquelled, but the crowd had broken up and was drifting back to the village as if nothing unusual had occurred. That struck her as the strangest thing of all that had happened so far.

"Stop!"

The protest had been registered, not by those who'd just thrown their neighbor into the plant—in a few moments all of them would be out of sight— but by the individual they'd sacrificed. He sat up and pushed two pairs of ministering hands away. Lysandra sat back, stunned again. She traded surprised looks with Goldberry.

"Why dost thou treat me," the man demanded, "in this manner so improper and unnatural?"

"My good fellow"—Howell stepped forward—"they were only trying to save your life."

"Saving it for what?" came the reply. "In saving my life, thou hast ruined it in ye process. My thanks," he added sarcastically, "for small favors."

Goldberry stood up. "Why, you ungrateful little—"

"Wait." Howell put up his mechanical hand to silence the leftenant commander, turning back to the victim. "Go on, man. How is it we've ruined your life?"

"I was to perform a service for my people"—he sniffed back a dirt-streaked tear—"which I, like every other within ye Realm of ye Selfquelled, was born to perform soon or late. My victory was proof that I alone was best suited. But now . . ."

The tear became a salty flood. Losing control entirely, the man burst out in wailing sobs.

"Why hast thou done this to me? What have I ever done to thee?"

Howell placed his hand on the man's shoulder.

"What is it that thou wishest—now he's got me doing it—us to do, instead? Must we leave you—"

"Leave me"—his face brightened with a look of ecstasy—"to ye worthy end which I and my people have chosen for me! It may yet not be too late! If so, I shall declare myself well satisfied and bid thee all a courteous and grateful farewell!"

"Well," replied the coyote, "that's clear enough."

Lysandra nodded, stood, and dusted her hands off, sealing her suit and joining Grossfuss and Howell, who'd backed away. Leaning against the leathery side of the plant-thing, the man climbed to his feet and began looking for footholds to carry him back to the still-open upper half. With a shared sigh, the three Confederates turned.

"Wait!" Goldberry cried. *"You cannot leave him here like this!"*

"We must, Goldberry," Howell told her sadly. "He has his ways, and we've ours. His is to cooperate with this brutal atrocity, ours to let him do what he will with his own life."

Grossfuss nodded solemnly, but said nothing.

"It would have been different," Lysandra added, taking Goldberry's arm, "if he'd been unwilling. We'd have fought the whole vacuole for him, if necessary."

"I understand you," Goldberry told them, "no better than I understand the Selfquelled."

She offered no more arguments, but let Lysandra and her friends lead her away. Even so, angry, injured tears streaked the leftenant commander's cheeks, just as they had those of the would-be sacrificial victim. She paused every few steps to look back. By this time the winner of the monathlon had made it to the opening in the top of the plant. He paused to shout and wave cheerfully at the four travelers and leaped in, making a hideous wet noise as he struck the inner surface.

The process of being digested by the plant must have been painful, for his screams—assaulted emotionally and philosophically, Lysandra was sickened to the center of her being—slowly diminishing in strength, followed them long after the plant-thing was out of sight. When they'd almost made it back to the *Victor Appleton,* Grossfuss collapsed and had to be dragged the rest of the way.

This time it was Obregon Grossfuss who lay trembling and unconscious in his cabin, while his fellow travelers conferred. Her father had been correct in observing that each individual experiences different and purely personal limits to his courage. Or whatever it was that had failed the powerful Himalayan.

In the galley, Howell looked up from his coffee. Only his daughter knew him well enough to be aware he was having trouble overcoming certain strong reactions of his own to what had happened.

"I confess," he told the two, "that this barbaric ceremony, or something like it, is what I've been expecting all along."

Lysandra nodded. "It's certainly a source of the surplus energy and organic chemicals you predicted would be necessary for life in this vacuole to continue as it does."

"Indeed. I wonder if you noticed, as I did, how rapidly anything organic that happens to drop on the 'ground' —Humility's entire hut as an example— decays. Certain questions remain regarding the efficiency of the process, how frequently sacrifices must be made, given that the sleeping Selfquelled are also tapped every 'night' in their plant-provided dwellings by those artery-seeking rootlets."

"How can you discuss this calmly?" Goldberry demanded, not coping well with her own nausea and horror. "I do not want to hear about it!"

"Changing feelings," Lysandra inquired, "about the ecotopia you thought we'd discovered?"

Howell placed a paw over his daughter's hand in gentle admonition.

"Try to be kind, my dear."

Nonetheless he ignored Goldberry's qualms himself to lecture the girls on organisms living in Earth's sea-floor thermal vents and creatures elsewhere that survived independent of a sun's energy. The vacuole, he argued, wasn't quite as pure a case as any of those. In many ways, it was considerably stranger.

"Which," he concluded, "leads me to a grimmer deduction. Humility speaks as if his culture were thousands of years old. I think the phenomenon's more recent, perhaps only a few centuries."

"How have you arrived at this remarkable idea?"

Despite her disgust and disillusionment, Goldberry had become interested in what Howell had to say.

"Well, as you'll recall, when we arrived in this macabre locale—was it only twelve hours ago?—the Selfquelled, through their spokesbeing, espoused a stringent equalitarianism of which you found yourself approving. It was, I gathered, considered an unforgivable breach to stand out from the crowd in any particular."

"Are we not born equal?" the leftenant commander asked. "Should society not reflect this fact?"

Howell shook his head. "It's possible, my dear, that we're all conceived equal. Although I remind you that genetic evidence militates against it. We begin accumulating different experiences from that point onward, and I rather doubt we're born that way."

"And by the time," Lysandra added, this being her specialty, "any of us has generated his first independent thought, equality's completely out of the question."

Goldberry pouted. "All the more reason," she

insisted, "that society is obliged to *make* things equal."

"By discouraging independent thought?" Lysandra asked.

"Equalitarians lament inequality so lugubriously," Howell continued as if his daughter hadn't spoken, "because they miss its principal feature. More than merely one or two (or one or two dozen) dimensions exist along which to measure any being's potential strengths and weaknesses. As you might expect, I'm rather an awkward tennis player. Whereas Elsie—forgive me, dear—*Lysandra* might have made a career of it. We're quite unequal with regard to tennis playing."

"Lugubriously?" Goldberry looked dubious.

"On the other paw, Lysandra usually relies on me to find food when, say, we're on a camping trip. I enjoy it, possess the nose and ears and legs for it. I'm also a better shot than she is, though I doubt she'll admit that. Thus we're unequal with regard to hunting, although the inequality in this case flows the other way."

"Trivialities," Goldberry argued. "I do not see where this recitation is leading."

"I'd hardly expect you to. You see, thousands, millions of endeavors permit the measure of a being to be taken. None of us will measure up the same way at any two. This is fortunate: it gives each of us a unique constellation of aptitudes; something to exchange against the equally unique—but differing —aptitudes of others."

"Individual differences are to be celebrated," Lysandra asserted, "not lamented. They're what make trade and every other achievement possible for intelligent beings."

"Quite so," agreed her father. "Thus, the one way we Confederates agree to be equal is in the right to remain unmolested while attempting to capitalize on those differing aptitudes."

"So, like us Antimacassarites, the Selfquelled are wrong"—Goldberry was unconvinced—"and you all-knowing Confederates with your money and fancy toys are always right. This is not news. You still have not told me where it leads us."

"She's persistent, the first prerequisite of a respectable intellect." Howell had turned to his daughter, and back to Goldberry. "Consider that, not long after they laid this claim to equalitarianism, the Selfquelled contradicted themselves—to your disappointment—by demonstrating, through the monathlon, that, in their own way, they're quite competitive. I believe the entire tangled truth about the Selfquelled lies in this apparent contradiction. It is, in fact, an outgrowth of other basic facts of life in the vacuole."

Lysandra nodded. "The one unavoidable economic fact is that the plant life must be fed."

"Yes," Howell agreed. "Equalitarianism is the most fundamental social characteristic of the Selfquelled. It probably brought them to Majesty, possibly separated them, in some long-forgotten dispute from whatever colony they were a part of. Competition was a later and, shall we say, ulterior, development, intended to solve their special economic problem in a manner consistent with their primary value—"

"Anonymous mediocrity," Lysandra supplied.

Howell sighed. "No less true for being bluntly put. The idea's to produce a warm body to satisfy the plant. The best and brightest—those who are most fit in a physical and mental sense, and therefore in a social sense least desirable—are detected by various forms of competition and sacrificed to the horror in the center of the vacuole to which all Selfquelled are enslaved by their dependence."

"Defensive customs have evolved," Lysandra pointed out, "such as sitting down and shoving the 'winner' over a starting line that is also the finish—in more ways than one."

"I'd guess," Howell offered, "the local plant evolved as a version of Earth's ant-lion, trapping prey, such as the can-can, by gravity—we nearly fell when we blundered through the wall—and chemical attractants. Now, as long as it's nourished by the Selfquelled—who may have begun their slavery seeking protection from wild beasts—it no longer requires these energy-consuming measures."

Both girls nodded, but didn't interrupt.

"I'm certain pheromones figure in it somehow. Recall how we fell asleep our first night in the hut? Had we been up a full day? Were we that tired? Do you believe that clumsy root could have attacked us if we hadn't been rendered helpless?"

"The second night," Lysandra said, "zipped in my suit, I was immune. Is that what you're saying?"

"What," Goldberry asked, "are pheromones?"

They explained to her that pheromones are organic chemicals that, in various ways, can alter behavior.

She bobbed her head. "You spoke of ants. As they scramble about, they lay down invisible trails for others of their kind to follow. I have watched them. Are those pheromones?"

Majestan ants were from Earth. Howell gave her an affirmative.

"I'd guess," the coyote told her, "the Selfquelled are regulated in every respect by the desires of this local manifestation of the sea. Helpless to resist its blandishments—I got a taste of that on the trek to the sacrifice—they devised means of appeasing it."

"If it were fed," offered the leftenant commander, "it would stop emitting attractants."

"And life," Elsie added, "could go on as before—for the survivors."

"Indeed. Now the attractant merely acts as a signal to the Selfquelled that the thing is hungry. At the cue it provides, they immediately declare some sort of competition."

Goldberry shuddered. "Ugh!"

"Pheromones aren't irresistible," Lysandra suggested, "not for us. We can be shocked out of it, as at the sacrifice."

Her father nodded. "Clearly the huts—and the plant-thing in the center—are a prime source. My guess is that the 'birds' propagate it or at least collect and distribute it.

"And what I took to be allergy, and cursed my shots for, was an assault not so much on our physiology as our will, accounting for the claustrophobia I've felt everywhere but in the subfoline."

"It worked to a degree," Goldberry told them. "It kept us where it wanted us and away from other places."

"I thought I noticed," he replied, "that the man-eating thing lay in a direction none of us thought to venture until it wanted us to."

He paused.

"This situation has gone on for hundreds of years. But between the plant's appetites and this culture's skewed ethics, a severe toll has been exacted. I invite you both to take a fresh look at what we know of the Selfquelled."

"At what, for instance?" Lysandra asked.

"For instance at the fact that, outside a range of prepared responses—which is relatively broad and fooled all of us at first—the Selfquelled simply aren't very bright."

Goldberry assumed a scandalized expression.

"Shocking, my dear leftenant commander, but true. Within situations normal to them, they appear at least, well, purposeful. Create a novel situation and they flounder—or ignore it altogether. I'd estimate the useful average intelligence of the Selfquelled to be somewhere between that of a Labrador retriever—one who doesn't enjoy my technological advantages—and a trained seal."

Goldberry opened her mouth and shut it again, permitting Howell to continue.

"More conspicuously, they're deformed, with diminished sight and hearing, flaccid limbs, and slow reflexes. We noticed this, but attributed it to inbreeding. However that may be, the situation worsened, in a shorter interval than inbreeding might have accomplished, by a process I'll call 'unnatural selection,' a system that rewards failure—or at least mediocrity—and punishes success."

"Only those," Lysandra stated, "who fail to win competitions on a consistent basis—the least fit—are permitted to live and produce offspring."

"Precisely. And the result is this state of physical and intellectual devolution we see around us. The situation isn't without precedent in the tax codes of primitive nation-states. Nor, I daresay, in civilized man's latest form of enslavement."

"I'll bite"—Lysandra sighed, recognizing her father's tone—"just to get it over with. What latest form of enslavement?"

A twinkle shone in the coyote's eye. "My dears, I realize you've labored all your lives under the illusion that—with notable exceptions—humanity represents a sort of summit of evolution, the highest, most accomplished life-form to arise on Earth."

His daughter shook her head: "Yes, I'd been laboring under that illusion—with notable exceptions."

"It's possible you're mistaken," her father asserted. "Another organism exists that doesn't walk erect, possesses no thumb, doesn't even have a nervous system, let alone a massive brain. It neither thinks nor works, and doesn't even have to *move*, in order to be nurtured, protected from natural enemies, maintained at the peak of health, while lying exactly where it is, giving nothing in return."

Lysandra yawned.

"And who," Howell continued, undaunted, "lavishes all this tender love on something that is no more than a burdensome parasite? That massivebrained species which fondly tells itself it stands at the apex of billions of years of natural selection! It also tells itself that this malignant growth is beautiful, or moderates environmental extremes. Yet, in those pitiable civilizations that suffer a universal fetish with regard to this loathsome excrescence, there are more beautiful things—sunsets, operas, Impressionist paintings—that receive less attention."

Goldberry opened her mouth.

"These fools," Howell rushed on, "could have done more to moderate the environment themselves, simply by abandoning the wheel, adopting hovercraft, ripping up millions of miles of asphalt and concrete, which turn summer into a sweltering nightmare and winter—when those treacherous materials become ice-coated or packed with snow—into lethal, surrealistic skating rinks for dense, high-velocity traffic.

"But I digress. I was speaking of the lawn.

"For centuries you humans fled the countryside and an unrewarding existence of laboring away your lives from dawn to dusk, which was imposed on you by barbaric tribal leaders in the first place, to the detriment of your health and longevity, for no better reason than the fact that a population of passive bucolics is vastly easier to control and steal from than one of hunters and warriors.

"You escaped by the millions to industrialized cities, afterward to suburbs, only to discover—to your perverse delight—that you were free to work a

full day at some dull, repetitive job, while anticipating the joy of trudging behind a noisy, foul-
smelling engine for no remuneration, sweating away
your leisure hours every week in backyard and
front yard, gathering a harvest of no value whatever.

"Meanwhile, your idle and inquisitive neighbors
were at liberty to evaluate your moral worth upon
no basis more rational than the condition of your
tiny pasture and your worthless crop, while city
governments, worthy successors to those barbaric
tribal leaders, enjoyed yet another excuse to annoy
and harass you if you failed to tend your fields in a
manner the law approved of."

"What," the leftenant commander asked, "is a
lawn?"

Lysandra laughed. "Your whole planet is a lawn,
Goldberry, in need of mowing!"

"My next point," Howell told them, "is more spec-
ulative, but vital to understanding what happened
here. I believe, you'll pardon a sentiomorphism, that
vampire roots and sacrifice have proven insuffi-
cient; the plant's need or greed has caused it, over a
span of time, to pull a sort of swindle, to fake a
quicker turnover of day and night than occurs in
the sun-exposed upper reaches of the planet."

"Sentiomorphism?" echoed Goldberry.

"Shorter years"—Lysandra saw her father's point—
"than on the surface?"

"Precisely," the coyote answered. "The pertinent
clue is what Humility told us about the light-dark
cycle occurring every day, *365 days each year.*"

"But," Goldberry complained, "there are 381 days
in the Majestan year—"

"Yes," Howell told her. "Earth has a 365-day
year, composed of 24-hour days, for a total of 8,760
hours."

"Actually, 365 1/4," Lysandra corrected, "8,766
hours."

"And 23 hours," Goldberry continued, "in the Majestan day."

"For a local total," Howell responded, "of 8,763 hours, making the Majestan year phenomenally close in duration-length to Earth's year, an astronomical coincidence often remarked upon in the appropriate texts."

"So the days are shorter," Lysandra observed, "but they have more of them. Where does that get us?"

"To my point," her father replied. "The vacuole, you see, cycles every 5 hours. Thus 1,753 such cycles are contained in the Majestan year."

"Actually, 1,753.2, but so what?"

"If you counted," Howell informed her, "365 such 5-hour cycles as a year—because that's how long the year was on the planet you came from—there'd be approximately 5 (all right, 4.8) such abbreviated vacuole years to every Earth year."

Understanding dawned in Lysandra's eyes: "I see, so when somebody down here claims he's 123, that means he's only 123 *vacuole* years old"—she referred to her implant—"times 365 vacuole cycle 'days.' "

"Times 5 hours," Goldberry offered, getting into the spirit.

"Which makes him 224,475 hours old, or, dividing by the 8,766 hours in a real year—"

"Prematurely aged," Goldberry interrupted, "his life truncated by the plant, Humility is 26 Majestan years old!"

"Actually, 25.6," Howell corrected glumly, "to be precise."

CHAPTER XIII:
The Council of Criticism

Legs folded beneath him, Humility the Mortified sat on the ground in the center of the ugly, blackened circle that had been his cottage. This was, perhaps, not the most pleasant of places to be sitting. Much of the remaining debris was of the more stubborn type, large chunks of hard-edged cellulose that imprinted themselves on his flesh, and even these were draped with an oozy gray-yellow evil-smelling slime of decay, somewhat similar in texture and appearance to lettuce leaves left somewhere warm and moist to rot for several weeks.

It was, however, the only way known among the Selfquelled that the new cottage, which would grow to replace the old, could accustom itself to its occupant's physiology and particular needs, tailoring nutrients and ingrown furniture to him.

As he sat, another of his people approached and sat nearby, taking care to remain outside the circle.

"May it give ye Benefactor"—Humility gave the newcomer a polite greeting—"ye intruders still cower fretfully within their traveling domicile?"

Howell's guess had been correct. The Selfquelled were extremely slow in a mental sense, although they weren't altogether witless. Everything they knew was the result of generations of long unquestioned habit and rote memorization, whereas new concepts were almost impossible for individuals among them to wrestle with. Moreover, they suffered the same problem any group of normal human beings does: their collective intelligence was that of the brightest person in the group—divided by the number of its members. As a consequence, the conversation that would have taken place in just a few minutes on the surface, among surface-dwellers, in fact occupied the better part of an hour.

"Yes, Most Normal," Ignominy the Unsatisfactory answered after considering the question for five minutes, and comparing it against memories not much older than that, which were already growing dim and hazy. "May Its pleasure nourish us, several among our number have been delegated to watch ye obscene, unnatural thing and to report should they again emerge from within its foul recesses."

Without otherwise moving, Humilty nodded. He could do this much without thinking it through, although a more detailed reply was a good deal longer in arriving.

"This is indeed pleasurable to ye Benefactor; we meantime must convene the Council of Criticism among ourselves."

"Well spoken, Most Normal."

Ignominy had replied with unusual crispness.

After a long pause for thought, it dawned on him he had something else to say.

"I have risked thy justifiable displeasure by anticipating thy wish and summoning ye others."

Such forethought represented an astounding intellectual leap for one of the Selfquelled—not for nothing was Ignominy the Unsatisfactory seated high in the Council of Criticism (and a fair candidate for some future sacrifice)—but he'd retire during the next dark period with a headache owing to his effort.

He added, "I myself, if thou wilt pardon ye impertinent initiative upon my part, have had ye thought that ye presence of these surface-creatures must seem an unconscionable disturbance to ye Benefactor, may Its pleasure ever increase."

"Indeed," a third Critic offered as he joined the first two—he'd been rehearsing this remark since he'd first heard the Council was meeting—sitting down outside the cottage-circle, "for it ith an unlawful opening of ye Thacred Thycle, may ye Benefactor which ith ye axith be kindly enough toward uth to keep it turning."

With some absentmindedness, Humility acknowledged the man's presence. He'd been laboring over a dim idea he didn't want to lose the subtleties of in the middle of expressing it.

"May ye Benefactor nourish thee, Inanity ye Halffinished. As I was about to say to Ignominy, however, there is even yet more to ye matter. Hast thou not noticed they are one and all a great deal cleverer than any among our own number?"

Five minutes passed before Inanity replied.

"I have, may it pleathure ye Benefactor," he responded, "thounder of limb and body, ath well."

Taking a mere three or four minutes this time, Humility pressed on in a relentless manner—for one of the Selfquelled.

"I ask it of thee: doth not ye very existence of these unconsecrated strangers constitute an unsufferable and unforgivable rudeness to ye Benefactor?"

Perhaps another five minutes passed before they all got the point. Eyes widening, Inanity put a hand to his open mouth as if he hadn't thought of this possibility before. Ignominy looked down at his feet and shook his head with a sad expression.

"I agree," offered a fourth voice, that of Repulsivity the Contemptible. "May ye Benefactor, in Its infinite and unquestionable wisdom, mercifully excuse my self-assertiveness in Its august behalf. Ye present crisis cannot be mistaken for anything less than a mighty impatience upon ye part of ye Benefactor."

"It ith even pothible," added a horrified Inanity, having had some extra time to think while Repulsivity spoke, "that by now ye Benefactor groweth angry!"

"How could we expect otherwise?" Humility asked. "After all, inferior sacrifices have been made to it, monathlon or not, ever since their arrival here."

Ignominy looked up.

"Why else would our latest sacrifice have been fetched back up in our faces?"

Although he'd never have admitted it, even to himself, he was scandalized that, even by implication, and even by the Benefactor, the Realm's Critics should be criticized.

"Indeed," Repulsivity agreed, "even now, he who was known as Unworthy ye Despised—"

"—and who," Humility intoned, "shall be called henceforward Unworthy ye Rejected—"

"—lieth disconsolate and inconsolable within his cottage, nursing ye Sacred burns upon his unworthy hide. His very purpose in life and reason for being having been eradicated, Benefactor only knoweth what shall become of him."

"For a fact, no one knoweth," Humility told them. "For no Song of Antiquity telleth what shall come to pass should ye Benefactor become truly angry."

"And no one wanteth to find out!"

After only thirty seconds this time, Inanity had almost screamed the words.

"Perhaps," his leader told him, "it is not too late."

"How tho?"

"Perhaps ye Benefactor might be pleasured to receive a special sacrifice of great quality."

Inanity frowned with the pain of an unusual intellectual spasm, and brightened.

"Ah! It might even manifetht Ith pleathure unto uth in thome thpecial manner."

"Doth anyone know what that meaneth?" Humility had adopted the sternest of expressions toward this latest—and most profane—suggestion, although he no longer remembered it with clarity. "Doth anyone want to find out, either?"

Inanity shook his head, but Humility waited until both of the others joined him. This reestablished their relative positions, and gave him more time to think.

"It is well. Do not attempt to cozen thy Benefactor. We must be careful, however. Surely it hath been lost upon no one that ye intruders are well capable of thwarting us."

"Would these irresponsibles thus presumptuously defend themselves," Ignominy asked, "depriving ye Benefactor of that which rightfully belongs to It?"

Repulsivity the Contemptible, who considered himself a realist and worldly sophisticate, took a full ten minutes to compose his response: he snorted.

"Sadly," Humility told Ignominy, "I suspect myself they would. Strong and clever though they may be, however, we of the Selfquelled still outnumber them."

This time vigorous assents were to be seen all around. No great feat of intellect was required of them to understand that brute strength is additive in character, whereas intelligence isn't. Lysandra or her father might have told them this had always been the central tragedy of human existence, but, they concluded in the same triumph of twisted logic that had launched many more than a thousand ships, and sent armies marching over the faces of a million planets, it appeared to be—and in all probability was—their one advantage.

"Without a doubt," Humility told his fellow Critics, "and at whatever loss to our own numbers, we shall in ye end succeed at overcoming these intruders. They shall be taken to feed our Benefactor in ye center of ye Realm!"

He might well have left it at that, but one of those occasional new thoughts that had made him a great leader among the Selfquelled occurred to him.

"And Unworthy ye Rejected shall find new purpose in his life, for he shall lead ye attack!"

CHAPTER XIV:

Lysandra's Last Stand

Howell felt the tap of a huge finger on the portion of his anatomy he thought of as his shoulder.

"Hey, Cap'n. Sensors say there's somebody outside tryin' t'get our attention."

The coyote focused his attention away from the power-plant readouts he'd been studying in his mind. The yeti had come around an hour or so after they'd gotten back to the subfoline, feeling as well as might have been expected in the circumstances. After further discussion, the four of them had decided—not without a feeling of considerable relief all around—to quit the Realm of the Selfquelled and continue their explorations and mechanical tests elsewhere.

"Thank you, Obregon, I see that now."

"Just thought you'd wanna know, Cap'n."

Howell's cerebro-cortical implant was showing him the same disquieting image the yeti had seen: half a dozen of the Selfquelled—Humility the Mortified somewhat conspicuous by his absence—standing in a group together beneath the *Victor Appleton*'s needle-sharp prow, waving up at its unseen occupants.

A handful of plant-birds circled overhead.

"Where," he asked, "are Goldberry and my daughter?"

"Why, down here in the boiler room," came Lysandra's implant-carried voice, *"harmonizing on au-*

thentic sea chanteys and shoveling Number Nine coal, exactly as you instructed, Captain Bligh. But I dinna think she'll e'er make Warrup Six."

"I wonder," the coyote told her, "if they offer a course at U.M.C. in Remedial Literature. If so, remind me to sign you up. I take it you heard Obregon's delightful news?"

He "heard" a mental sigh: *"And passed it on to the leftenant commander. They make a pretty picture down there. Too bad we don't have flamethrowers. We're on our way forward."*

Howell could see his daughter coming toward him along the vessel's single short corridor as she thought the last few words at him. For several hours, as part of their general preparations for departure from the vacuole, she and Goldberry had been checking the subfoline over, inch by cubic inch, looking into every nook and cranny for any trace of the sabotage the threatening note had implied.

She plopped herself down at the galley table and made room for Goldberry beside her.

"Well, I have to admit," she told her father, with a look of frustration, "that if anybody anywhere did anything unsavory to our trusty ship, we sure can't find it."

She glanced at the leftenant commander for confirmation.

Goldberry's expression was one of disgust.

"What do you suppose *they* want?"

The yeti joined them at the table, as usual folding one of the chairs away (although melting might have been a better expression) and sitting on the floor.

"T'say good-bye, I hope."

"From your mouth, abominable one"—Goldberry grinned up at the Himalayan—"to Her ears."

Grossfuss' jaw dropped.

"Well fry me in peanut oil, I do believe this here Antimacassarite's developin' a sense of humor!"

Howell chuckled.

"So it would appear. Well, I expect I'd better go up and see what it is our former hosts want. Lysandra, to descend to the vernacular, would you care to ride shotgun for me? And I'd greatly appreciate it if you two"—with a nod he indicated Grossfuss and Goldberry—"would remain here below, merely as a precaution."

Grossfuss frowned, although, as with most of his expressions, nobody could see it.

"Aww, them nakes is all wimps, Cap'n. We oughta—"

Abruptly, Goldberry stood up.

"We shall do as our captain orders!" she told the yeti, softening her tone to add, "In this way we can act as reinforcements, should they be required."

The Himalayan gave her a hand salute Lysandra had last seen someone use in *Duck Soup*.

"I-hear-and-obey-Leftenant-Commander—*sir!*"

Either the two were becoming friends, Lysandra thought, or they were going to kill each other before this voyage was over with. Tactics settled, however, she and her father checked their weapons and stood on a portion of the deck that extruded itself upward until their heads, their shoulders, and so forth, had penetrated the ceiling.

At last they were standing on the hull, looking down at the small gathering below.

"Howell ye Nahuatl," one of the Selfquelled shouted up at the coyote, "Humility ye Selfquelled lieth in a mortal state, next to deceasement. In this extremity, he requesteth your kindly presence and that of all of your *Victorappleton* people, that we might all, before the end, understand and forgive one another."

Howell looked up at his daughter, a twinkle in his eye showing both suspicion and resignation.

"We can hardly refuse," he told her, "can we?"

"Ask me, why don'tcha!" the implant circuit crackled in their brains.

"Ask me!"

Lysandra grinned behind the facepiece she'd zipped into place, and shook her head.

"And the voice of the chicken," she misquoted, "is heard in the land. Father, I don't think it can hurt anything to go take a look, as long as we all—"

Noise filled her implant again.

"Keep our powder dry? That's what you told us the last time, cookie, just before the human sacrifice. An' you can bet I'm gonna do exactly that, an' the leftenant commander here agrees with me! Too bad I left my grenade launcher in my other suit!"

"Don't call me 'cookie'!"

Despite their trepidations, it was only a few minutes before the four travelers were on their way back to the Selfquelled village. As they walked along, they communicated by implant, reassuring Goldberry with an occasional remark in her direction.

"Hey!"

Lysandra was lying flat on her face in the mossy undergrowth, stunned and confused, before a dull throbbing pain spreading across her shoulder blades told her something had struck her in the back. She rolled over just in time to avoid being hit again by one of the green plant-birds, swooping on her like a hawk.

"Elsie, look out!"

As her father shouted, the vegetable beast plowed into the ground and stopped.

Its neck was broken.

"Hey, you ding-busted whatchamacallit, leggo!"

Grossfuss was shaking one of his arms in desperation, trying to detach another of the avians that had alighted there, seized him in its long, curved talons, and was shredding his smartsuit and the fur underneath with its razor-sharp beak.

Its green, eyeless face was streaked with scarlet.

A loud multiple blast split the air and Grossfuss was free, although parts of the bird still clung to him. Lysandra holstered one of her Walther UVPs, but kept the other in her hand as she began to struggle to her feet. Before she had quite made it, something else hit her from behind, and she found she had 150 pounds of inept but enthusiastic Self-quelled attacker to contend with, climbing on her back with both arms clamped tight around her neck.

A canine snarl and a human yelp told her her father had been assaulted, but the individual who'd done it was already regretting his impetuosity. Judging from noises all around her, Grossfuss and Goldberry had their problems, too.

Lysandra whirled, trying for a hold on her assailant, leaped up, powered by nothing more than adrenaline, and landed on her back. She heard a *whoofing* sound and the dull crunch of ribs breaking. The stranglehold loosened, but before she could take advantage of it, two more of the vacuolites had landed on her stomach and legs.

"Okay," she gritted between her teeth, "it was *your* idea!"

She pressed the business end of her microcaliber electric pistol into the side of the nearest head and pulled the trigger, seeing the flare at the muzzle as the trajectiles began to heat up with air friction, feeling both the recoil and the resulting mess splash against her suit-face. Something tried to seize her arm as she wiped it across her face, but she shot the person lying on her legs and was back on her feet before this could happen, surrounded with Selfquelled three or four rows deep, all climbing over one another to get at her.

Plant-birds circled thicker than they'd been at the human sacrifice, diving to strike a blow here, impale someone with a beak there, lash out with talons where they could, seeming not to care what punishment they inflicted on themselves or their allies. Lysandra put several trajectile bursts into the flock, thinning it for only a moment before it formed a solid deadly cloud once again.

Beneath that, and over the heads of the Self-quelled, she saw Howell's mechanical arm shoot upward, its three-fingered hand grasping the rounded, checkered grip of his antique Rockola .230 machine pistol with its big half-circle magazine, which, until now, had rested hidden but ready in his knapsack. The long-barreled weapon roared and crackled, a blue-pink fireball a yard across blossoming at its perforated muzzle as it spat half a dozen soft-cored, aluminum-jacketed bullets toward whomever had assaulted the coyote.

Goldberry, a professional soldier, was no stranger to fighting, and acquitted herself with brave aplomb. Her odd magazine revolver generated a flatter, less spectacular noise, and a good deal less muzzle-flash, but she used the weapon to good effect, firing it within inches of her hips and legs, peeling the clutching hands—and those they belonged to—away from her as if she wielded a saber.

Impressed, Lysandra began to follow her example, shooting into face after face, only to see them replaced by others, as in a nightmare, their expressions—like her own, if she'd known it—growing more desperate and savage by the second.

Mighty Grossfuss had a weapon in each great hand. Firing his Sebastian Mark IX, one well-aimed shot after another, he also swung his enormous gleaming Rezin back and forth, clearing a blood-soaked zone of death about him as he waded toward the six-foot space between her and Howell, attempting to close their ranks.

At one point, Lysandra thought she saw a head with a startled look fly past her on one of the yeti's extravagant backswings, but she might have been mistaken.

Perhaps.

She wondered if the beseiged Himalayan still thought the Selfquelled were all wimps.

Lysandra discovered she experienced peculiar moments of clear-minded hyper-awareness—almost like little windows in the battle—mixed in with all her fear and anger and confusion. Whenever she or one of her friends managed to kill—or perhaps only injured—one of the Selfquelled, a peculiar thing happened. Green snaky tendrils—horrible reminders of the vampire root—reached up through the mossy covering to pull his (or her) mangled body through the soil and below, into the ground, which closed up without a furrow afterward.

So much, she thought, concerning her mental questions about funeral customs in the vacuole.

She was shooting with both pistols, now, since someone had tried to remove her spare from its charge-holster, kicking hard at whatever her trajectiles didn't obliterate—remembering to use the balls of her feet, their edges, her heels, but never her toes—fighting with her suit-protected knees and elbows, even the backs of her gloved hands, trying to close the gap herself. By now she could see their stubborn enemy was attacking in waves, waiting for the surface-dwellers to exhaust themselves a bit more each time before they closed in again for the kill.

The kill?

With this half-thought, she realized—with a sickening start—that the efforts of the Selfquelled all seemed aimed, not at killing their victims, but at grappling with them, pulling them down and capturing them. In this moment she knew, without the slightest doubt, the idea compelling the Selfquelled was to sacrifice the four travelers, perhaps as revenge for interfering with the aftermath of the monathlon, to the hideous plant-thing in the center of the vacuole.

And to think—just minutes ago, although it seemed like much longer—all she'd been worried about was some tasteless practical joker's stupid threatening note.

This must have been what Ferdinand Magellan and Captain Cook had felt like!

She turned and smashed the barrel of one of her weapons against someone's head, and stomped on them—somewhere, she wasn't certain where—when they'd fallen, horrified that she enjoyed the feel of breaking cartilage and bones underfoot.

Just a moment later, she discovered, to her utter dismay, that they had much more than just the Selfquelled to contend with. Beneath her feet she felt a quivery shaking, something like an earthquake, and felt herself lifted her own height into the air. The "ground" itself—part of the vacuole, she realized, and the hungry plant-thing in its center—was rising up to fight against the travelers. The sheer mass of their enemies had been too much for them in the first place. Now this.

They were in danger of being overwhelmed.

"Father!"

She realized Goldberry had gone down beneath that mass.

At the same time, Grossfuss had become nothing more than a huge, angry, swarming mound of vicious human beings with an angry Himalayan yeti at its core.

Turning to catch a glimpse of her father, Lysandra was struck a sharp, resounding blow on the head.

She thought she'd felt her skull crack through her suit hood, fell to her knees, tried to shoot everything she saw about her into bloody rags, and tipped over on her face, still semiconscious, but unable to move.

It seemed like a long time went by.

Something—somebody—rolled her over, prodded her here and there, and abandoned her.

She wondered, idiotically, if she were dead.

At first she thought perhaps it was the press of the enemy, living and otherwise, which kept her motionless, but, as this weight was lifted from her body by unseen hands, Lysandra discovered she still couldn't move even a single muscle.

That last blow to the head, she thought, must have done something pretty serious to her.

Helpless, she watched her friends being tied with some local rope she hadn't seen before—why she thought of this or cared, she didn't know—and dragged off toward the center of the vacuole, to a hideous sacrifice, she was certain.

And knew why she cared about that.

Before they and their captors had altogether disappeared from sight, more green tendrils, much like the ropes, slithered up from the ground all about her. The ground beneath her body softened until she felt like she was floating on a bed of gelatin. Believing she was dead, she thought—if *believing* was the word to use—the vines pulled her down into the unknown depths.

But not before unconsciousness had claimed her.

And darkness.

CHAPTER XV:

The Second Expedition

Utter silence fell across the Realm of the Self-quelled.

In the vicinity of the H.S.P. *Victor Appleton,* it was no less silent. The unique vessel lay abandoned, half its hundred-yard length thrust through the vacuole wall, the other half projecting into the sea it had come from, its needle-sharp prow angled like the bowsprit of a sailing ship, into the still, humid, pheromone-laden air.

Without warning, a tentative but insistent series of scratchings could be heard—if anyone had been around to hear it—beside the bristled hull where it emerged from the wall. A hardened leaf fell with a clatter. The irregular scrabbling went on a few more seconds, stopped, started in a different place, inches higher or lower, stopped again, and started all over in the place it had begun. From time to time, at the extreme edge of audibility, muffled by dense vegetation, an eerie, high-pitched whistling accompanied this odd phenomenon.

Within minutes, a slim, tapering protrusion could be seen—if anyone had been around to see it—insinuating itself between hull and broken wall-edge, similar in appearance to the thirsty roots in the Selfquelled dwellings, as it was to the grasping vines that had disposed of their battle dead, but with certain differences. The most noticeable was that it wasn't green like everything around it, but bluish gray in color (or grayish blue) shading to a darkened version of the same hue at its tip. Rather than any of the various vegetable textures displayed by aspects of the single organism that constituted the vacuole, its surface gave the appearance of fine-napped velvet.

The apparition moved with intelligence and purpose, wiggling this way and that, up, down, sideways, extruding itself further through the narrow aperture created in the wall by the subfoline. The whistling came again from outside, louder this time, pitched just right, so that a human being with unprotected ears would have slapped his palms to the sides of his head and yelped out an involuntary complaint.

The soft-textured tapering object, not unlike the tail of a laboratory rat in all but color, or perhaps a velvet-covered garter snake, withdrew. It was replaced by the glittering, double-edged, hollow-ground blade of a spade-pointed spear which, like its organic predecessor, sawed this way and that, up, down, sideways, this time scattering wall-shavings and larger fragments on the "ground" below.

When it had done its work, the blade backed away, and the previous object manifested itself again. This time it kept coming, growing longer and broader until a yard of the thing had intruded into the vacuole, followed by the alien presence it was a part of.

Resembling nothing more than an attenuated three-legged starfish (Earth's deep-sea brittle star might have made a good comparison) an impressive seven feet from tentacle-tip to tentacle-tip, the creature was notable not for its fuzzy blue-gray tentacles, but for its eye. It possessed only one, but anyone would have agreed it was more than enough. The size of a basketball (some explanation would have been necessary to make this likeness understandable to the individual whose eye was being discussed), it occupied the center of the alien, constituting the majority of its bulk. What was most remarkable was that it formed a transparent crystalline sphere, transfixing (in a less poetic sense than usually intended by reference to the eye) the creature's body, so another person could have looked straight through the owner of this massive organ, his own vision obstructed only by the presence of a black, softball-sized object (requiring more explanation), the sensitive outer surface of which served as the pupil, and interior of which was, in fact, the creature's capable brain.

Without turning (and who could have told whether it had turned or not except another just like it?), this latest intruder into the Realm emitted one of its ear-penetrating whistles and moved away from the subfoline. Warbling and chirping, a second giant three-legged starfish emerged from the battered foliage, followed by a third, a fourth, and a fifth. The passage they squeezed through grew easier with each new entrant. Before long, a dozen of the peculiar organisms had joined the first, each clutching three or four deadly-bladed spears in its tentacles, twittering and staring around in astonished curiosity.

Like the others, the leader of these alien beings stood balanced on the end of a single tentacle (no greater an accomplishment than the way human beings stand on two feet—many nonhumans throughout the galaxy wonder how they manage it) using the other pair of appendages as arms. Unlike the others, in addition to its clutch of spears, it wore some sort of medallion, a gleaming gold in color, strapped around the base of one tentacle close to the gigantic eye.

On another tentacle, in a flapped fabric military holster identical to the one leftenant commander

Goldberry MacRame had been issued by her Anti-macassarite Leafnavy, it wore a blunt-muzzled pistol which that particular holster had never been intended for, and which, in turn, had never been intended by its makers, back on Earth, for use by any but a human hand. On a broad, anchoring strap, the leader's third tentacle bore a small supply of spare ammunition.

Having assured itself its followers were all accounted for, the creature whistled to them again, issuing an order of march. At once the readily comprehensible anatomy and stance of the alien warriors were transformed into a blurred, bewildering pinwheel spectacle of whirling limbs and glittering blades as the intruders began cartwheeling over the ground at a respectable rate, tentacle-tip following tentacle-tip in a circular motion, each limb passing its burden of spears back to the one following it, before meeting the ground.

The creatures had traveled at least several hundred yards in this manner, at perhaps twenty-five or thirty miles per hour (they were all accustomed to a much more circumspect pace across the treacherous and broken surface of the Sea of Leaves and found the higher speed permitted by the firm floor of the vacuole exhilirating beyond words—or whistles), when they halted again for a look around.

Without warning, a sudden deep rumbling came to them, frightening the warriors who, out of long-established martial reflex, backed themselves into a dense circle bristling with razor-sharp spearpoints. Their leader, holding all of his spears at the vertical in one tentacle, drew his pistol with another, searching for a likely target over its front sight of blaze orange plastic. Beneath their tentacle-tips, the ground had begun to bulge and swell in an ominous manner.

They'd just begun to relax—evidenced by their

resumed, if somewhat nervous peeping—when, with a rude and titanic spitting noise, the ground burst open at their metaphorical feet, ejecting a dark and bulky object at a tremendous velocity high into the air, and closing up at once behind it. The ascending object hit the peak of its trajectory and started down again, landing with a tremendous thump right in the unprotected middle of the scattering warriors.

When the dust—every bit as metaphorical as their feet—had settled, they saw a sight they at least recognized. Stretched out on the ground lay a smartsuited human figure that rolled over onto an elbow, groaned, and looked up at them through the paratronic medium of its blank-featured sealed facepiece.

Turning up into a seated posture, the figure lifted a gloved hand to open its hood.

"Fancy meeting you here," it told the creatures. "I'm Els—Lysandra Nahuatl. You must all be *taflak*."

A confusing minute or two were required before things and people began sorting themselves out. The taflak, of course, being intelligent creatures (and therefore, in a manner of speaking, only human) held a hurried conference among themselves. When in doubt, as the old saying goes, organize a committee and hold a meeting. To Lysandra it sounded just as if she'd fallen into a bushel basket full of soft, hollow toys—rubber duckies—with squeakers in their navels.

She used the interval to sort herself out.

Once she'd been pulled by those tendrils below the surface, she'd discovered, to her immense relief, she hadn't been paralyzed at all by being struck on the head. Instead, her automated smartsuit had hardened itself—to a much greater degree than she'd ever realized was possible—to protect her. It had been a lot like wearing a body cast, on every square inch of her body.

It had been dark in those depths, and, despite the fact nothing had happened to her down there, more frightening than anything she'd ever been through.

During the terrifying time she was unable to move, however, she didn't give up. Having learned something from what she thought of as her "electrifying experience" with the vampire root in Humility's cottage, she'd experimented with her cerebrocortical implant, letting just a trickle of current flow across her smartsuit's surface until she found the precise amount of power necessary to give the vacuole that had swallowed her a thoroughgoing "stomachache."

She wished her father and Grossfuss were here now—and Goldberry too, she supposed—if only to hear their protests when she informed them with a smug expression that the results of her modest experiment had exceeded all reasonable expectorations.

Feeling stiff and sore all over, she climbed to her feet, trying not to groan again.

She was most unhappy about one thing. Both of her holsters were empty. Shrugging, she realized some small chance might exist, anyway, that her electric Walther UVPs hadn't been swallowed with her after all, or carried off by the victorious Selfquelled. Flipping down the cover of her gunbelt buckle (this system, for various tactical reasons, couldn't be accessed via implant), she manipulated the miniature control buttons on its back, and turned this way and that until, to her surprise and delight, she heard a faint beeping noise.

Stepping off in the direction of the strongest beeps, she heard the signal grow stronger and stronger, the pulses become more frequent, until they merged into a single, continuous tone. Stooping down, she picked up one of her compact .01 caliber weapons from where it lay unmolested on the ground, reloaded it at once from a pouch of trajectile magazines on her belt, and reholstered it so that it would replenish itself with energy as soon as possible. She reset the mechanism within the buckle, and soon discovered her other pistol, still lying where it had been dropped during the furious and confusing fight.

Meanwhile, the taflak seminar had broken up, and the obvious leader of these genuine Majestan natives approached her, taking great care, which amused and touched her, not to move in too abrupt a manner and perhaps take the chance of startling her into using one of the powerful and deadly weapons she'd just recovered. She noticed at once that it—he, she reminded herself, or she—was wearing a pierced Confederate coin strung onto the broad base of one of its tentacles, a massive, solid-gold two-ounce chunk of common currency known as a *superlysander* after the same President of a century earlier she'd been named for, and whose bearded countenance graced one side of the thing.

He was carrying a stubby-handled long-bladed spear, almost a guardless sword, which would have looked at home in the hands of a Zulu warrior, but he also wore a Confederate sidearm of some sort—perhaps a Brown & Brown slug pistol, it was hard to tell, just looking at the weapon's floorplate—crammed into an Antimacassarite military snap-flap holster. Lysandra had always regarded covered holsters as a bit imprudent since they slowed the draw, but considering how the taflak traveled (something she'd seen in her studies aboard the *Tom Sowell Maru*), they made better sense for this particular species.

She decided it was wisest to let him speak first.

"I say, old fellow, terribly astonishing, discovering you down here like this, what?"

Lysandra jerked back with surprise. Although its

voice had been high-pitched and a bit squeaky, the creature had spoken to her in perfect English—extremely *English* English—with an accent that seemed familiar to her somehow.

She cleared her throat.

"Yes, well, I guess I'm somewhat astonished, myself. I thought you people were all surface-dwellers. And by the way, no offense, but I'm not a fellow, I'm a girl."

"Dear me," replied the taflak, and for a moment he sounded just like her father—if Howell had been breathing helium. "Is my face red, speaking figuratively, of course. With all due respect, Madame Lysandra, I rather doubt you're capable of pronouncing my given name, don't you know, my tribal dialect being what it is, and so forth. But members of your species, among others, have previously referred to me as 'Middle C,' no doubt for the pitch and quality of my voice, and I find this quite pleasing and entirely satisfactory."

Middle C's accent, Lysandra realized with a start, after listening to it long enough, was Fodduan. An interesting theory began taking form in the back of her mind, having to do with the boy and the lamviin she'd seen back in Talisman. If circumstances permitted, she'd remember to ask Middle C about it later on.

The taflak spoke again.

"Kindly be good enough to allow me to introduce my henchmen—is that the correct word? Henchmen? Somehow it doesn't seem quite— *Associates.* Precisely the word I want, I believe, *associates.* Allow me to introduce my associates, 'Siren'—"

To her immense pain, Lysandra learned how this taflak had received his name.

"—and 'Glassbreaker.' "

"Pleased to meet both of you!"

She jumped into the conversation, seizing their

blue-gray tentacles in turn and shaking them before the second "henchman" could demonstrate the quality for which he'd been named. Finding both of her Walther Electrics was one thing, a stroke of luck. She felt even luckier to have retained her glasses intact through the fight with the Selfquelled, and didn't want them spoiled now.

"As they are you, my dear young human female, although they don't speak a word, sorry to say."

She also wanted to get things moving—consistent with the interpersonal and interspecies politeness which intelligent praxeology calls for in "first contact" situations—since too much time had passed since the vacuolites had carried her friends off.

She sat down on the ground, and the three taflak warriors followed her example to the best of their anatomical ability by coiling up their supporting tentacles like snakes or furry bedsprings, thus lowering their great eyes to her level.

Off to one side, a few yards away, the rest of the party posted guards and relaxed.

"What brings you down a thousand feet below the surface of the sea, if you don't mind telling?"

"As you may be aware," Middle C informed her, "a great battle took place several days ago."

Lysandra nodded. She knew the battle in which Goldberry had also fought, although, not knowing how the lines had been drawn, she wouldn't mention this aspect of it to these people.

"We warriors are searching," the taflak continued, employing simpler words than he'd used before, "for those among our people who, after that infamous fight, disappeared beneath the surface, sucked into the Sea of Leaves."

"Pardon me for saying so," she replied, "but so much time has passed. Do you think—"

Middle C leaned closer.

"To be perfectly frank, Miss Nahuatl old girl,

we're also doing a bit of exploring for its own sake, don't you know, something I've dearly wished to undertake for many years, but have never quite been able to persuade my fellow tribesbeings was worthwhile until this rather convenient excuse presented itself."

Lysandra grinned at the adventurous warrior, realizing that, whatever else it signified, the "infamous" battle on the surface was about to become an unprecedented turning point in the history of Majesty for people of all species.

"We've been following," he explained, "a sort of weakened line of least resistance in the fabric of the sea, as it were, which led us straight to this peculiar place."

"Straight, I'll bet," Lysandra replied, "to the stern of our subfoline—our vehicle, I mean, the *Victor Appleton*. We've been exploring, too, Middle C—my father, a couple of friends and I—but I'm afraid something terrible has happened to them."

Hoping she still had time, Lysandra proceeded to recruit the taflak to help save Howell and the others.

CHAPTER XVI:

Three-Legged Calvary

"Hey! Wait for me!"

Lysandra had intended leading Middle C and his tribesbeings into the center of the vacuole, but, as it turned out, she had a hard time keeping up with the cartwheeling warriors.

Plant-birds flapped their dry wings overhead.

Lysandra made sure her smartsuit was well sealed, to avoid the biochemical compulsion the nasty creatures seemed to exert on behalf of the Realm of the Selfquelled. Unlike Earth beings, the Majestan taflak seemed immune to the vacuole's pheromones, which had never been tailored for their benefit.

The whirling natives disappeared with many a *whoop* over a low rise in the distance.

By the time Lysandra had arrived in their wake at the ritual site, they already appeared to have the situation well in tentacle, experiencing less trouble with the Selfquelled—or possessing fewer scruples—than the Confederates and Antimacassarite had. They'd surrounded the devolved humans with a tight bristling circle of spearpoints until their two-legged "leader" could catch up.

The prisoners, however, appeared to have prisoners of their own. Much taller than any of the genetically impoverished Selfquelled, the leftenant commander was visible, standing near the middle of the Selfquelled crowd not far from the carnivorous plant-thing, still alive, unmistakably indignant, but almost mummified in what seemed to the Earth girl like miles of vacuole-grown rope.

Lysandra realized, feeling an odd, hollow sensation in her chest—as if her heart had switched to a different time-signature—that she could also hear her father, arguing with his captors. She couldn't make out individual words yet. The remainder of the Selfquelled seemed to be standing around waiting for something.

As it turned out, before the taflak had arrived, Grossfuss had just been given to the plant-thing.

Heedless of any possible risk, a grim and determined Lysandra strode through the line of spear-brandishing alien volunteers, elbowed her way past dozens of dispirited vacuolites, and joined Howell, who seemed to be wearing even more rope around his body than the leftenant commander. Even as this occurred to her, his mechanical arm popped out between wrappings, poultry shears in hand, and snipped a long row of coils, which fell to the ground and squirmed away.

"Why, hullo, dear," the coyote greeted her. "Glad to see you made it after all—and with new friends, how delightful! This appositely named specimen's Repulsivity the Contemptible, this afternoon's master of ceremonies, and a sort of stand-in for Humility the Mortified, who, I gather, was either a casualty of our recent confrontation, or has more important matters to attend to."

"Mmmphl!" commented Goldberry, one of her restraints being wrapped across her mouth.

Without a word, Lysandra drew both her Walther Electrics and pointed one at each of the man's eyes. The "ground" beneath her feet began to revolt again, rumbling, quaking minutely, threatening to swallow her as it did before, until she thumbed the safeties off the ultravelocity pistols; their ready-lights glowed hot and bright, and a suddenly sweating assistant Selfquelled leader motioned to the huge, squat growth they all stood beside, somehow calling it off.

The quaking subsided.

"Articulately put, my dear," Howell approved. "I was attempting to persuade him myself that further resistance is hopeless. I'm devastated to inform you they did manage to have their way with poor Obregon, before our newfound allies manifested themselves, which is what's occasioned the delay. I'm sure he takes some satisfaction in knowing he's a larger meal than this disgusting object of worship's accustomed to, and is proving rather difficult to digest."

Lysandra was shocked to hear her father talk this way about a friend who'd met a hideous fate.

"Why should he care anymore?" she complained, astonished she'd grown this fond of the Himalayan without realizing it. "Don't you understand, he's dead!"

"Like Lysander's braided beard I'm dead," her implant crackled. *"Get me outa here!"*

"He volunteered to go first," her father chuckled, "realizing his suit would protect him. Goldberry and I let him, since neither of us happened to be wearing one."

"It is evil," asserted Repulsivity the Contemptible, "to deceive and deprive the Benefactor!"

"Mmmphl!" Goldberry insisted angrily.

"Say"—Lysandra grinned—"a great idea, Leftenant Commander! Wish I'd thought of it myself!"

She holstered her pistols.

Using both her small hands, she pried a couple of the living ropes apart where they encircled Goldberry's narrow waist, and, with a wiggling motion, withdrew the enormous kitchen knife that the Selfquelled—not being a weapons-oriented people in particular—had somehow overlooked, and which the Antimacassarite, most likely in the desperate confusion of the battle, had forgotten all about.

The Earth girl turned, plunging the long blade full length into the plant-thing, slashing down.

Ignoring Repulsivity's hysterical screams, and the accompanying tearful moans and wailing sobs of the rest of the Selfquelled, the taflak waded in and followed Lysandra's example, wielding their sword-like spears, chopping the "Benefactor" up like a cabbage before it "knew" what was happening and had a chance to retaliate.

They'd almost been required to hack it down to ground level before Grossfuss popped out of the middle of the green and red and yellow mess, covered everywhere with vegetable pulp and noxious-smelling slime, but suited up to the top of his shaggy sagittal crest and otherwise none the worse for the bizarre experience.

Reeking, he stretched a leg, climbing onto level ground while everybody who could move backed away.

"Hiya, Goldberry," his voice came through a suit-amplifier. "Guess we'll talk when you aren't all tied up."

He turned to Lysandra.

"I never believed you was dead, cookie. I knew you and your little dog Toto here'd figure a way t'rescue ol' Obregon 'fore I disintegrated or ran outa air."

"Mmmphl!"

Goldberry's eyes were no longer quite sane.

"She's right," Lysandra told the yeti. "Don't call me 'cookie.' "

"Item 529," the coyote declared in his official copilot's voice, "flux capacitor."

"Flux capacitor check," the yeti answered.

To the ear, the interior of the subfoline *Victor Appleton* had already begun to bear more than a close resemblance to an aviary, full of whistling, twittering, and jostling. Lysandra slid into her accustomed place in the jump seat behind her father.

"Well," she told him, "I finally found out where Humility was during the festivities."

A well-showered Grossfuss in the pilot's chair, and Goldberry, long since untied and restored to her dignity in the other jump seat, listened, both of them, like the coyote and his daughter, anxious to be on their way out of the vacuole.

"His old cottage died, as you recall—"

"The captain killed it," the leftenant commander corrected, "for which I thank him."

Lysandra grinned, although the memory of that "night" still caused her stomach to tighten.

"So he did. Anyway, when Repulsivity the Contemptible got over his distemper enough to talk, he informed me Humility's occupied hatching a new cottage. It seems he's gotta sit right where it's growing while it biologically attunes itself to him or something. Otherwise, he'll be allergic to it."

"Or it to him," suggested Howell, flipping switch after switch on the control panel and reading off results as he and the yeti worked their way through the checklist. "Item 555 . . . it would be a great pity, after all, if it had to contend with food poisoning at every meal—I do rather wish you hadn't gone back to the village, my dear . . . primary ignition commencer."

"Check."

Behind them, another spate of high-pitched noises and what sounded like turkey gobblings could be heard as their passengers made travel preparations of their own.

"I had to," Lysandra argued. "You know as well as I do this could well be Confederate praxeology's last and only chance to record the folkways of the Selfquelled."

"Item—"

The coyote and the yeti swiveled to stare at her. They were joined in the expression by Goldberry.

"I know of no such thing, my dear girl," Howell stated. "You mean, I trust, no Confederate in his right mind would willingly come down here again? Where were we, Obregon? Oh yes, here it is: item 566, metalune interociter."

"Check."

Lysandra shook her head.

"I mean the Selfquelled are desperately afraid the vacuole will die. Just as Humility's cottage did."

Around her, eyes widened even further.

"It does make a demented kind of sense, I guess. The monster Brussels sprout that swallowed Obregon was sort of like a giant vampire root, built inside out."

The yeti shuddered.

Howell interrupted his business with the controls to lay a consoling paw on the Himalayan's massive arm.

"Anyway," Lysandra went on, "I offered them our regrets—only slightly insincere—and told them we could give them a ride to the surface, in relays, if necessary. But I also explained, in twenty-three words of one syllable or less, that this disaster would never have happened if they'd just treated their guests more decently—at least refrained from initiating force against them—or simply warned us not to trespass into their vacuole in the first place."

"Hmm," her father answered, but the rest of his reply was buried in the rising level of cheeping, peeping, beeping, and warbling from the galley and parts aft.

"I said"—he raised his voice—"we're pretty full up as it is. What did Repulsivity say to that?"

Lysandra tossed a quick glance over her shoulder; she turned back to face her father.

"He told me the Selfquelled—or rather their Council of Critics—had decided to stay in the vacuole no matter what. They believe it's better to die with it, than to inflict—how did he put it?—the 'evils of a profane world upon the virtuous.' "

The coyote sighed a mental sigh, conveyed to the others by means of paratronics.

"He means rather than leave the deadly—and now uncertain—security the vacuole once offered them. Well, I wouldn't want to wish them anything they'd consider bad luck. Perhaps the infernal thing'll grow back, like Humility's cottage."

The distraction at the rear of the vessel's living quarters was now continuous. Goldberry frowned back, expressing a disapproval she believed she had special justification for.

"I, for one," she offered, "have learned what all of you attempted to teach me at the first sacrifice—"

"Which, by the way," Lysandra interrupted, "also turned out to be a dud. The filthy thing spat him out the second time, the same way it did me, more or less. His fellow Selfquelled are all calling him 'Something-or-other the Rejected.' He even tried to compensate by leading the charge against us at the Battle of the Vacuole, but managed to survive that, although he isn't happy about it."

Grossfuss grinned, and ran a huge paw over a long bank of push-buttons, but waited until a slight lull in the racket from the galley allowed him to speak.

"You think maybe they oughta start callin' him 'Somethin'-or-other the Unkillable'?"

Goldberry opened her mouth.

"Or at least," Howell suggested with a twinkle of humor in his eye, " 'Something-or-other the Inconsolable.' Item 666, positronic synapsifier."

"Check—gee, lookit the colors. Pretty neat. I didn't know we had one of them."

The leftenant commander tried again to get a word in edgewise, but whatever she'd intended saying was drowned out by a chorus of ear-splitting whistles, more twittering, and the sound of bodies jostling for room to rest on the crowded deck.

"Or 'Something-or-other,'" Lysandra added during the next lull, not to be outdone, " 'the Inedible.'"

"As I was saying!" Goldberry shouted into a sudden silence, then continued, embarrassed and annoyed: "Henceforward, I shall be more than willing to leave the Selfquelled People to their chosen fate, whatever it turns out to be."

A blue-gray, elongated, sinuous object slithered across her shoulder, causing her to jump.

"I say, Miz Leftenant MacRame Commander, old thing, deucedly generous of you, what?"

Middle C turned to Howell, who, having completed the checklist, had folded his spare arm away.

"Captain, we've finally settled among ourselves who'll sit on whom, and are now ready to depart."

They all glanced back at the galley, where a dozen taflak warriors were crammed together into an indistinguishable mass of tentacles, razor-sharp spears, and eyeballs.

"Frightfully sorry about the noise," their leader continued. "With all due respect to you and your kind offer of a lift, none of them are accustomed to being pent up like this. I shall be most grateful when we're all home, safe and sound."

Goldberry mumbled something under her breath.

"Excuse me, what was it you wished to say," Howell inquired, "Leftenant Commander?"

She looked down at the floor and shook her head.

"I think it was somethin'," Grossfuss told him, "about hitchhikin' cannibals."

"By the bye," the taflak added, "Glassbreaker found this in the loo—hope it wasn't anything important."

Middle C extended his blue-gray furry tentacle toward them. For the first time, Lysandra noticed the end of the taflak's manipulative organ could be splayed into several dozen slender—almost hair-fine—foot-long tendrils.

What they held was another scuffed and dirty scrap of notepaper. There could be no way of telling when it had been left in the subfoline's head, or by whom.

She suspected it hadn't been one of the taflak:

YOU HAVE IGNORED THE WARNING.
PREPARE NOW TO PERISH.

CHAPTER XVII:

Captain Nemo Himself

The voyage to the surface of the Sea of Leaves was uneventful, right up until the end, in the same sense lost things are always found in the last place—by definition—you look.

At Lysandra's semi-professional insistence, they didn't just back out, turn the *Victor Appleton* around, and go back the way they'd come, but, consistent with Middle C's estimate of the location of his people's village—the warriors, he informed the Confederates, had traveled a fair distance on the surface in their perfunctory search for survivors—struck out on a different course, which was more direct and, at the same time, took them into new territory.

For all of that, however, the young praxeologist-turned-reluctant-biologist failed to catalog a single new species of Majestan wildlife, and the leaves, of course, were always the leaves, fascinating in their own way, but too much of a good thing.

Aloud, she'd made some comment to this effect.

"Game's indeed been frightfully scarce in these marches, as long as any of my tribe remembers."

The leader of the native warriors kept her company in her cabin, sitting, after a fashion, on a folding chair with a tentacle coiled under him for support.

"It's an ill Turning of the Sea," he added, "which brought my village here this season."

Before his one great eye, the curved outer wall of Lysandra's personal sleeping quarters had been converted for use by non-Confederates as a viewscreen, just as it had been for Goldberry on the subfoline's outward voyage.

Looking at Middle C and his companions up close, the Earth girl wondered if it would ever be possible, even in theory, for the taflak leader, or any of his fellow Majestans, to adapt to cerebro-cortical implantation, with his brain floating like that at the center of his giant eye, coated with pitch black optical pigment. In good light, she'd discovered, it was possible to see nervous and circulatory connections between his floating brain and triple-tentacled body.

Outside, a creature designed by a sadistic lunatic "swam" by, all sharp-clawed legs and underslung serrated jaw. Lysandra had seen a thousand of them on the previous trip.

"I understand already," she told Middle C, "that your villages—huts of tightly woven sea branches—are built together on a sort of raft made from the same material. One article compared it to a shredded wheat biscuit, if that means anything to you. But I didn't know they were free to drift across the surface like that."

He gave her a brief, upturning whistle she'd already learned to interpret as a chuckle or smile.

"Where might they anchor themselves otherwise? As my people often say, upon the Sea of Leaves, nothing stands eternal except change. This is most important to remember in a moral sense, since it also implies nothing evil can ever last—"

"Nor anything good," Lysandra put in.

"I confess it," replied the taflak, with a gesture she thought was a shrug, "my people are cynics. And primitives on top of that, so what do we know? But it also means that, in extremity, we can tow our village elsewhere, as I believe we shall have to do before it drifts much farther in this direction."

Lysandra laughed. Middle C's people, to any extent they were primitive—and not just adapted to the particular circumstances they found themselves in—wouldn't stay primitive for long. Not if most of them were at all like this charming, bright, and witty individual who led their hunter-warriors. She'd also noticed the way his thick Fodduan-influenced Oxford accent seemed to be fading as he became acquainted with the crew members of the *Victor Appleton*.

She nodded.

"Well, I think I can explain the lack of game easily enough," she told him. "Grossfuss took these holos as we orbited the outside of the vacuole wall, at my request—okay, call it a tantrum, if you insist—just before we left. It looks to me like the Realm leads a secret life the Selfquelled don't know anything about."

The light within the cabin changed in color and intensity. On the viewscreen, the real-time image of the nearby sea-depths faded, only to be replaced by the three-dimensional polychromatic pictures Lysandra had promised.

She almost regretted it.

If a golf ball had been painted green, and each of its dimples housed a pair of powerful, boneless, saw-edged manipulators—not unlike the vampire root, what she'd started calling the "undertaking tendrils," or even the tentacles of the taflak, but with built-in teeth—somewhere between an eighth and a quarter of an inch long, it would have been a perfect miniature model of the vacuole, taken as a whole. As they watched, a can-can larger than either of them had ever seen before shuddered through its final moments of life, locked in its deadly embrace, fell motionless, and was dragged to the surface.

Similar manipulator pockets were already busy digesting other prey no less impressive.

A faint, involuntary answering quiver passed through Middle C's entire body, beginning with the rimlike torso in which his eye was set like a great jewel, and rippling out to the ends of tendril-tips which reminded Lysandra of corn silk.

"I don't complain, but this isn't the pleasantest of sights, praxeologist friend."

"That thing's a thousand feet across," she told him, "and all appetite. Apparently it just drifts, chewing its way through the Sea of Leaves the same way it chewed its way, metaphorically speaking, through the normal Selfquelled population. Those tentacles are over fifty feet long, about seven times the full span of a large male taflak. No wonder your hunting parties can't find any game here."

Middle C regained control of himself.

"The wonder, my dear female human person, is that neither you and your otherwise impressive vessel nor I and my small hunting party were captured and destroyed."

Suppressing an unprofessional shudder or two herself, Lysandra nodded her agreement.

"We caught it napping, I think, or less innocently preoccupied during one of the periods when it's dark inside. And afterward, your party approached it from an angle we'd probably desensitized with the *Victor Appleton*'s penetration."

She decided it was past time to clear the viewscreen and change the subject.

"If you don't mind my asking, Middle C, where did you learn to speak English?"

The taflak warrior brightened, if she'd become any judge at all of his species' body language.

"From my great and good acquaintanceship . . ."

He "fingered" the medallion on its cord about the base of a tentacle, pulled it off, and handed it to her. On one side was the expected portrait of the bearded hero for whom she'd been named, on the other, data concerning the weight and purity of the coin, the identity of the company, North American Express and Van Lines, which had minted it, along with their motto, *"Don't leave without home."*

". . . exploring Majesty just like yourselves, young Berdan Geanar, a Confederate human boyperson afterward known by the war-name he took in my village, MacDougall Bear—"

"I see," Lysandra answered, disappointed her guess about Middle C's accent had been wrong.

"And one Epots Dinnomm *Pemot,*" he added, "xeno-praxeologist and scholar—although he claimed to prefer the sobriquet *taflakologist*—late of the University of Mexico, as he told us, at Mexico, in Mexico, a gentlelam of the Imperial Fodduan persuasion. They met here, in my very village, don't you know, the distinguished lamviin scientist and the boy pursuing something called the 'bright suit'—an affair to redeem family honor—and someone, the relative in question, I gathered, who was part of a 'Hooded Seven' conspiratorial society. The result, as you may be aware, was a battle most gloriously spectacular. Tell me, Lysandra, old sentient being, is that Mexico conceit a joke?"

For a moment, the girl froze. That second threatening note, the one Glassbreaker had found in the head, hadn't been signed the way the first one had, but the writing was the same, and she didn't doubt for a moment who—or what—it had come from. Then, realizing the taflak warrior's startling revelation would have to be pursued wth elaborate care, preferably in the presence of her father, she relaxed. Middle C wasn't going anywhere, and they had nothing but time.

"Yes," she laughed, handing the coin back, "and literally true, as well. The name of Earth's greatest open marketplace of learning, the ancient city it's located in, and the region, once a nation-state, where they're both found. I went there myself, although don't ask if I knew this Pemot. At least a hundred thousand other students did, too, of a dozen or more species, when I was attending."

"I think I should like very much to see that marketplace someday," replied the taflak, "and perhaps even to trade in it somehow. What's a nation-state?"

Here we go again, Lysandra thought, maybe I should call Goldberry in here to explain. The leftenant commander was up forward, she knew, with Grossfuss and Howell, learning to navigate (foligate?) the subfoline with the help of her smart-helmet circuitry. Lysandra hoped the yeti and her father had healthy, steady nerves.

"A large tribal grouping," she answered, "something like the First Wavers' Securitas or Antimacassar. I've been told that's not really the way taflak politics work, and we don't tolerate them on Earth anymore, either."

Somehow she knew Middle C nodded.

"You've indeed been told correctly, old— My word, what's that up there?"

He pointed his spear at the viewscreen where the subfoline's computer had outlined the traces it detected of some massive, rectangular object lying on the surface.

Lysandra grinned.

"I think it's your village, Middle C, from a perspective you've never seen before."

"It's entirely possible," the native admitted. "I myself have burrowed beneath my village raft many times to effect repairs upon it, and that looks about right. But if it be so, will you be so good as to kindly tell me what *that* object is?"

The Earth girl stared at a cluster of symbols lying perhaps half a scale mile from the village.

"I don't—yes I do! Those are summaries of pressure indications, Middle C—not an outline of any material object creating the pressure, if you follow me, but sort of what it feels like when big, soft wheels are being driven slowly over the leaves. We saw something a lot like this on our way out here. I think this is another Securitasian crankapillar, headed straight toward your village!"

Alarmed, the warrior gripped his spear, perhaps a futile gesture, but a comforting one Lysandra could identify with. Her first thought had been for her Walthers.

"Tell me, Lysandra, old mentor, does some way exist in which we might see above the surface?"

Howell popped his wolfish head into the stateroom, startling both of them.

"Oh, sorry. Watch the spear, will you please? I see you've noticed it, as well."

His daughter passed on the taflak's latest question. The coyote shook his head.

"No indeed, Middle C. Among the other things I neglected, I'm going to recommend to Hellertech the installation of a periscope. However, that won't do us much good now. In case you're curious, we're three hundred feet below the surface, angled gently upward and making perhaps fifteen miles per hour in this loose stuff. I'd estimate we're still a good five miles away from your village."

"Twenty minutes," his daughter told the taflak, not knowing how well he appreciated feet and miles, "and I don't know what we're going to do when we get there."

"Well, I've one small idea right now," offered the coyote. "Since we don't happen to have a periscope, and can make even better speed closer to the surface—"

He turned, his head vanishing through the door membrane, leaving behind the corner of one shoulder.

"Obregon, take her up at full speed, if you please, until her decks are just—"

He turned back to his daughter.

"Well, ship's linguist, can you perhaps suggest a Sea of Leaves analogy to *'awash'*?"

Lysandra shrugged. "Until they just need raking?"

"Fine help you are. Let's go out on deck as soon as it happens, whatever we decide to call it, and get a better idea of what's going on. Middle C, if you'd care to join us?"

The taflak indicated his assent and filed out of the cabin behind his hostess.

By the time the three had assembled, with Goldberry, at the proper place just forward of the control area, the Himalayan had brought the subfoline up to a position just below the surface. Now, at Howell's nautically worded request, he leveled the vessel off and let her rise another foot, so her passengers topside wouldn't be swept off in the peculiar current she created as she moved along.

"Great Albert's ghost!"

It was Howell who'd exclaimed, despite himself. They'd emerged to a scene of red-orange flames and greasy black smoke dirtying the cloudless sky above the village. A mile or two away, uniformed and armed troops wearing moss-shoes had leapt from the crankapillar and were trudging at their best speed afoot, approaching the village under a barrage of arrows and tentacle-cast spears.

Lysandra and her shocked companions could hear taflak screaming and the flat *chuff* of the Securitasians' smoothbored percussion muzzleloaders, returning fire. She had never understood how that technology had lasted long enough for development into more efficient forms, and thought personally she might prefer the natives' theoretically more primitive weapons, with their higher rate of fire.

However, it was clear to the travelers, from where

they stood, that the floating taflak settlement was already in peril from a far deadlier menace. Those left aboard the crankapillar had turned their flame-throwers on the village. It was only the short range of these crude weapons, plus the danger of inciner-ating their own advancing troops, that accounted for its not already having been destroyed.

"Obregon, please take her down again, at once," Howell told the yeti over his implant. *"Maintain maximum speed, and anything extra you can squeeze out of her."*

"Aye, aye, Boss."

"Everyone," he informed his daughter and Gold-berry, "should be sure to strap themselves down in as secure a manner as possible. We're going to undertake whatever we must to save our new friends' families from those barbarians."

The girls nodded and started below.

He turned to the taflak.

"Middle C, pass the word to your warriors. This vessel doesn't have any other weapons, aside from her reinforced and pointed prow, so we're going to ram the blasted thing!"

"Yes, old canine Captain."

"And may the anarchistic spirit," Lysandra in-toned over her shoulder, "of Captain Nemo himself watch over us."

CHAPTER XVIII:

Fire to Frying Pan

"Stand by t'ram!"

Lysandra caught herself bracing for the anticipated impact long before it was necessary, and tried, without any particular success, to force herself to relax.

The Securitasian crankapillar stood frozen on the viewscreens of the H.S.P. *Victor Appleton,* a broad and easy target for the Himalayan pilot at the subfoline's controls. The Confederate ship herself ran silent, and it was only the slow, steady growth of the picture of her victim-to-be that gave her occupants any sense of motion.

"The power plant's indicating 115 percent nominal," Howell recited to the world at large. "All other systems showing solidly in the green."

Even though her offworld pursuer was unarmed, no defense she could put up would save her. The surface-machine's flamethrowers, located in her after-section only, must have been installed for the primary purpose of keeping the slaves at work on the crank from revolting against their masters. Given their predilection for raids into Antimacassarite territory (if Goldberry's stories were to be believed), they must also come in handy while attempting to evade or discourage pursuit by swifter craft. Now, like junk cars in the demolition derbies of old, these machines did their best, most destructive work while backing toward their enemy.

Which was how the crankapillar was oriented with regard to the taflak village.

"Okey dokey," Grossfuss replied, his enormous hairy hands firm on the vessel's controls. "By popular request, an' much against my better judgment, here we go!"

The *Victor Appleton* didn't accelerate—she was already running at her top-rated velocity and then some—but burrowed closer to the crankapillar at a pace that amazed even her operators. This close to the underside of the green, leafy surface, a much greater speed was possible than in the depths, where she'd been forced by friction, the sheer physical resistance of the Sea of Leaves itself (not to mention a certain measure of prudence which, even so, hadn't spared them the surprise of colliding with the vacuole), to proceed at a crawl.

Now, however, three hundred feet of superconductor-powered subfoline, an unstoppable juggernaut the size of a previous century's small oceangoing freighters, tens of thousands of metric pounds of ceramic, metal, and smart plastic, hurtled toward the Securitasian galley at twenty-five miles per hour, an absurd speed, Lysandra thought to herself, until you calculated the kinetic energy involved. Let's see: E's equal to the mass in pounds, times the velocity—that had to be in feet per second, not miles per hour—squared . . .

Leaning hard into her lap and shoulder restraints, Goldberry sat forward, at the edge of her jump seat, her eyes glittering, an avid expression on her face as they came closer and closer to her nation-state's traditional enemies. Lysandra realized it was an ironic twist—the leftenant commander herself had suggested doing something like this when they'd sighted a crankapillar on the outward voyage; they'd all informed her she was being silly and they couldn't interfere—what a difference a little Securitasian initiated force made!

And how lucky for them all the aggressor wasn't an Antimacassarite screwmaran. The Earth girl, cynical about First Wavers, believed it was a matter of pure chance.

At Howell's order, Grossfuss set his imaginary sights just forward of the decked and railed command section of the jointed First Wave vehicle, where the least injury might be inflicted on its helpless involuntary occupants, while maximizing damage to the portion of the primitive vehicle attempting to roast Middle C's hometown. Someone on the crankapillar's afterdeck must have seen the *Victor Appleton* coming in the final moment, for a wash of red and orange flame filled the viewscreen.

Taken in by the three-dimensional image on the viewscreen, Middle C, or one of the other taflak, shouted out loud—and followed with a mumbled and chagrined apology.

In the instant before impact, Lysandra had a terrible thought for a moment like this: what if whoever had left those threatening messages had sabotaged the subfoline, perhaps weakening her structure in some manner that wouldn't show on the readouts?

"Excuse me, Cap'n," came a voice from another quarter, "I sure hate t'mention it at a moment like this, but what if whoever left those threatenin' messages—"

"Shhhh! Not now, Obregon!"

"Thar she blows!"

With a grunt of effort, the Himalayan pulled back on the wheel, raising the subfoline's needle-sharp prow. Lysandra, heart pounding, her bloodstream filled with adrenaline, saw and felt everything that happened after this—she'd noticed much the same phenomenon occurring during the battle in the vacuole—in slow motion.

First came the odd, musical twang of the prow's first penetrating contact with the woven gunwales of the crankapillar. This was followed by a familiar screeching, tearing, grinding noise—she realized it was the old fingernail-on-the-blackboard enlarged in scale several orders of magnitude—which dropped in pitch as it increased in volume, until it became a prolonged, deep-throated rumble. It was only the *Victor Appleton*'s automated safety systems—Lysandra realized in this moment how much those extrusions were like the tendrils of the vacuole she'd battled—and the preparatory strapping-in Howell had ordered that saved them all from being dashed and broken against the forward bulkhead.

"Hull stresses maximizing!" shouted Howell above the mechanical din. "Engine load at 102 percent!"

The Earth girl tried not to imagine she could also hear the screaming of the Securitasian officers as they were smashed to pulp along with their frail craft, or, if they were lucky, pitched over the side to crisp and bubble in the spilling fuel and flames of their own weapons, or to struggle and die in the jaws of eager sea denizens that had somehow sensed this mortal conflict and now swarmed just below the top layer of leaves to take predatory advantage of it.

A peculiar vocalization, somewhere between a whimper and a growl, seemed to emanate from Grossfuss, although nothing was coming over his wrist synthesizer.

Another long, unbearable series of rending noises, and the subfoline was free, slowed by just a fraction of her original speed, and already turning about under Grossfuss' hands for another pass through the flimsy vehicle if it proved necessary. Noise also filled the *Victor Appleton* once again from the inside, as the sight of the broken, burning Securitasian vessel came onto the viewscreen, and the taflak warriors set up a mind-splitting cheer of hoots and whistles.

A glance at Goldberry told Lysandra the Antimacassarite girl was close to tears of joy.

This crankapillar would destroy no more villages.

Middle C, closer to Lysandra than the rest of the taflak, whistled at a frequency somewhere near the upper edge of her perception and thumped her on the back.

She turned and looked a wordless question at him.

"Frightfully sorry," the warrior apologized, a blush somehow conveyed by his voice. "I quite forgot myself."

She took his tentacle and squeezed it hard and grinned.

Grossfuss turned the subfoline again, to take the war-chief and his companions home.

Grossfuss maneuvered the subfoline alongside one shelving edge of the rectangular village raft-platform. For her own part, Lysandra couldn't have felt any better if they'd been landing at Talisman, ready to Broach up to the Fleet.

Dashing through the checklist once again, the yeti and Howell powered the vessel's peculiar vibrational engines down—they'd performed far beyond reasonable expectation—and joined Goldberry and the coyote's daughter on the improvised deck topside.

"I believe," Howell suggested to the others, "it's the local equivalent of a ticker-tape parade!"

Middle C was already on deck with his comrades, waving his tentacles and brandishing his spears for the benefit of a cheerful, noisy crowd that had gathered at the edge. Grossfuss couldn't resist grinning and waving as well, and soon his friends, even

Goldberry, were bouncing up and down, raising interlocked fists over their heads and, in general, acting as if they were the winners on a telecom quiz show.

Howell gave a series of mental commands that, among several other things, lowered a treaded ramp to the woven floor of the village. He waited as the dozen taflak warriors, the two human girls, and his gigantic Himalayan pilot stepped down onto the tentacle-made surface. Following what he understood to be a long nautical and spacefaring tradition, he himself was last off the ship.

Goldberry looked around with a bewildered expression, half ecstatic—she'd been raised, after all, for no other purpose than to achieve military victories and celebrate them afterward—half unsure of herself in strange surroundings.

The villagers closed in on all the travelers, each one, big and small (at least half the population of the place seemed to consist of what Lysandra assumed were children), shrilling delighted congratulations and satisfying a healthy, unsuppressed curiosity—in contrast to their overdecorous reception by the Selfquelled—regarding the weird-shaped beings who'd returned with their hunting party.

Middle C, acting as their host, explained that his people's jubilation concerned more than just a violent and satisfying end to the threat the crankapillar had represented. Nor would it matter a bit that the hunters hadn't come back with the survivors of the earlier battle they'd first been hunting for.

This, according to Middle C, had been no more than a long shot from the beginning.

Lysandra grinned. She'd gotten the impression the first moment she'd seen him that the adventurous warrior would have welcomed any excuse to go exploring.

A gang of his people would be out on the Sea of Leaves by now, he told them, trying to rescue castaway galley slaves and making prisoners of the surviving Securitasian officers.

If any.

Howell chuckled. "And if so, we'll never hear about it? It doesn't look as if you've any facilities here, even if you had the inclination, for keeping prisoners."

The warrior shrugged, acknowledging the truth, if not the justice, of the coyote's words.

"Aww, they wouldn't knock off enemy troopies," Grossfuss insisted, "as wanted t'surrender, would they?"

Goldberry had stiffened at the beginning of this conversation. Now she launched into a lecture—at the top of her lungs and still for the most part inaudible against the riotous background—on civilized conventions for the treatment of prisoners.

Braced against the ear-penetrating noise, and ducking slap-happy tentacles, Lysandra looked around. Middle C seemed to be tendering more personal greetings to a smaller taflak—the girl couldn't tell a male Majestan from a female, as yet—and a pair of tiny ones. Not much else of the native village could be seen through the press of sentient beings all around them.

She got a vague impression of dozens of cylindrical thatched huts, woven of the same material as the supporting raft—and looking, just as she'd been informed, a lot like one of the processed cereals she refused to eat for breakfast every morning—and an open common area. In many respects, Lysandra thought, the place looked like a neat and tidy, sanitized Hollywood version of an African *kraal*. Washed by a steady wind from the Sea of Leaves, it even smelled clean.

Behind her, the extruded boarding ramp began

sliding back into the substance of the subfoline's hull—a safety precaution against innocent, curious tendrils, Howell was telling the taflak leader, and no offense intended. The smaller villagers in particular seemed fascinated with the coyote, and he, in turn, permitted them to touch him, pet him, even scratch behind his ears, an indignity he'd suffer at the hands of no known Earth organism.

The crowd closed in even tighter around them.

Grossfuss had planted his broad fundament on the village floor, and was tolerating, with the good humor often characteristic of the Himalayan (although, Howell had maintained in private to his daughter, this was a rare quality among yetis), many of the same liberties being inflicted on his captain.

Before the Earth girl had quite realized what was happening, the innermost layer of taflak all around them was bristling with gleaming spearpoints. In another instant, or so it seemed, the travelers had been relieved of their weapons by what seemed like a hundred agile, quick-moving tentacles.

"What did I tell you?" Goldberry screamed, her voice rising with hysteria. "I told you about these animals, did I not? And did you listen? No, you—"

"Leftenant Commander, *shut up!*"

It was the first time in her life Lysandra had heard her father use this particular pair of words.

"I'm indeed most frightfully sorry to have to do this to such good and proven friends."

Middle C seemed apologetic as he attempted to explain to the four what was happening.

"But you understand, don't you, we can afford to make no exceptions? Ours is a primitive subsistence economy, and we were a hunting party, after all—no offense intended."

The alien crowd swung open before—but not behind—the astonished travelers. Lysandra could see into the common area she'd noticed between the huts.

At its precise center, a bonfire had been laid but not yet lit.

Atop this woodpile was an enormous, big-bellied cooking pot.

CHAPTER XIX:
Frying Pan to Fire

Middle C urged his four victims forward with a short, threatening thrust of his spear.

"Be careful about that one, fellows," he told the other warriors, for some reason of his own putting the words in English. "Remember how she escaped last time."

Judging from the number of deadly, gleaming points that materialized about her at those words, there'd be no escaping this time for the leftenant commander.

As they approached the huge, brightly decorated container, Lysandra could see it had been hand-made from some sort of pottery. Her analytical mind pursuing its own interests to the last, she recalled reading somewhere that the natives extracted clay from some mineral-concentrating organ of the single species of plant life making up the Sea of Leaves. This might be of some interest to archaeologists, someday—in particular when they found human, yeti, and coyote bones inside—but she couldn't have explained why she was thinking about it now.

Forced at spearpoint, a grim-faced Goldberry was the first of the four to stumble up the random steps provided by the firewood—thick branches from a good distance below the surface, hacked up into yard lengths—and into the water. Lysandra followed her, wondering how long her smartsuit's cooling system would hold out when the water began to boil. Altogether too long, she thought, if it meant she'd have to sit and watch her friends being cooked to pieces.

Her father hopped with ill grace over the lip of the pot and joined her with a splash, but she failed to notice this. She came back to herself at the noise of a greater weight of water spilling over onto the ground. The mighty Grossfuss displaced a lot more volume than the taflak had anticipated. A considerable amount of angry shouting and scurrying followed this accident. Some of the firewood had gotten wet and needed replacing. Middle C, an ordinary Confederate cigarette lighter in his tendrils, bent down and lit the kindling.

As the four travelers sat together in the pot, smoke curling up around them, Lysandra came to a decision.

"I don't know what you guys are going to do, but I don't intend to be the entree. Weapons or not, in about ten seconds I'm jumping out of here and taking as many of these savages with me as I can before they get me. If I can just grab a spear—"

"I couldn't agree more wholeheartedly," her father told her. "Let's count to five and jump out together. That way, perhaps, we'll preserve the element of surprise."

"Well, while you're countin', Cap'n, count me in. My mama didn't bring me up t'be no billa fare!"

"Which leaves you, Goldberry," Lysandra told the Antimacassarite. "Are you with us, or—"

The leftenant commander assumed the most disgusted expression she was capable of.

"How could you have considered otherwise, child?"

Lysandra nodded. "We'll discuss that crack later, if, by some odd chance we both happen to live through the fun we're about to have. Grossfuss? Father?"

"Let's make it all together now, if we can," the coyote announced in a calm voice. "Ready?"

"Five!" they all shouted.

They began to swarm and scramble up over the slowly warming lip of the cooking pot, trying not to get in one another's way and not succeeding. To their utter surprise, Middle C materialized through the curtain of surrounding smoke, four pistols, two knives, and a large pair of poultry shears proffered in his tentacles.

"I say, old half-stewed companions, if you wish to shoot your way out, you may want these."

All motion stopped for an instant.

Lysandra and Grossfuss were out of the pot, stamping out the flames and helping Goldberry and Howell, who had no smartsuits to protect them, past the coals.

A small, high-pitched taflak giggle came from somewhere near the back of the crowd, perhaps a child who just couldn't maintain self-control any longer. This spread to one or two of the adults who began laughing, and soon the entire village had caught the infection, falling to the woven floor, rolling all over themselves, entangling their tentacles with those of their equally helpless neighbors, hooting and whistling in a convulsion of uncontrollable mirth as the travelers stood, cold and dripping, in front of the defunct cooking fire.

Grossfuss, his white fur soaked and matted to his hide, shook his head slowly.

"Well I'll be boiled in oil, or some reasonable facsimile, it's a rotten practical joke!"

A corner of his mouth turned up, pulling the rest of his features into a grimace. From that point on, he was lost. He chuckled. This turned into a giggle. That became a laugh, but soon became a guffaw. He put his hands on his sides, threw his head back, and roared. In a few moments, he was rolling around with the taflak.

"Come . . . now . . . Lef . . . tenant . . . Commander" —Howell managed to get the words out between convulsions—"it ought to be at least twice as funny for you-hoo-hoo-hoo . . . as . . . for . . . any . . . body . . . else-hee-hee! Oh dear, I can't stand it!"

Goldberry grinned—it looked like a painful expression under the circumstances—still holding back what Lysandra suspected the girl feared would be insane laughter if she let go. The Earth girl shrugged —a cold, wet, squishy gesture—and it was this, and a certain amount of relief after thinking she'd been about to die a horrible death, which broke her own self-control. She chuckled, caught herself with a hand over her mouth, and chuckled again.

It was like an uncontrollable fit of hiccups. She looked from the dozens of taflak surrounding them, to her friends in various states of soggy disarray, to the oversized cooking pot behind her, down at herself, and began to laugh, collapsing against the pot—cold again, since the fire had lasted only a few seconds—until she couldn't breathe and tears were streaming from her eyes.

Middle C slapped her on the back with a fuzzy tentacle, somewhat tentatively, as if waiting to see her reaction to the gesture. For her own part, Lysandra, more helpless now than when she'd been buried in the vacuole, seized the tentacle, pulled against the native for support, and went on laughing.

For some reason this seemed to please the warrior. He seized the two-ounce gold medallion he'd been wearing, untied the fine cord holding it to the base of his tentacle, knotted a larger loop in it, and dropped it with a ceremonious flourish over Lysandra's head, so that the heavy coin lay at the base of her throat.

This accomplished, he fell down beside her and surrendered to his own hooting convulsions.

When the hysteria had subsided a bit, the travelers were asked to hide in huts surrounding the village common, and encouraged to watch the fun as the same joke was pulled, over and over again, on the dazed surviving galley slaves as they were brought in a dozen or so at a time by taflak rescue parties.

The villagers demonstrated no sign of ever tiring of it, and even looked forward to working it, over and over again, on the growing influx of Confederate visitors.

During a lull between batches of victims, Middle C explained that, in the case of the Securitasian slaves—as the taflak had learned after the recent battle—more than just humor seemed to be involved. When first pulled from the Sea of Leaves—sometimes from the jaws of hungry predators—they seemed apathetic and listless, unhappy at the prospect of being set free, preferring the mindless, dull security of their positions at the crank (and the comfort of always knowing what to do because somebody was always around to tell them) to the many frightening uncertainties of individual liberty and self-ownership.

"I understand exactly what you mean," the coyote answered the warrior. "Freedom was once defined, after all, as the choice between working and starving."

The taflak cannibal joke, however, seemed more reliable than anything at snapping the slaves out of it, reminding them in the most graphic and convincing manner possible that it was good to be alive. They'd be on their own, of course, from now on—but better able to accept it and do something with themselves.

Most of the liberated slaves would prefer, the warrior chief predicted from his previous experience, being taken to one of the Confederate settlements at the planet's poles to start a new life under that offworld culture's easy lack of rules. Her own past experience told Lysandra that some of them, at least, would be running their own businesses within a couple of years, most likely sending Confederate tourists out to be thrown into a taflak cannibal pot.

In fact, Middle C told them, thanks to a previous business arrangement and a homemade spark-gap transmitter left them by a previous explorer, the lamviin Pemot (she reminded herself that she must speak with her father about that boy MacDougall Bear—she was sure she'd seen him at the South Polar terminal—pursuing the Hooded Seven), a number of hovercraft had already been summoned. When they got here the next day (it was a long trip; the taflak village lay almost precisely on the equator), neophytes among the drivers would be treated to a dunking while their better-educated companions stood by, sniggering.

What followed, when the last slave had been "processed," could only be described as a party, with plenty of hot, spicy food—none of it the flesh of any sentient being, but native delicacies from the Sea of Leaves—a number of different aromatic drinks the travelers were dubious about, and the taflak equivalent of eardrum-penetrating singing and enthusiastic dancing. Lysandra and the yeti joined in the latter, leaping and stomping about the raft-platform, while her father did his operatic best to contribute to the former.

It appeared to his daughter that he'd at last found a willing and appreciative audience.

Somewhere during the proceedings, Lysandra found she hadn't just been made an honorary member of the tribe, but had been adopted, with Howell's cooperation, as Middle C's younger sister. She looked down at the gleaming Confederate coin he'd given her earlier, wishing she could pronounce her taflak name, but it was impossible. To her uninformed ear, it sounded something like an ill-tuned shortwave radio. Instead, she recorded her new brother's voice as he pronounced it, and played it back whenever ceremonious introductions—something else the taflak never seemed to tire of—became necessary.

Night fell, genuine, cool, moonless, black-skied, starlit nighttime, as opposed to the stifling and dangerous half-darkness of the Realm of the Self-quelled, far below.

Lysandra's suspicion that the taflak were a far more sophisticated people than Middle C had admitted was confirmed when she discovered how well they understood the mission of the *Victor Appleton*. It was hoped by Confederate scientists, they informed *her*, that subfoline would help solve the mystery of Majesty.

They even seemed to appreciate the fact that opinions about the planet and its remarkable sea varied a great deal throughout the galaxy, from the cold, objective theoretical debates of academia (which, more often than the general public realized, approached being settled over steaming coffee and smoking pistols by the dawn's early light), to their own homegrown and more romantic legends.

But what really lay in the stifling heat (or was it Plutonian cold?) and darkness—hardly anybody disagreed about that—at the bottom of the leafy biomass? Was it nothing more surprising than the bizarre, toothy, glow-in-the-dark creatures adapted to living in the blackness and incredible pressures on the Earth's ocean floors? Or might traces be discovered there, as taflak stories would have it, of an ancient civilization that had overstepped some preordained boundary and been punished for it by unnamed inhuman (and untaflak) agencies?

Some of those legends were recited for the girl and her father by the firelight, which seemed a perfect setting. Local variants seemed less concerned with arrogance on the part of the mythical civilization than with a certain sloppiness, somewhat humorously reported. As if the ancients had constructed a vast garbage disposal system and absentmindedly put themselves down it.

Lysandra heard, in the rapid-fire translations Middle C offered them, some vague hints, perhaps, at miraculous flying machines, something which might have been electric power, even dark portents of a great and all-destructive war. But she failed to let herself be carried away by these interpretations. Earth had ancient legends, too, in particular from India and Tibet, which, to a technological mind, hinted at similar nonexistent accomplishments.

In the meantime, the only way to unravel Majesty's mysteries was to go down there and find out. Soon they'd wander back aboard the subfoline for a long and much-needed sleep. But for the moment, Lysandra was more than content. Out on the surface of the sea, small creatures leaped, soared, and plopped back into the leaves, reminding her of flying fish. Torches and firelight flickered, and the festivities continued until everyone lay exhausted, trying to decide if they could manage one more drink, or one more bite of deep-fried morsel.

The Earth girl lay half-propped against the outside wall of a hut, conversing with Howell and Middle C and enjoying a cool breeze, when Grossfuss stumped up to them.

"Well, folks," he told them with a tone and expression of disgust, "Goldberry's gone."

"Dear me," the coyote answered, getting to his feet with a slight stiffness. "She needn't have done this. I intended taking her home tomorrow. I thought she accepted the whole charade with every appearance of good grace, but I was wrong. I suppose she fabricated herself a pair of moss-shoes and struck out on her own again."

Lysandra shook her head. "Some of those Securitasian officers and troops had moss-shoes, I think."

She couldn't be certain. None of them, it appeared, had survived their own attack.

"You both got it wrong," the yeti told them. "I guess we know, now, where all them threatenin' notes came from. Sure wish you'd never given her that smarthelmet, Cap'n, or taught her t'use it. The leftenant commander took the *Victor Appleton*."

CHAPTER XX:

The Crimsoned Pirate

Leaping to their respective locomotory extremities, Howell, Lysandra, and Middle C rushed to the edge of the village raft where the subfoline *Victor Appleton* had been "docked" earlier that day. The Himalayan giant who'd discovered the vehicular theft in the first place (and was still a bit distended from a volume of native food and drink that might have supported the entire population of that village for a week) followed at a somewhat more measured pace.

Firelight cast their long, wavering shadows out across the surface of the Sea of Leaves. One of them whirled, end over end, like a child's pinwheel in the wind.

"Gone, of course!"

Disgusted more with herself than anything else, Lysandra stood at the break of the platform, hands clenched into fists at her sides, looking out over emptiness. Home, or at least the first stepping-stone toward getting there, was a quarter of a world away, the distance, as some crowlike thing no doubt flew at migration-time on Majesty, from this equatorial *ultima thule* to Talisman, the First Wave settlement and Confederate starport at the planet's south pole.

It was going to be a long, long walk.

This, however, wasn't the principal item bother-

ing the girl (although *bothering* would have been
too mild an expression for anyone aware of the
present physiological readouts of her smartsuit).
Despite her negative first impression—and her second and third, as well—she'd learned to trust the
Antimacassarite leftenant commander to a degree,
had even begun to learn to like her.

And now this.

In the distance, firelight reflecting from its scaly
body, one of the flying fish creatures leapt from the
depths, skimmed the surface, and disappeared.

Aloud, Lysandra used a word she'd never heard
her father use, although quite a number of his
friends—that American private investigator, if she
believed just half the unlikely stories she'd been
told about him—used it all the time.

An enormous shadow superimposed itself over
her own.

"Such language for a little girl," Grossfuss chuckled. "Don't worry, cookie, we'll go home with the
hovercraft, tomorrow—and yeah, I know: don't call
you 'cookie.' "

Close to tears, she whirled on the yeti, stamping
one small, angry, rubberized foot on the woven mat-
ting, producing no sound—and achieving no satisfaction—whatever.

"You can scratch 'little girl' from your list, as
well, you great big overstuffed—"

They heard a throat-clearing noise.

"If you're both finished," Howell intervened, before his "little girl" could give the Himalayan mechanic another lesson in irregular Anglo-Saxon verbs
he didn't need anyway, "I'd appreciate a bit of quiet
for just a moment."

Stepping, in his characteristic delicate manner,
to the extreme edge of the raft where just a few
leaves reached up and lapped over, he emptied his

mind, pouring every bit of concentration he was capable of into his cerebro-cortical implant.

A few yards from the platform, the vegetation began stirring, and the coyote's companions were treated to a sight and sound they'd never experienced before, having been inboard the subfoline whenever the opportunity presented itself.

With a sort of modest grandeur—and plenty of astonished whistles and exclamations from the platform—the *Victor Appleton* arose from beneath the Sea of Leaves.

The party descended through the hull back-to-back, Walther Electrics, Sebastian Mark IX, and long-bladed taflak spear pointed outward to cover all directions.

Howell alone hadn't drawn his pistol.

Inboard, they found Goldberry at the subfoline's controls, smarthelmet in place with its tiny, glowing pilot lamps, her mouth hanging slack. What showed of her face beneath the visor was ghastly white. The terror filling her eyes inside the helmet was repeated on the screen before her. She was also entangled, from her slim ankles to her graceful collarbones, in the vessel's tentacular safety restraints, tied up in as neat and effective a manner as anything the Selfquelled had managed. It was possible this had been unnecessary: she seemed frozen in a kind of deadly fascination with the horrifying images.

"Someone's reversed the motion of the holos I took during our voyage to Middle C's village!"

Holstering her pistols, Lysandra peered at her father with suspicion, a bit horrified herself.

"She thinks she's headed back to the vacuole!"

"On autonavigation," Howell admitted, "and quite unable to do anything about it."

Middle C displayed one of his rippling shudders: "And I thought we taflak were jokers!"

The coyote reached to flip a switch at the back of the helmet. Goldberry slumped a moment, turned as far as her restraints permitted, and stared at the four standing behind her. She opened her mouth, but Howell raised a mechanical finger of admonition.

"A moment, Leftenant Commander. Listen, if you please. No doubt you're grateful to see us here, to see yourself here, rather than where you thought you were going. At the same time, naturally, you're angry and embarrassed at having been deceived."

All of this was true beyond question, judging from the girl's complexion, now a chagrined shade of pink. At the same time, Lysandra could tell by the fire in Goldberry's eyes that she wasn't at all apologetic for what she'd tried to do.

"How . . . ?"

"This particular arrangement," the coyote informed his prisoner, indicating the viewscreen and the booby-trapped pilot's chair, "was the last thing I attended to, paratronically, just before we left the *Victor Appleton* earlier today."

The taflak gave an interrogative whistle: *Why?*

Howell turned to the warrior, the yeti, and his daughter.

"Because, as the old saying goes, even paranoids have enemies. Goldberry and Obregon both required code-keys, you see, hers programmed into the helmet we provided."

Middle C repeated the musical question.

"Well, had Lysandra and I perished in the vacuole, for example, Obregon and Goldberry, deprived of access to the subfoline, would have been marooned and likely killed. Nevertheless, this is a most expensive toy for which to be held responsible, and, with all due respect to Obregon here—even to Goldberry—this easy access had always made me feel rather *un*easy. This morning I provided that should anyone, in my absence, attempt to set a course for anywhere but Talisman—without an additional password—the trap would spring."

Again he addressed Goldberry.

"Of course, those 'Hooded Seven' missives were a factor. And you'll forgive me, I trust, if I regarded your interest in learning to pilot this vessel with some suspicion. I also saw your face light up when we rammed the crankapillar."

"I was impressed," she admitted in a voice that spoke more of lifelong military self-control than any genuine calm, "with what this merest of your machines did to those bandits! I wish to continue this practice on a regular basis."

"So I'd rather imagine. But your planning started a bit earlier than that, didn't it, Leftenant Commander? Lysandra dear, could you trip the swivel-release and turn her chair around so the rest of us can sit at table? Much better. You might also relieve her of her pistol and the kitchen knife if you can get to them. Obregon, will you kindly make us a pot of coffee? Now where was I? Ah, yes: otherwise you wouldn't have left those silly notes about."

Goldberry shook her head. "I did not write those notes."

"Come now"—Howell returned a canine shrug—"Leftenant Commander—"

"On my captain-mother's pince-nez, I swear it! I do not know who did, but I did not, you . . . you dog!"

Grossfuss looked up from his struggles with the coffee maker: "She called you a dog, Cap'n."

"I am a dog, Obregon."

"Yeah," the yeti nodded, looking down at his feet in embarrassment. "I kinda forget sometimes."

Lysandra shook her head and grinned despite the

anger and disappointment she was feeling. "So do I."

Examining the edge of his spear with a judicious tentacle-tip, Middle C shrugged.

Howell sighed. "Why bother denying it, Goldberry, now you've been caught? It's over, understand? All that remains is a decision concerning what to do with you."

"An' what might that be, Cap'n?"

"Yes, tell us." Enthusiasm colored Middle C's voice. "This is an aspect of civilization I'm most curious about. Will you shoot her? Shall we warm up the pot? I'm uncertain it can withstand the heat, and the firewood's begun to dry-rot."

"MacRame, Goldberry, no middle initial," the trussed-up Antimacassarite officer recited in a flat, fatalistic tone. "Leftenant Commander, serial number 2–3—"

The coyote frowned. "Goldberry, nobody cares about your serial number. Please let me think."

"Whatever you decide," Lysandra told her father, joining him at the table where she tossed Goldberry's weapons with a clatter, "make it *good*. After all, we scraped her up off the beach, we gave her a job— practically a home—and now look!"

"I see." Howell nodded, accepting a cup of coffee from the yeti. "Well, what do you say we begin with an anecdote? For some reason I'm reminded of the old story—perhaps it was a folk song—of an old lady walking in the woods one winter day who found a small snake, stiff with cold and almost dead, lying in her path. She took the frozen reptile in, warmed it on a blanket beside her fireplace, and, when it began to stir, offered it a saucer of milk."

"A saucer of milk?" Lysandra wrinkled her nose. "For a snake?"

"Hush, or like all literary nitpickers, you'll miss

the point. When she bent to place the saucer beside the snake, it reached up and bit her on the arm. As she lay dying—I did mention it was poisonous, didn't I?—she demanded, 'Why did you do it, snake, after I saved your life? I took you in, warmed you, offered you something to eat, and this is how you repay my kindness?' And the snake said—"

"It's a *talkin'* snake?"

"Hush, Obregon. The snake said, 'What did you expect, lady? I'm a snake.' "

He paused, waiting for a reaction.

Lysandra made a face. "That's a disgusting story."

"Yeah," agreed Grossfuss, sitting beside the table with his mixing bowl and a cup for the Earth girl, "an' none too complimentary to the leftenant commander, here."

It was perhaps unjust that it was the yeti Goldberry chose to glare at over that.

"What," asked Middle C, dipping a cautious tentacle into a cup Grossfuss had offered him, "is a snake?"

"And how," Lysandra asked, "does this dumb story help us decide what to do with *her?*"

"Well, consider why you're so angry with her," Howell replied. "In the beginning, of course, we all suspected she wasn't altogether to be trusted, being a confirmed statist, and perhaps—after we found the first note—somebody's hired hand. Yet, as we journeyed on, especially after that evil night in the cottage, it appeared she was wholly with us, a good comrade to have at your back in a fight."

He focused all of his attention on his daughter.

"Tell me, my dear, isn't it Goldberry's inconsistency which rankles worst?"

Lysandra snorted. "How about the insignificant matter of our stolen subfoline?"

"We have our subfoline intact," Howell began.

Lysandra insisted, "And no credit to her!"

"And no harm done the subfoline. Moreover, from the first moment we saw her, Goldberry has, in fact, acted with remarkable consistency, remaining a good naval officer every minute, alert to advancing the interests of her native Antimacassar."

"Get me a barfbag"—Lysandra made exaggerated motions, blind hands reaching—"I'm going to be—"

"A terrible praxeologist," Howell interrupted, "if you don't get this straight. Obregon, we're being most rude—it's terrible stuff at first, isn't it, Middle C?—can you contrive to get some coffee for the leftenant commander? I won't maintain that Goldberry shouldn't be blamed for being what she is."

"A snake." His daughter dropped her hands. "You chose the analogy yourself, Father."

The Himalayan freed one of the Antimacassarite's hands and placed a steaming cup in it, for which the young woman gifted him with an almost grateful look.

Almost.

"My dear," Howell answered his daughter, "we all have choices to make in life, however constrained, and we make them whether we believe we're making them or not. However, it's indisputable that she is what she is, whoever's responsible, and I, for one, can't imagine how anyone can profit by punishing her for it."

"Pretty squishy." Lysandra offered a final protest, "How about the next person she victimizes?"

"Self-defense means just that, my dear, *self*-defense. Let the next person be prepared as we were. Let Goldberry understand the Confederacy isn't Antimacassar, where only an elite may own and carry weapons—it might be lethal force next time, instead of clever tricks. I'm simply saying I won't be a part of punishing her now for performing what she mistakenly conceives to be her duty."

Goldberry opened her mouth to argue, but must

have thought better of it, sipping at her coffee instead, her brow furrowed with new ideas, acute pain, or both.

"And?" his daughter asked.

"And we'l! just ship her off to Talisman with the rest of the slaves. After all, it's what she's been all her life, you know, a slave. A self-made slave."

"All slaves're self-made," Grossfuss observed. "Ask anyone who's ever carried a credit card."

"Quite. From there, like the rest of the former slaves, she'll be on her own. Perhaps she'll even find a way to get back to the Antimacassarite fleet and re-enslave herself."

A mixed expression altered Goldberry's face, half scandalized outrage, half confusion of a sort Lysandra thought she recognized as the beginning of an open mind. She was certain she knew what the Antimacassarite was thinking: she'd fought battles beside these people—Grossfuss, Middle C, Howell, his "child" daughter—and knew their ferocity matched hers point for point. Yet now, when she'd betrayed them, they were letting her go, so to speak, with a warning. To a power-oriented mind like hers, this spoke of confidence and terrifying strength.

"Or better yet," Lysandra speculated, "the next time we hear about her, she'll have recruited a complement of those former slaves (some of whom, of course, are prisoners of war from her own nation-state) and become a hovercraft pirate!"

And Lysandra knew Goldberry was thinking it wasn't such a crazy idea, at that.

CHAPTER XXI:

The Sudden Stop at the Bottom

"Hard about, Obregon, bring her hard about!"

"I'm tryin', Cap'n! We ain't got the power nor room t'turn!"

Whole sections of the panel *flashed, flashed, flashed,* the panic-color of fresh blood, dazzling Lysandra with refractions in her spectacles. Harsh bells jangled, klaxons hooted in her battered ears. The subfoline shook, bow to stern, with stresses she'd never been built to take. A jumble of fur and struggling motion roiled before the helpless girl as the frantic beings at the controls fought to get the vessel's nose up. But worst was what Lysandra saw and heard in her implant.

More than a mile below, even as the *Victor Appleton*'s three passengers prepared themselves for a grim and terrible death, they glimpsed the hazy outlines of a legend.

Having disposed of a would-be hijacker, and bidden what they hoped was a temporary farewell— they intended returning to the village in a few days—to Middle C and his people, Howell and Lysandra, with Grossfuss as their pilot, item-mumbled and switch-flipped through the dreary checklist, to continue their shakedown cruise. As she'd been designed to do, the subfoline would penetrate the peculiar vegetation of the Sea of Leaves, burrowing closer toward the planet's real surface, six miles below. This time, they'd take her all the way.

As they did, they encountered little known, weird, fearsome species of animal life inhabiting the single species of vegetation of which the sea was made, among them a few even more threatening and hideous than those which, like the can-can, had earlier endangered the craft, although none quite so terrible as the vacuole. Lysandra's favorite was a predatory blob of emerald protoplasm a hundred yards across, a giant amoeba that oozed its way among the leaves, catching smaller creatures thousands at a time in its viscous pseudopods and absorbing them. On rare occasions—overcast nights in particular—it came to the surface, had been reported from time to time to disbelieving Confederate zoologists, and was known as Shea's Leviathan. Another, rarer, and more like a vast, hundred-armed squid, she'd heard called Wilson's Shoggoth.

For a while, the yeti, the coyote, and his daughter were occupied, physically, mentally, emotionally, testing the subfoline, surveying life and times in the tangled darkness beneath the surface, and—the hard work they put in helped—recovering from their previous adventures. As they began to settle into a routine, father and daughter at last found private time to talk over some of the things that had happened in the vacuole and the village, with special regard for one Leftenant Commander Goldberry MacRame, late of the Antimacassarite Leafnavy, and even later of the subfoline *Victor Appleton,* which she'd attempted to steal. Lysandra—or perhaps Elsie—had always been an "ugly duckling" in her own view, and her self-consciousness about her looks had worsened in association with the tall, well-shaped, beautiful First Wave officer.

"Moewyt' myxedhinn, nethu, what a *zoddiv* she turned out to be," the girl exclaimed to her father.

They weren't speaking English, having chosen to discuss the personal items in Lysandra's life in Fodduan. Howell sighed, but it wasn't an unhappy sound.

"Ediil, I hope you've begun to learn, not only that beauty's merely skin deep, but that exercising quick intelligence and a pleasant, unique personality are better and longer lasting."

Lysandra made a sour face.

He persisted: *"Emna, yl uai'h vedo sa roed etasrod siidisiir,* a rarer kind of beauty's found in energetic motion, directed by that intelligence and personality, radiating outward from the inside."

"Yl uai'do semvytp ekais fo, Lesrod." The girl folded her arms in front of her body. "You make me sound like a room deodorizer."

He couldn't help chuckling. *"Fu hoedons,* I can't be less honest with you over this than about anything else."

Lysandra's frown faded. *"Y niigoed ku fu mylo eth fu mabo al ys,* I wouldn't want you to be, Father."

He nodded. *"Srot essoth, A lofemo heipiirsod,* this is difficult for a child to learn, let alone a parent to teach. A little girl's indoctrinated by her solicitous mother, grandmothers, sisters, aunts—especially when those well-meaning relatives believe she won't grow up to be pretty, something you'll never need to worry about, believe me or not—until she accepts it as background noise, no different from a fan oscillating in a bedroom window or commercials blaring from the telecom. And no better heard, once a young mind's decided to filter it out."

Lysandra affected a shocked expression. *"Nydder,* would I ever do that?"

The coyote raised his eyebrows. "Do little pigs live in brick houses? A distinction does exist, however subtle, between those old bromides (which I assure you are true, for all that they're bromides), and a greater truth: people's impressions of a person depend more on certain individualistic virtues than on any popular and ever-changing standard of what's pretty and what isn't."

"And furthermore," Lysandra answered, nodding, "an individual's perceptions of herself, *lad gres sreu'do gadsiir,* are more important than anybody else's."

"*Nesynlevsadu,*" Howell told her, feeling pleased. "I'd hoped you'd come to understand that, but never pressed you, not desiring to be categorized with oscillating fans, telecom commercials, and the bromide-dispensing mother you never knew."

"And never missed."

Lysandra understood all of this as well as she could at this time and place in her life. To her dismay, understanding seemed to concentrate at the intellectual level, where it didn't do much good. Observing Goldberry, she'd seen (as an example of the kind of insight which didn't help) that, far from building "men," the military preserved people in a dependent state, past the age when they should be making mature decisions for themselves. It was accepted in the Confederacy, if nowhere else, that responsibility can't be taught by denying people opportunities to exercise it. But she knew, nonetheless, it was the pretty ones—whatever their level of intelligence or maturity—who were taken most seriously.

"I appreciate what you're saying, *doemmu,*" she added, feeling shy (saying it in an alien language helped), "*eth Y mabo uai lad ys.* You're the best father anyone could wish for. As long as I can remember, I've had you to rely on. I don't know what I'd do without you."

"I won't have done my job, if you can't do without

me. Just remember what I said about intelligence, and personality, and—"

"And 'energetic motion'?"

"Uoer," Grossfuss commented in an offhand manner as he passed the table on his way to the head. *"Nriviin, vaavyo,* the idea's not t'give 'em time t'notice whether you're pretty or not. Just encourage 'em t' find reasons t'see that you're beautiful."

Lysandra pushed her glasses back: *"Sretiiviin,* Obregon, but don't call me *'vaavyo'*—"

She stared, mouth open, at her father, at the yeti's retreating form as he disappeared down the corridor, and back at her father again. They hadn't been speaking English.

Neither had Grossfuss.

However kind the manner in which Grossfuss had concurred with Howell's attempt to quell Lysandra's self-doubt, it had been a shock when, for no accountable reason, he'd proven able to understand the Fodduan they'd been using for private conversation. They couldn't follow him into the subfoline's small bathroom (she had trouble enough wondering how he squeezed in there by himself), demanding to know why he was familiar with a language rare in the galaxy, spoken only by the few Sodde Lydfans who'd begun traveling in the Confederacy and a smaller number of Confederates who'd visited their planet long enough to learn it.

"You musta been mistaken," he told them, once he'd returned and they'd found a polite way to inquire about it. "You was thinkin' so hard in that jabber, you just thought I talked it, too."

"It appears to me," Howell told Lysandra over the encoded circuit they'd established in the vacuole, *"he's telling the truth."*

Lysandra shook her head. *"He wasn't aware he was speaking another language?"*

"Precedents exist," her father replied, *"so-called*

'idiot savants' who add, subtract, multiply, and divide enormous numbers, even tell you what day of the week a date will be on a thousand years from now. Not that I'm saying our friend's an—"

"Then again"—the yeti shrugged, his hands leaving the wheel a moment—"I been around a lot, this mudball an' that. Y'pick up all kindsa weird talents in a varied an' adventurous life, could be without even knowin' it, sometimes."

At last the subfoline and her occupants approached within a mile of the bottom of the sea, as she'd been designed to do. However, the results of testing, analyzed by the vessel's own systems, consisted of anything but good news.

"Well, Cap'n, here it is, in black an' white."

In fact, the columns of figures were rendered in whatever color and on whatever background the owner of an implant desired. It didn't change what the figures added up to.

"Yes," the coyote answered. "Unfortunately, I must concur. Vegetation density increases more rapidly with depth than anyone expected. As a result, this vessel, whatever her revolutionary efficiencies, consumes more power than anticipated."

In her mind's eye, Lysandra examined the numbers. "In these conditions, we turn out to have a more limited range than they'd hoped at Hellertech. You know what this means?"

Her father nodded in grim silence.

"It means," the Himalayan answered with less self-control, "we don't know where the point of safe return is! We don't even know if we can get back right now!"

Howell shook his head. "Those figures are some sort of average, Obregon, obtained by sensitive instruments from orbit. Unless they're completely mistaken, they imply the path becomes easier ahead for some reason, not more difficult."

"Yeah? I know how pararadar works with the leaves—lousy! We oughta turn back right now!"

Howell turned to Lysandra. "What do you think, my dear, should we be persuaded by Obregon's—"

" —cowardly objections?"

"A vile an' base canard!" the yeti complained.

"I know many people who play violin," replied the coyote.

"But not a one," his daughter finished, "who plays the bass canard."

The Himalayan covered his face with his hands. "Jokes," he moaned. "At a time like this, jokes."

"Or shall we take our chances that the figures are reliable in aggregate and press on?"

"Hey," the yeti complained, "is this a game show on the telecom or somethin'? Whatever happened to— *Oh my achin' sacroiliac, the figures were right!*"

An emergency program in the computer had wiped the columns of numbers from their inner eyes, replacing them with graphics. Grossfuss and the orbital projections were correct. After slogging through a mile of ultradense vegetation no one had expected, just as unexpectedly, the "bottom" had dropped out of the Sea of Leaves.

"Hard about, Obregon, bring her hard about!"

"I'm tryin', Cap'n! We ain't got the power nor room t'turn!"

The control panel *flashed, flashed, flashed,* in panic colors, dazzling Lysandra. Bells jangled, klaxons hooted. The odor of overworked machinery began to fill the subfoline as a jumble of fur and motion, the coyote and the yeti, fought to get the vessel's nose up. Even as they all prepared themselves for death, they glimpsed, more than a mile below, the hazy outlines of a legend.

The dense tangle of leaves and branches that had

retarded progress had been replaced without warning by a giant forest of unspeakable, enormous vertical trunks. These might have been scaled on foot, but the travelers hadn't made any preparations for mountaineering more than a mile in pitch blackness. The worst thing was that, no more than a dozen feet below her keel, nothing remained, to keep the subfoline from falling thousands of feet to the surface.

In their minds, and on the screen they hadn't thought to dispose of after disposing of Goldberry, tucked like toy blocks between the trunks—although the travelers were in no mood to appreciate the view—were what might have been vast buildings and other unnatural works. If so, it was a bewildering architecture no creature born on Earth could have dreamed of, executed on a scale even the Confederacy had never dared. Or it might just have been the bedrock below, littered with the detritus of an unknown biology—the Cyclopean equivalent of fallen leaves, seed casings, bark fragments—and distorted into weird shapes through stress imposed by a living mass no other world had ever borne.

What they saw, what their implants and the ship's instruments recorded below them, bathed in the powerful floodlights they were attempting to point in any other direction, were delicate, transparent spirals half a mile in diameter, miles long, stretching like glass coil-springs between drum-shaped cylinders of frozen lace tilted on their narrow rims, so it seemed any cantilever long enough to balance them must extend halfway to the core of the planet.

Here and there the eye-shocking jumble was punctuated by huge shining masts, pulsing with their own light, adorned with complex cross-spars and what looked like guy wires running the wrong direction, set at absurd angles, serving no apparent purpose. Broad as a starship, lakes of some fantastic bluish liquid were fed by glowing streams that appeared to run uphill. These wound between great piles of what looked like bowling balls, thousands of them, complete with holes—if bowling balls were manufactured egg-shaped, a hundred feet in diameter, and could be stacked so the pile was broader at the bottom than the top—leaning out and casting whatever was below it into shadow.

Everywhere, tangled networks of wire and piping might have served an entire planet if they hadn't looped around, shorting themselves, feeding back into one another (or sometimes humping over and passing on), as if some nineteenth- or twentieth-century house builder had integrated plumbing, electric wiring, and gas lines, indiscriminate of any physical laws or mechanical logic the travelers knew. Although nothing, aside from the blue liquid, could be seen to move, they sensed an overall sort of movement, as if the entire scene were swarming, covered with millions—billions—of insects, too small and far away to be seen.

"Bristles reversing now! Down t' 10 percent power!"

'We'll make it or we won't," Howell replied, "in which case we'll see what's down there at close hand."

Inch by hard-won inch, they recovered control, slowing the subfoline, reversing her in time to keep her—and all within her—from plummeting into the chasm. For the first time they heard her straining power plant, felt unbalanced vibrations in her bristles. Backward she climbed, toward the light five miles above. For an hour her headlamps brightened whatever lay below, swinging away from those fantastic sights only after the leaves had closed in again beneath them.

"Ain't the fall that kills ya"—Grossfuss pressed his eyes with the heels of his hands—"it's the sudden stop at the bottom!"

"Jokes," Lysandra moaned, "at a time like this, he makes jokes!"

Howell was too tired to reply, although the yeti had done the work. Lysandra was exhausted, and she'd just sat behind them, wondering why her life wasn't passing before her eyes.

"I believe," the coyote suggested when their pulses were down to only three or four multiples of normal, "it might be good to power down and call it a day. The superconductor can recharge from potential differences in the surrounding leaves—too bad we're too deep for electrical storms—and we can get some sleep."

The yeti nodded, not answering, but obeying with a yawn. In minutes, all indicators were on standby, alarms had been rigged to detect large predators. Even so, at least two of the travelers were allowed only temporary respite. They'd just survived terrible danger, as they'd survived it before on Majesty, but it was nothing to compare with the danger the subfoline and her passengers had been in since beginning the voyage, although, aside from vague, melodramatic warnings, which they'd attributed to Goldberry MacRame, they had no way of knowing it.

Before they were ready for it again—this being the nature of violent adventures—another disaster occurred. Prepared to resume the upward voyage after a few hours' rest, Howell and Lysandra awakened in their cabins to find themselves tied up.

Just as Goldberry had been.

CHAPTER XXII:

The Trojan Sasquatch

"Father?"

Lysandra awoke with a sweaty start in the dim quiet of her cabin, to discover she was unable to move more than her fingers and toes. Peering down the silver-gray length of her smartsuited body, she found she'd been tied up with extrusions of the subfoline's safety system, the same way Goldberry had.

"Grrrh!"

Growing heated in the face, and seeing tiny purple flashes before her eyes, she wondered if it was possible for someone her age to burst something, struggling like this.

"Right," she whispered to herself. "*Two* conspiracies want to steal Hellertech's baby before we can get her back to the surface. Or two agents working for the same conspiracy."

A knock sounded on her cabin doorframe. Grossfuss lumbered through the membrane and stood over her.

" 'Scuse me, cookie."

As easily as if he were reaching for the table salt, he seized her by her bonds and lifted her. It hurt her back. She gritted her teeth, refusing to make a noise, even to tell him not to call her "cookie." He carried her like a suitcase into the corridor where he'd hauled her father, and dumped her on the floor beside him.

"You two can stay in galley where you can see what's goin' on an' I can keep an eye on you."

The instant his back was turned to fumble with the subfoline's controls, they struggled to get free, straining against their bonds with more than blood in their eyes. Lysandra desisted when the purple flashes started again, but Grossfuss, occupied with whatever he was doing to the vessel, hadn't noticed—although he began to speak to them, tossing his words back over his shoulder.

"The idea," he explained, "—superconductin' subfoline though she might be, an' pretty valuable—ain't t'steal her like the leftenant commander had in mind, but t'do for her altogether."

How many individuals out of a thousand would have asked why? Lysandra asked, "How?"

He turned, smiling. "I'm plannin' t'precipitate"—he put emphasis on the first syllable—"this here bucket to the bottom of the Sea of Leaves, cookie, that's how."

The yeti was setting the vessel on an automated course that would take her back the way she'd just come, and drop her a mile to the surface of the planet.

Lysandra looked at Howell. He was unharmed, but it was the first she could remember seeing him speechless with anger. Grossfuss—or the ship's safety systems—had bundled him like a bulldogged rodeo calf, his four legs bunched together, and had also taken the precaution of depriving them of their weapons. She could see them, if she cared to exert herself, straining against complaining stomach muscles and cramping her neck, where they lay piled on the galley table.

"Guess you'll both feel better if y'go out knowin' there wasn't nothin' wrong with her, vegetation or not. It was just my way of tryin' t'turn you back 'fore it hadda come t'this."

The Himalayan straightened and came away from the controls. Violating what Lysandra thought of as true villainous tradition, he didn't gloat over the helpless, trussed-up bodies of his victims. Instead, he seemed apologetic.

"I'll feel a lot better, myself," he told them, "if you understand this ain't personal. You both been good friends. I'm only doing what I been programmed for by the folks who sent me."

"The Hooded Seven."

Howell had spoken.

The yeti grinned. "You got it, Cap'n, an' on the first guess too. They mean t'stop what they call a malignancy from spreadin' through the entire universe."

"Meaning the Galactic Confederacy . . ." Howell began.

"Or humanity?" his daughter interjected.

". . . or simply the spread of progress?" Howell concluded.

Grossfuss shrugged. "Beats me. It's kinda strange: sometimes I feel like I know, but other times, well, maybe I just wasn't programmed very good. Too bad, me bein' one of the principals, like I'm s'posed t'be. 'Course, you've figured out by now I'm the one wrote those notes. You called that one wrong, but you had reasons. Hoped it'd scare you off, abort the run, so I wouldn't hafta do this."

"Programmed? One of the principals?" Howell mused. "Tell me, Obregon, if you don't mind, what will you be doing, while we're plummeting to our deaths?"

"Gee, it's nice of you t'ask. Don't worry, I plan escapin' at the last minute. We're in a sorta pocket, here. Nothin' like the vacuole, or what's down at the bottom, but a person can get off if he wants. I got friends waitin' t'welcome me."

Grossfuss turned his back and was busy for a

moment at the panel. He rose, shambling over to the coyote and his daughter. Despite being tied, disarmed, and, to appearances, helpless, they could think, which, of course, meant they were still dangerous.

"Well, Cap'n, cookie, I gotta say g'bye, now. I'm sorry things turned out this way."

Although warned, the yeti had forgotten Howell was a dog and had failed to deprive him of a dog's weapons. Knowing her father would attack, Lysandra furnished a diversion.

"How often do I have to say don't call me 'cookie,' you murderous, flea-bitten abomination?"

Howell lurched and sank his teeth in the Himalayan's leg. This produced an immediate, violent reaction. Shaken like a rag on a clothesline by the screaming, bleeding Grossfuss, the coyote held on while Lysandra levered herself up against the bulkhead, hopped across the corridor, got her back to the table, and snatched the first weapon her hand brushed. It was the outsized pair of shears her father had carried in his rucksack since the night in Humility's cottage.

Meanwhile, the yeti had regained enough control to draw his pistol, point it at his own ankle, and shoot. Noise of the discharge filled the subfoline, echoing off walls. For a moment no one could think of anything else. Grossfuss had aimed at the coyote's head, but, in the struggle, sent the bullet through his body.

With a snarl that would have done Howell justice, Lysandra leaped with the shears held like an icepick in her hand—although she'd been taught better technique—but being stronger than the girl and her father put together, the yeti batted her out of his way as if she were a mosquito, and departed forward.

"Father?"

She raised her head, lifted herself to her elbows, and tried to get up, cracking her head on the underside of the table where the yeti's blow had tossed her. Her shoulder hurt. It was possible, from the way things felt, she'd broken a rib.

"Father?"

As she crawled from under the table, she noticed the shears still in her hand. Gratified to see a large tuft of scarlet-stained white fur, she cut through her bonds. In one corner of her eye, the Himalayan was making good his escape toward the ceiling and out through the permeable hull. She was torn between pursuit and seeing to her father, who lay injured and hadn't answered her.

Concentrating, she ordered the hull closed around the yeti's body, using her original code-key, which took priority over those given Grossfuss and Goldberry. He bellowed as the molecules of the subfoline began to mingle with his own, and the retreating column of extruded flooring left his hairy legs dangling and thrashing. Howell lay panting on the deck in what was no less a pool of blood for all that the expression was a cliché. It astonished her there was so much of it. He lifted his head as she cut away his bonds, and licked her hand.

"I'm not hurt as badly as it looks," he told her, struggling to his feet. "Get Grossfuss. I'll change courses or stop the vessel. And don't forget your little gun, dear."

Having no choice, Lysandra rose, turned, and seized both Walthers from the table, only to discover that the hanging legs were gone. She ought to have killed him, but had only slowed him down. He'd known secrets other than Fodduan. Holstering her left-hand gun, she exited the subfoline the same way the yeti had, pursuing him out onto the hull. As her head cleared the decking, she saw Grossfuss

running the length of the vessel toward its needle-
prow.

At the same moment, the fleeing Himalayan
turned, eyes widening as he saw Lysandra's head
and shoulders projecting above the hull, shot at
her, and missed. As her arm cleared the hull, she
shot back at Grossfuss, a larger target, and connected. The half-dozen ultravelocity trajectiles caught
him like the bumper of a hovertruck. His body
distended for a moment, like a blowfish, then, more
like a marionette with cut strings, collapsed in an
unnatural-looking manner.

Fearful of what she'd have to look at when she
got there, she crept forward, following the muzzle of
her pistol, along the top of the now-motionless
subfoline, pushing random leaves and branches out
of her way, to investigate the remains. As the girl
drew even with the inert form of the yeti, a dozen
small dark forms scurried away from his body and
into the leaves. Scavengers were fast down here,
she thought, to sense death and be on the scene so
soon.

However, they'd been disappointed scavengers.
Nothing was left of the yeti but a thick, heavy pelt,
soaked with blood and lubricant, filled with lengths
of titanium framing and the few bits and pieces of
machinery her trajectiles had left recognizable. What
she'd thought of as a living, breathing, creature
had been in reality only an empty hulk. The "remains" began smoldering, burning fast and hot like
celluloid or smokeless gunpowder—around them the
leaves wilted and yellowed—consuming themselves,
until nothing was left but the yeti's gunbelt, heat-
ruined weapon, and a pile of fine, white flakes.

Her father, now lying unconscious—even dying—in
the copilot's seat, where he'd succeeded in bringing
the vessel to a halt, had been right all along. He'd
insisted yetis were shy creatures. They'd avoided

contact with other sentients for tens of thousands of years. Even now, they were never known to do much traveling or socializing, let alone outright villainizing.

"Guess I'll have to tell Howell," Lysandra commented to herself as she turned to go back inboard the subfoline, "that Grossfuss made a complete ash of himself."

She bound her father's wounds—one bullet, entrance and exit—as best she could and made a bed for him on the galley table where she could take care of him and handle controls at the same time. In one way, she felt lucky: how many other fifteen-year-old girls could lift their fathers and carry them the dozen steps required?

But Lysandra's troubles had just begun. Her early concerns about getting back to the surface turned out to have been well founded, although for different reasons than she'd have guessed. She hadn't practiced operating the *Victor Appleton* much, having left this to her father and the traitorous Grossfuss. Now she'd have to rely on its built-in instructions and what she remembered.

Meanwhile, outside this pocket lay the densest, most difficult and dangerous level of the sea to navigate, one filled with giant predators and other obstacles.

As a bonus, the sabotaged propulsion system was threatening to break down, and so was life-support. Whomever he'd been working for, Grossfuss had done his job.

Resigning herself to days of struggle against nature and machinery, Lysandra seized the wheel.

She would manage to survive.

CHAPTER XXIII:

Lysandra Alone

This place, as with all such places, reeked of alcohol and disinfectant. Its slick-floored corridors echoed with screeches, squeals, and moans of abandonment and despair, and of bewildered pain no one could ever explain to the victims.

The girl stood over the still form of her father, her glasses in one hand, wiping her tear-streamed eyes with the other, trying without success to stifle the gurgling noises that ripped themselves from her body against her will.

"So I said, 'Don't worry, Father, I'll get you to a doctor right away.' And you said, 'Take me to a vet: they're more competent, more honest about what they don't know, and work a lot cheaper. If you were hurt, I'd take *you* to a vet.' "

In fact, it took her longer than that to get the words out. In the end, she pressed her free hand over her aching solar plexus and sat down on a chair beside the bed, wondering if it was true a person could laugh herself to death.

"Dear me," her father replied. "People make peculiar demands, full of adrenaline and endorphins, not to mention bullets. I don't remember a word. Nor powering down the subfoline as you assure me I did. But here we are, Pixel's Pet Hospital, Talisman-on-Majesty, alive and in good comfort. I've no complaint. Except that I *itch*."

Howell lay in a shallow wall-niche, wrapped in rubbery gray bandages, with inset pilot lamps and miniature controls, from neck to hips. Lysandra had persuaded the proprietors to remove the bars enclosing the niche, to refrain from putting patients in the dozen other niches the room offered, and had assured them lining it with papers wouldn't be necessary. Her father had been housebroken long before she (or the veterinarian, for that matter) was born. She hadn't had the courage yet to tell him the itching meant his body had been shaved to the skin and it would take him months to grow his beautiful pelt back. She hadn't had the courage to tell him about something else, either.

"Yes," she answered, "and speaking of peculiar demands, while you were in surgery this morning, I got restless and went back to the *Victor Appleton* to search the quarters of the thing that called itself Grossfuss. I found this voice-letter—"

She closed her eyes and concentrated, transferring it via paratronics to his implant.

"As you can see, it claims to be from some faction of the taflak, objecting bitterly to mechanized exploration of Majesty's biomass. Father, I thought the natives were rational individuals. Now it looks like they may have been Grossfuss' bosses, and what's worse—and even less explicable—their objections appear to be on religious grounds. It's a textbook fact that religion never got invented on Majesty. They seem to prefer practical joking."

"On the other paw," her father argued, "we came here to put new facts in the textbooks, didn't we? And perhaps remove some old ones. I confess, this one strikes me as odd. I—"

He was interrupted by a set of knuckles rapping on the doorframe, followed by a chimpanzee in medical greens coming halfway through the membrane.

"Mr. Nahuatl? Please forgive me—we're not ac-

customed to having patients who can talk back—
you've a visitor waiting to see you, just outside."

Howell turned to Lysandra, who shrugged.

"It must be someone from Hellertech. Please ask
them to come in, Doctor, and thank you."

The veterinarian nodded and ducked out . . . and
in through the membrane walked Obregon Grossfuss.

"Hold on a minute!"

He raised his hands, an appropriate gesture, considering that the muzzles of two pistols—not to
mention that of a snarling coyote—were pointing
straight at him.

"I don't know you people! You only think you
know me! I just wanted t'talk so y'wouldn't shoot
me if y'ran across me in Talisman. It ain't that big
a town."

A reluctant Lysandra put her guns away.

"Very well, sir," her father told the yeti, "kindly
come in and be seated."

The creature nodded, looking relieved, and accepted the coyote's invitation.

"I just spent several real bad days," he complained,
"locked in a tool crib in a vacant warehouse, after
bein' drugged an' kidnapped. Took m'gun an' all
m'clothes. I escaped—that's another story—an' got
a 'com call from Hellertech when y'filed your report. Thought I'd better come see you right away."

"They also accessed your implant"—Lysandra noticed he wore a brand new gunbelt and a different
greasy coverall—"learning enough to imitate your
personality."

"I was the original mechanic," he told her, "an' I
don't care what it says in that report, I don't drink.
Except occasionally. For medicinal purposes."

"We all wish—I assume it's Grossfuss?" Howell's
tone, Lysandra knew, indicated a grin. "We all wish
to consider ourselves unique individuals and to have
others acknowledge it. I believe the robot developed

enough character of its own to hint indirectly that it was a replacement. It was confused in other ways as well."

"It wanted"—the yeti was sarcastic—"t'be appreciated for itself?"

"Precisely. Though I must admit, with no offense, they did an excellent job of imitating you."

"Yeah, but 'they' who?"

"Why," Lysandra answered, "the Hooded Seven."

"That's only a name, y'know."

They discussed the report Grossfuss had read—and Howell and Lysandra had lived—wondering who could be behind the actions of the artificial yeti. The coyote mentioned the evidence his daughter had found in the robot's cabin, and her consternation over its apparent violation of the accepted facts about Majesty.

"I was about to remind her," he told Grossfuss, "that a planet—and a people—are much larger and more complicated things than ordinarily appreciated. Yet it's often the case that an entire planet's characterized by a single phrase. Sodde Lydfe's a 'desert planet' although it also has oceans, mountains, icy poles. To those born elsewhere, Earth's an 'ocean planet' although (with the exception of our native cetaceans, naturally enough) this feature's often the least significant to those who grew up on Earth's continents."

Lysandra nodded, pushing her glasses back into place.

"I'm ashamed I had to be reminded. And in the same way, disagreement and dissent of one kind or another seem to be an unavoidable fact of intelligent life. You may recall, Father, the Fodduan saying which, loosely translated, means 'Only the ants are unanimous.' Brochures—and textbooks—often picture a uniform culture and set of attitudes among the natives of a planet, especially when, as on Majesty, they're not chopped up into nation-states. But this is as inaccurate and thoughtless as characterizing an entire planet by a single climate zone."

Grossfuss, not knowing Lysandra as his predecessor had, was astonished at all these words tumbling out of her.

"A 'surprising' number," her father added, "of conflicting parties and differing points of view compete, even among the 'primitive' taflak. And as contact with the Confederacy continues, and they're exposed to more variation, this will be increasingly true."

Mouth hanging open, the yeti's head had swiveled to watch the coyote as he spoke. Now it swiveled back—as if he were watching a tennis match—to Lysandra.

"The phenomenon's seen, too, among the First Wave human colonists: left-leaning Antimacassarites, whose primary concern is social welfare; right-leaning Securitasians, a tribe of paranoids who'll sacrifice anything to 'national security.' Each has its own internal factions who might favor or oppose what was done to us. In addition, a growing number have, for a complex variety of reasons, abandoned their nations-states to mingle with Confederates at the Poles."

"Confederate immigrants," Howell suggested, "now share the planet with both sorts of natives, having originated in a culture advanced both technically and philosophically. However, certain harmful deviations are an unavoidable tax levied by any open, pluralistic society, and, moreover, crime can be a measure of a society's health, indicating the level of its 'gumption.' Thus, we're not without our own leavening of suspicious characters and genuine criminals."

"But that means," Grossfuss made the dismal deduction, "anybody could be t'blame."

She nodded. Despite similar feelings of futility, she was determined to continue this, to track down those responsible for Howell's close encounter with death. Schooled in field praxeology, she vowed to go wherever the search took her, beginning with the taflak and the apparent contradiction with the textbooks. As long as she could recall, until she'd piloted the subfoline alone, Howell had been someone to lean on in a crisis, to offer love, help, and advice. Now, for the first time in her life, she must strike out on her own. Although she hadn't noticed it yet, her personal problems and self-doubts were forgotten in the press of more important matters. Perhaps this is one definition of growing up.

The Hooded Seven: if what the phony yeti had implied was correct, only Six remained. Or Five, if what Middle C had told her, about MacBear and Pemot, could be relied on.

Meanwhile, she'd get what information she could out of the real Grossfuss. She and her father finished telling him their story, including certain matters it hadn't seemed relevant to write into the report. The Himalayan didn't seem happy—in point of fact, he looked sick—as he listened to Lysandra's description of her destruction of his mechanical look-alike.

"Oh," was his only comment. "Rats!"

Lysandra was concerned. "What's the matter, Mr. Grossfuss?"

"Call me Obregon. Nothin's the matter, those were just rats you saw. Come t'Majesty with the First Wave, five thousand years ago, an' adapted better'n anything or anybody else. Vicious buggers, an' there's millions of 'em down there. Maybe billions. Didn't nobody warn you about the rats, cookie?"

"Don't," she told the yeti, realizing she was starting all over again, "call me 'cookie.' "

Grossfuss' eyes widened.

"I should have warned you, Obregon," Howell told the yeti, "she's sensitive about that."

"And before this goes any further," Lysandra informed the coyote, "I've got something to tell you, too."

Howell cocked his head. "And what might that be, my dear?"

"Hey, cook—Miz Nahuatl"—Grossfuss tossed a thumb at the door—"you want I should step outside?"

The girl shook her head.

"Call me Lysandra. And I don't think it'll be necessary, Obregon. If you're here, maybe I won't get lectured about how I'm just fifteen, or how I've never been out in the world on my own before, or how what I intend might be dangerous."

The Himalayan raised his eyebrows. "Oh?"

"Yeah. Father, I also booked passage for myself aboard the *Tom Jefferson Maru* this morning, while you were in surgery. I have to get after this MacDougall Bear or his lamviin friend Pemot while their trail's still hot. I'll probably be back before you're ready to check out of this place, but I mean to find the people—or whatever the Hooded Seven are—who did this to you."

After a brief silence, Howell grinned.

"Yes, dear, I know."

L. NEIL SMITH has been interested in "rockets, missiles, and space travel" since the age of eight and grew up reading science fiction and scientific nonfiction: astronomy, physics, chemistry, and biology. Currently he lives in Fort Collins, Colorado, with his wife Cathy L. Z. Smith, their cat Eris (named after the Goddess of Discord), and their African Grey parrot, Sedrich.

Mr. Smith is the author of the North American Confederacy series, including the Prometheus Award–winning *The Probability Broach*, *The Nagasaki Vector*, *The Venus Belt*, *Their Majesties' Bucketeers*, *Tom Paine Maru*, *The Gallatin Divergence*, and *A New Covenant*. A new chapter in his North American Confederacy was begun in the first volume of the MacBear/Lysandra heptalogy, *Brightsuit MacBear*, available from Avon Books, and Mr. Smith is at work on the further adventures of MacBear.